A Seniors Bedtime Reader Volume I

Seven stories to help while away your evenings.

Christopher Oelerich

A Seniors Bedtime Reader

Cover design: Renae Killen
Content editing: Steve Mehling
        Tom Tallarito

Email – chris@aseniorsbedtimereader.com

Copyright © 2018 Christopher Oelerich
All Rights Reserved

ISBN-13: 978-1986987288
ISBN-10: 1986987280

Dedication

For you Sweetheart.

Contents

Acknowledgments

To my family, friends and enemies; past, present, living and dead. Thank you all for your friendship and inspiration.

Without each of you, I would not be living the rich life I have been blessed with today.

A special thanks to Steve Mehling for his invaluable advice and direction.

A Chance Encounter

Conspiracy theories abound regarding age-old secret societies, organizations and groups of elites that control politics, banking, corporate enterprise and even illegal activity.

Saturday April 5, 1975.

It was one of those very rare days in spring when the sun manages to burn through the thick gray mid-west overcast. At 9:00 a.m., the doorbell rang at the Bachman's condo in the quiet middle-class suburb of Wheeling, Illinois. Marty and Nadine had already been up for several hours packing up the last of their belongings before the movers arrived. The couple had just closed on their new home in Columbia, MD and on this bright sunny day they could not have been more excited. The risk Marty had taken, leaving the accounting firm for a job with Global, Ltd. ten years before, had paid off handsomely with his recent promotion to Vice President of Accounting and move to corporate in Washington. After finding the accounting discrepancy that caught the large transfers to unknown numbered accounts, he was congratulated and rewarded with the new position.

Global, Ltd. a privately held holding company with a board made up of former world leaders, financiers and global elites. Rumored to be one of the largest companies in the world. With those rumors came tales of its ability to influence elections, depose governments, manipulate currency and determine when and where wars would begin and end, among other things. Martin Bachman had heard all the stories and wrote them all off to wild conspiracy theories.

Their Schnauzer, Sid, barked once and went to Nadine's side as he always did when there was someone at the door. Nadine looked briefly through the peep hole to see who was there. It was a man who looked to be of medium height and build, dressed in a dark business suit with rather grayish looking skin. She called to her husband.

"Marty are you expecting anyone?"

"Yes, there are some papers being delivered from the office this morning that I have to sign off on."

As she opened the door, the first shot from the suppressed Smith & Wesson Model 10-38 Special killed the dog, the second shot killed Nadine Bachman. The gunman entered the apartment. As Marty was running into the living room, he fell next to his wife. The assailant shot each of them one more time, picked up Marty's briefcase and cell phone, put on a fedora, sunglasses and gloves, closed and locked the door as he left the condo, walked down the stairs to a nondescript white sedan waiting in the parking lot. The car pulled out, turning right onto River Road heading south and drove away.

John Golden, Personnel Director for Global Ltd., was taking a last look through some of the week's paperwork on Friday, April 4th before leaving for the weekend when he noticed a search request for VP of Accounting. It had to be a mistake. Marty Bachman had just been named the new VP of Accounting and was scheduled to begin work at corporate the following Monday. He would straighten it out after the weekend when he saw Marty in the office on Monday.

Monday April 7, 1975.

John Golden arrived at the offices of Global Ltd. as he always did, one half hour before the rest of the office, to give him a head start on the day. It also gave him a chance to get a cup of fresh coffee and scan the Washington Post. He was sitting down when he saw the small heading on the lower left of the front page, VP of Accounting for Global Ltd. murdered. The article went on to say it was an apparent robbery gone bad, that the only items taken were a brief case and a cell phone. There was no evidence left behind and the police were investigating. Almost to the second, at 8:00 a.m., John Golden's phone rang.

"Good morning, this is John Golden,"

"John, this is Bill Layton at Layton/Brown Executive Recruiting."

"Yes Bill, what can I do for you?"

"John, we received a search request via fax over the weekend for a VP of Accounting, I thought it was a little odd since you named a new VP a month ago."

"Did you read this morning's paper?"

"No, I haven't."

"Our new VP of Accounting was murdered over the weekend."

"He was what?"

"He was murdered, apparent robbery. Look, hold off on the search for a day or so while I look into this, I'll get back to you on how to proceed."

"Thanks John."

After two tours in Vietnam as an Army Ranger, John Golden went to work for Global Ltd. He had a knack for picking good people and was especially adept at reading them. These two qualities, along with his being a team player, helped his quick rise to Director of Personnel.

There was something odd about the request he saw on his desk the previous Friday afternoon. It could have just been a clerical mistake, but the fax request to the recruiter was not. Someone had to deliberately send it. John Golden decided to do some discreet investigating on his own starting with the Wheeling, Illinois Police Department. He contacted the Wheeling Police and was directed to a homicide detective named Jim Pattison.

"Homicide, Pattison speaking."

"Detective Pattison my name is John Golden, I am director of Personnel at Global Ltd.

I'm calling to see if you can tell me anything about your investigation into the Bachman murders over the weekend? Martin Bachman had just been promoted to VP of Accounting here at Global."

"Right now, we don't have much to go on. There was no evidence other than the slugs retrieved from the bodies and it's my guess the gun will never be found."

"Was anyone seen leaving after the shooting?"

"There was a man spotted in a dark suit carrying a briefcase wearing a hat, sunglasses and gloves. He was spotted getting into a car and driving off. Very generic looking, that's all we currently have."

"Thanks for your help detective, I don't imagine anything will come up here, but if it does, I'll pass it along,"

"Thanks."

To satisfy his curiosity and hopefully put this unfortunate mess to bed, he decided to check through personnel records. Even though John Golden was the Director, he had to sign in to access the company's files. He went directly to accounting and when he pulled the drawer open it took less than a second to see that the personnel file for Martin Bachman was gone. John closed the drawer and for some reason took his handkerchief and wiped the cabinet clean where he had touched it. He signed out and went back to his office shaken somewhat by what he had just witnessed.

At 4:00 p.m., John's assistant came in and told him that she had just spoken to Norbert Berman, Executive Vice President of Global. He was on his way down to see John.

"John, I don't think I have ever seen him in this part of the building before, do you have any idea what he is coming here for?"

"No, I don't Carolyn, just show him in when he gets here."

There was very little movement at the top of Global Ltd. The makeup of the senior staff was primarily European and American. Norbert Berman was Austrian, spoke with a thick accent and had been EVP for as long as John had been with the company. Shortly after his assistant Carolyn left, Norbert Berman knocked on John's door. He got up and greeted the EVP,

"Mr. Berman, I'm John Golden, what can I do for you sir?"

"John, the loss of Mr. Bachman is very unfortunate, and we would like to have you find a suitable candidate as quickly as possible."

"I will get right on it sir."

"Was there any specific reason that you were checking with the police in Illinois?"

"No sir, I just wanted to close out his file properly."

"According to the police report, it was robbery and nothing more."

"That's what they said sir."

"Oh, and one other thing, you were in the file section today?"

The first thought that came to John's mind was 'I smell a rat.'

"Yes sir, it was just some routine checking.,"

"John, move quickly to find someone and keep my office informed."

"Yes sir."

John Golden went directly to file storage, signed in, went to the bank of file cabinets, opened the drawer marked personnel and removed his file. Upon hiring, all employees were required to have their fingerprints taken and attached to their individual file. If his experience and ability to read situations had taught him only one thing in his lifetime, it was John Golden must disappear or John Golden was going to die.

John left his office with only his personnel file in his briefcase. To avoid raising any suspicion, he did not pack any personal items from his desk or office. He was tempted to call his wife Gloria, but knew it was best to wait until they were face to face. He started the drive home preparing a mental list of tasks he believed had to be accomplished within the next twenty-four hours. As he was going through an intersection, he noticed a car rental agency. He stopped in, took a one-week rental telling them he was going on a road trip and parked his car in their lot. When he arrived home, John noticed that Gloria was just beginning to start dinner.

"John, I thought I'd make chicken marsala tonight. We haven't had it in a while. Oh, and by the way, the telephone repairman was here waiting when I got home."

"What time was that?"

"Right at 4:00 p.m., he said they had a line issue and wanted to make sure everyone had service."

"How long was he here?"

"Just a couple minutes. He took the phone off the wall, looked it over, did something with the handset and left. Why?"

"Oh, nothing. Look you haven't started yet. Why don't we run over to Leno's tonight and have dinner there?"

John put his index finger to his lips and waved his hand gesturing his wife that they should go.

"Johnny, I like your plan, dinner out sounds good."

Gloria Golden knew something was not right and that home was not the place to talk about it. Leno's was four blocks from their home and would give them ample time to talk. He told her what had happened to Marty Bachman and his wife, the conversation with Berman, the missing personnel files and what he knew they had to do.

"John are you absolutely sure we have to disappear?"

"As sure as we are walking down this street and we have to leave tonight."

John and Gloria Golden took a quiet booth in the back of the neighborhood Italian restaurant where they could talk. They would pack minimally as they would have to change their overall appearance immediately. They would walk back after dinner, get their things ready and then leave sometime in the middle of the night.

"We are going to see Bill Whitten first."

"Our Bill Whitten?"

"Yes, he works at the records repository in St. Louis. I have to get access to my military records and think he may be able to help."

"John, will he be in any danger?"

"If it looks that way, I won't go forward. It will just make things a little dicier for us, but far from impossible."

Packing took only a few short minutes, each had a small overnight bag with just enough clothes for a change and several of their most cherished mementos. At 10:30 p.m., they were ready but decided to wait until after midnight to leave. They would drive to Philadelphia and catch the first train to St. Louis. They wouldn't need any ID's and could remain anonymous. At midnight, there was a knock on the door. Without making a sound John looked out one of the front windows and noticed a male figure at the door. There was a white sedan halfway up their driveway with a man in the driver's seat. The couple sat quietly while they heard the deadbolt being worked first. John took up a position to the left of the door with a baseball bat, a Louisville Slugger signed by the great Frank Robinson. John counted himself one of the greats' biggest fans. As the intruder finished working the second lock, the door began to open slowly. The first thing John saw was the business end of a suppressed Smith & Wesson Model 10 – 38 Special followed slowly by a man with a medium build in a business suit.

When the would-be assailant had cleared the door, John swung as though he was going to drive one over the center field wall and out of the park. The last thing the shooter saw was the autograph as it smashed into his forehead. He fell to the floor on top of his revolver, dead. John rolled him over, picked up the gun. Running out the front door and down the drive, he reached the sedan before the driver could start the motor and shot him twice through the open passenger-side window. He ran back to the house, wiped the grip clean, cocked the hammer back, wrapped the recently deceased assailant's hand on the grip, put his finger on the trigger, then fired once up into the ceiling. John Golden looked at his stunned wife,

"This was just to help confuse things a little. We have to go right now."

They locked the front door and carried their bags into the garage, opened the garage door backed out in the rental. John walked to the sedan, pushed the driver to the side, started the car and drove it into their garage, closing the door when he was back in the rental. The Goldens' headed out for Philadelphia, not looking back.

"John, how much time do you think we have before they find those two and where did you learn how to do those things, not that I'm upset that we're alive?"

"Honey, I was an Army Ranger. I led my own teams and as far as I can figure, we may have two days if we get lucky."

It took only one day for the bodies to be discovered by the Montgomery County Police Department after an anonymous tip. Orders came down from the Justice Department that it was to be treated as a John Doe investigation. Within a day, the bodies were picked up as well as the impounded vehicle and all collateral materials.

John and Gloria paid cash for their tickets when they booked an economy sleeper, allowing them to get a little privacy and some rest. Thirty-six hours later, they were in St. Louis. The first order of business was to contact Bill Whitten. Gloria took a cab to the repository. At the entrance, she told them she was there to see Mr. Whitten and gave her maiden name, Gloria Morrell. Bill Whitten had been in their wedding party and when he heard the name came right away to the entrance. Gloria handed him a note from John telling him to call a payphone at The Park Plaza Hotel from a payphone. Twenty minutes later, the phone at the Park Plaza rang,

"Is that you Blue six?"

"Yes, it is Blue one."

"Why the secrecy?"

"I'll fill you in when I see you. Can you get me access to my military records?"

"Yes, I can. When do you need to see them?"

"As soon as possible. Can it be done this afternoon?"

"Yes, I will arrange it."

"Can it be done without you having any connection to it?"

"I think I can do it, yes."

"You have to be absolutely sure, I can't have anything come back to you."

"I'm sure, be here at 12:00 p.m. sharp."

At 12:00 p.m., John and Gloria arrived at the repository. Gloria having gone from brunette to blond and John from brown to black. Gloria waited in the lobby area while John went with his old friend to look at his records. He explained to Bill Whitten what had happened and when the records were brought up, he removed the fingerprint card. He asked one more time if he was sure he couldn't be connected to his being there and was assured everything was ok. He thanked his old friend for what he had done, shook hands for the last time and left with his wife to start new lives.

Monday June 7, 2010.

Murray had just celebrated his sixty-ninth birthday and was getting used to, as he called it, being kind of retired. Estelle was several years younger, ok eight, and still wanted to work partly for the social contact and for the additional income it provided them.

The Waxman's paid their taxes, qualified for zero financing on their new car, bought a new bedroom set on time and just recently closed on a new home in one of the newest fifty-five and over golf course communities in Las Vegas.

Murray and Estelle had owned their own business, a small specialty manufacturing company. Their income allowed them to max their contributions to Social Security and 401K. These coupled with some modest investments helped to ensure that their later years would not be too difficult. However, there would have been no future had Murray not invested the twenty-thousand-dollars on new identities and minor plastic surgery for Estelle and himself thirty-five years ago. It turned out to be golden.

Though both Murray and Estelle were just average golfers, they both loved to play. One of the most important must-haves on their wish list for amenities was a golf course at any development they moved to. They ended up buying at Mountain View Estates an age restricted community with three golf courses. Two weeks prior to moving into their new home, they booked their first tee time, 12:20 p.m., on Monday June 14th at the Palm

View course. It didn't matter that the Las Vegas heat would be more than ninety-nine degrees to mid-westerners the heat was welcomed. Murray and Estelle were handing their receipts to the starter when a cart with a man and woman pulled up alongside them. The man asked if they would like to go out as a foursome and to have possible company for Estelle. Murray readily agreed. They introduced themselves as Jack and Lori Harding. The two couples played eighteen holes and couldn't have had more fun. When they were walking off the eighteenth green, they exchanged information and agreed to play again in the future. Jack and Lori told them they would be out of town for a month and would catch up when they got back.

Murray and Estelle decided to play a local public course on Wednesday July 14th. They called for a 9:00 a.m. tee time and to their surprise Jack and Lori pulled up alongside them as they were stepping onto the first tee. They went out as a foursome and again had a terrific time.

Murray and Jack had a chance to talk while they were playing and as they talked about their pasts found they had very similar military backgrounds. Murray and Jack had both been in Vietnam at roughly the same time. Murray had flown as a private pilot for years after leaving the service, while Jack had stayed in the Army reserves and had flown there. Murray had owned his own small manufacturing company for years accumulating most of his flight time for business. Jack worked for the government and told Murray he was getting ready to retire after thirty years. Murray and Estelle had been married for thirty-seven years and so had Jack and Lori. Estelle and Lori had similar conversations and were surprised they had so many things in common. They decided to start playing on Saturdays which would be convenient for both couples and Murray said he would arrange for a morning tee time.

On the drive home, they had a chance to talk about the game that day and their new friends.

"Estelle, that was really something running into Jack and Lori this morning."

"It sure was. I had a wonderful time. We have so much in common I'm looking forward to next week."

"So am I sweetheart."

"When we finish next week let's see if they want to catch lunch with us. It's nice to be making friends."

On the drive home, Jack and Lori had a chance to talk about their new 'friends', Murray and Estelle.

"Jack, do you think they suspect anything?"

"No, I don't. They have been living in these identities for so long and have put so much distance between themselves and their past. I doubt anyone they ever associated with would even recognize them if they saw them today."

"Honestly?"

"I don't even think any facial recognition programs out there today could make a connection, whatever work they had done was perfect."

"Murray seemed to be very interested in what I have done. I kept it benign, how was Estelle?"

"She was very open and we seemed to have a lot in common. She was also very interested in what I have done, but she didn't appear to be overly inquisitive or suspicious. Jack, have you given much thought about how they will react when you confront them?"

"You mean is there any chance he would resort to violence or run? I'm guessing no. Lori, they are very smart and disciplined. They wouldn't have lasted this long if they weren't."
"When are you going to file your report about finding them?"

"I want to talk to them first to confirm I have the right people. There is something about this that just doesn't seem right."
At lunch Friday July 16th on the patio overlooking the crowded practice green, Murray and Estelle were just taking in the afternoon.

"Murray, I've been thinking."

"What about sweetheart?"

"Doesn't it seem like a strange coincidence that we ran into Jack and Lori today?"

"A little."

"Murray, do you think we have been away from our past for so long that we have become complacent?"

"No, I don't. We have always been careful and at this point in our lives, I don't think the odds are good that we will ever run into anyone or be recognized. We've been away for a long time. We worked on the Chicago accents and have kept ourselves fit and most importantly have kept our noses clean. We haven't even gotten a parking ticket since we ran."

"If there is something, I don't want to tip them off."

"Let's see how the game goes next week. If you still feel odd, we'll cool things with them for a while."

"That's fine, Murray, I don't want to seem overly cautious."

"No Estelle, you're right. We have managed to have a good life and this is not the time to get sloppy."

The ride home was quiet to say the least. Both Murray and Estelle were running the events of the day through their minds looking for anything that would indicate there was something amiss.

"There doesn't appear to be anyone following us. I have been checking since we left the course."

"We looked over our shoulders for years and I really don't want to go back to living that way again."

"Neither do I."

"Let's go to the range tomorrow. We haven't been there in six months or better. It's in our best interest to make sure we can both hit something if we are forced to. I'll get the guns out when we get home".

"Murray, I think we should keep the shotgun in the bedroom until we see where this is going."

"You're right, but I don't want to make it a habit. We have worked hard to have a real life."

Jack Harding, considered a top investigator, was tasked with finding John and Gloria Golden, however the assignment did not follow any normal procedures. He was told he would be working directly for a Special Agent Vincent Davidson, a man he had never heard of before at Homeland Security. When Jack asked his station chief, Inspector Murphy, about Special Agent Davidson, he was told orders had come down to him from the highest levels at the Justice Department and they were to cooperate fully. The day after Jack was given the assignment of tracking down John and Gloria Golden, he was in his office starting the process of reviewing the case files. They had been forwarded to him the night before when a man claiming to be Special Agent Vincent Davidson showed up unannounced, requesting to meet Agent Harding.

Jack was briefed by Special Agent Davidson at that meeting. He was told that the people he was looking for were 'terror suspects' from the mid 70's and that the government felt they still posed a credible threat to national security. Jack was prohibited from discussing the case with any of the other investigators he worked with all the way up through and including his superiors. He was to report only to Special Agent Davidson as the case progressed. When their meeting ended, the two men shook hands as a formality. Jack Harding watched Special Agent Vincent Davidson as he was walking down the hallway and thought to himself, 'that is the most coldblooded individual I have ever met.'

He reviewed the case files making a note that a 2005 ballistics comparison during a cold case review showed the gun that fired the bullets into the driver of the car found in the Goldens garage and the slug from the ceiling of their home in Darnestown MD was identical to the one used to kill a Martin and Nadine Bachman in Wheeling, Illinois several days earlier. They worked for the same company, but no connection could be made as to why the same hit team that had killed the Bachman's were found at John Golden's home seven-hundred miles away. And who did the killers work for? The deceased were handled as John Doe's and no identity was ever associated with either of them.

John Golden's military and work history were not consistent with terrorists. Neither was that of his wife who had a degree in finance and worked for an investment company. He made the decision not to give any pertinent information to Agent Davidson until he was able to determine who he really worked for and more importantly, what this whole case was all about.

Agent Harding forwarded his weekly reports to Agent Davidson for almost a year without ever giving any indication that he may have tracked down the Goldens. Jack had established a relationship with a young software developer several years prior and was using a revolutionary new recognition program he had developed. All his dealings with Bill Stanley were by direct contact and this day was no different.

"Bill, it looks like your program worked better than expected, it found the people I have been looking for. The various recognition and aging elements worked just the way you said they would."

"Thanks Jack, I'm glad I could help. Where do we go from here?"

"I have to file a report first and then I can let you know how we will proceed. In the meantime, under no circumstances should you discuss this with anyone. We'll talk soon."

"Lori were you able to get a tee time for this Saturday?"

"Yes, I did. We were able to get 10:00 a.m., will that work?"

"Yes, it will. I think it's time to have a talk with Murray and Estelle, they aren't fugitives in the strict sense and I need to find out what they have been hiding from for the last thirty-five years."

Saturday July 24th Murray and Estelle pulled up at the golf course to find Jack and Lori waiting for them inside the clubhouse.

"Murray, can Lori and Estelle go out as a twosome and we will follow them? We need to talk." As the two men rode along in the cart, Murray knew the jig was up.

"I'm guessing it's not about golf?"

"No, it's not." Murray took the upper hand immediately.

"Jack, the only thing I know about you for sure is who you don't work for, so please listen to what I have to say."

Inspector Jack Harding made a feeble attempt at playing dumb after being confronted with Murray Waxman's blunt statement.

"Murray, I don't understand?"

"Jack, what you do after today is up to you. Do you have a friend or neighbor that has a car you can borrow?"

"Yes, but what does that have to do with anything?"

"Maybe nothing as far as you and Lori are concerned, but it is more than likely life and death for Estelle and me. Have Lori borrow a car, park it at the closest busy supermarket to your home away from the front door. Go to the store after dark and park away from the borrowed car. Take jackets and baseball caps in a bag to the store and put them on when you go through the checkout. Take the borrowed car and meet us in the parking garage of the Luxor tonight at 10:00 p.m., on the third level along the southwest wall. Make sure you are not followed."

"Murray, what is this?"

"Jack, we're not stupid. Meet us tonight at Luxor and make sure your cell phones are turned off."

The two couples played as twosomes and left for home afterward. On the ride home, Murray and Estelle immediately began to formulate their plan.

"Murray, we have had thirty-five great years and I for one don't want it to end here."

"I don't either. We will meet with them tonight and get a lay of the land. If we have to run, we have our contingency."

"Do you think they work for Global?"

"No, not directly. If they did, I think they would have moved on us already."

"Who do you think he works for then?"

"I have no idea, but I think he suspects something and is being very cautious about just turning us in."

As they were pulling into the development, they took extra time to see if there was anyone surveilling their home or following them. When they were sure they were in the clear, they pulled up to their home, into the garage and began to prepare for the meeting. Estelle had become as meticulous a planner as Murray over the years and the two worked as though they read each other's minds.

"Murray, let's stop and have something light on the way down to the Luxor."

"Good idea, it will give us an opportunity to see if we're being followed."

"Are you going to take the roundabout way there tonight?"

"We'll leave right at dusk, work our way down, park at Excalibur and walk over to meet them."

"Don't forget hats and jackets."

At dusk, they left according to plan and drove around until they were sure they weren't being followed. They parked at Excalibur and were outside the parking garage at 9:00 p.m., waiting for the Harding's and watching to see if anyone suspicious followed them in. When they spotted them pulling in, they waited for a few minutes and made their way to the southwest corner of the garage. There, they found Jack and Lori in a borrowed car, a relief to Murray. Jack saw them and got out of the car.

"Murray, you seem to know what this is about."

"Yes, I do. More than you may think."

"What do you mean by that?"

"Let's all take a walk over to our car and we can talk when we get there. By the way did you check to see if anyone was following you?"

"Murray we are the 'police', but I think you already know that."

"You may think you are, but I can assure you that if the people I believe are running this investigation, you and Lori are in as much danger as we are, maybe more."

They walked to the lot at Excalibur, Jack got into the front with Murray while Estelle and Lori rode in the back. Murray drove out onto Tropicana headed west to the I-15 north ramp.

"Where are we headed Murray?"

"We are going to drive north maybe as far as Mesquite. It'll give us time to sort things out. You're not carrying any tracking devices, are you?"

"No, as a matter of fact, we made sure we were clean when we left the house."

"So, it appears you know who we are?"

"We believe you are John and Gloria Golden."

"You are right on that count."

"You aren't criminals. The bodies found at your home thirty-five years ago indicated that one man killed the other and was then killed by some kind of blunt force trauma, more than likely in self-defense."

"A baseball bat to be exact and it was self-defense."

"Why didn't you just call the police, you weren't in any trouble?"

"Because they were sent to kill us, and we needed time to get away."

Murray then related the entire story about the Bachman murders, his investigation and meeting with the EVP of Global Ltd. He described the similarities in the description of the killers and the men who showed up at his home.

"Disappearing was the only option we had. They would have had the police hold us until another hit team could be dispatched." Estelle went on to explain.

"We have followed Global over the years. They have done a masterful job of concealing what it is they really are. Little bits leak out now and then about their activities and whenever anyone blows a whistle they conveniently turn up dead from accidents, suicide, random murder or just go missing altogether."

Murray turned to Jack and asked,

"Do you work for Global?"

"No, I'm with Homeland Security."

"Then who is heading up this investigation?"

"His authorization comes from the top levels of the Justice Department."

"Who do you report to?"

"The agent we were told we have to work with and only him"

"Can you tell us his name?"

"Yes, Vincent Davidson. Have you ever heard of him?"

"No, we have been hiding for the last thirty-five years."

Murray thought it was time to ask the sixty-four-thousand-dollar question.

"Jack, have you told anyone you have identified Estelle and me?"

"No."

Murray openly breathed a sigh of relief while Estelle came out with, "Thank God."

Murray suggested they stop at one of the local bars along the road to make sure they were not being followed.

"There are a couple of redneck bars a few miles ahead that will be packed tonight. We won't have any problem staying out of plain sight. Jack, turn your cell on. We'll be able to see if they are tracking us."

At the Mustang Bar, Murray told Jack to turn his phone off. He pulled to the back of the overcrowded lot, backed in between two tricked-out lifted pickups making his sedan almost invisible and started his watch, while whispering,

"Slouch down in your seats. We're going to be here for a while. I don't have any intention of giving myself and my wife away until we have had time to talk."

They were sitting quietly and watching when twenty minutes into their wait a black SUV followed by two non-descript looking sedans slowly drove through the parking area. The vehicles stopped several times and they could see the drivers looking over the lot. On their last pass, Jack seemed to get anxious when the last sedan went by. All three vehicles turned out onto the highway and headed in the direction of I-15. Lori was the first to notice the change in her husband's demeanor.

"Jack, is there something wrong, did you see something?"

"I recognized one of the drivers from Homeland Security, and the sedans are ours." The statement caught Murray off guard.

"Those are your people?"

"No one knows about this operation other than me and my immediate supervisor."
"Did you recognize either of the other drivers, especially the one in the SUV?"

"He is Special Agent Vincent Davidson from the Justice Department."
Murray Waxman turned and looked at his wife of thirty-seven years sitting in the back and from her expression he knew he had to finish the conversation they had started earlier.

"What I know about Global is thirty-five years old, but I don't believe they have changed their methods one bit. Which is why I will say that your lives are in grave danger if you give us up."

"What are you suggesting?"

"I say, we see if we can get them to show their hands."

"And what if I say you are just proposing this to save your skin. What's in it for Lori and me?"

"If we are wrong, they kill me and Estelle which is what we believe they are out to do and you and Lori go on to live long happy lives. On the other hand, if we are right, they are going to kill me and Estelle, then take care of you and Lori in short order."

"It's not in their interest to kill Lori and me?"

"It is, if they don't want any witnesses. They leave no loose ends. Absolutely nothing can ever be traced back to them. They are literally untouchable."

"Murray how can anyone or a group for that matter be that ruthless?"

"I don't know. I can only speculate how long they have had this apparatus in place."

"Are you saying you want to try to bring them down?"

"Absolutely not. At this point I do not believe that is possible. I just want to go as I have been for the last thirty-some years."

"I still can't believe that anything like what you are describing even remotely exists. I need to take some time to think about what you've said."

"Jack, you saw your own people. What does that tell you?"

"I know, I know."

"Jack, as I said before, I'm willing to try to get them to show their hands. But we have to move quickly."

"Where are you suggesting we start?"

"First, we need to get hold of that recognition software. Do you think you can get it?"

"I'll call the developer."

Jack turned on his cell to make the call when Murray put his hand up.

"Wait, we have to get a handful of burner phones first. We are only a half hour out of Mesquite and we can pick them up there and start calling on the way back to Las Vegas."

"You're really serious, aren't you?"

"I'm serious about living."

The stop in Mesquite took less than half an hour. Jack, Lori, Murray and Estelle each purchased a phone with cash wearing baseball caps while keeping their heads down. The less they showed their faces, however poor the resolution on the security cameras, the better. On the ride back, Jack made the first call to Bill Stanley hoping to make arrangements to secure the recognition program, the phone rang twice.

"Hello, Inspector Harding?"

It wasn't Bill Stanley. Jack ended the call and opened the window, removed the battery from the phone and tossed it onto the shoulder of the road.

"Someone else answered the call and asked for me."

Murray didn't so much as flinch.

"I'm guessing he's dead. I wonder if they got the software from him?"

Murray had barely finished talking when Jack Harding's cell rang, it showed Bill Stanley.

"Bill, where are you?"

"I'm in my car on my way to St. George."

"I called your office. Someone answered and asked if it was me."

"What?"

"Did you talk to anyone and mention we were working together?"

"Absolutely not."

"Let me call you back."

Jack called Bill Stanley back using another of the burner phones.

"Bill, it's Jack Harding."

"Yes, Jack."

"My cell is probably being monitored and I'm guessing yours will be soon since they were in your office and you called my cell with yours. Where exactly are you?"

"About three miles from the Moapa truck stop."

"We can meet you there in fifteen minutes. Park out of the way in the lot. I'll find you. If anyone approaches your car drive off quickly. Turn your cell off as soon as we end this call."

"Murray, he probably has his laptop with him. I hope we are ahead of Davidson by enough to get the software."

The fifteen-minute drive seemed like an hour. When they finally pulled into the parking lot, Murray drove to the back and Jack spotted Bill Stanley.

"Wait here while I run over and talk to him. I have to give him enough information so hopefully he can avoid falling into Davidson's hands."

Bill Stanley was getting out of his car as Jack approached him.

"Jack, what is going on here?"

"I don't know for sure, but what I can say is that we are all in danger. Do you have the software program with you?"

"Yes, on my laptop."

"I'm going to have to ask you to let me have it. You are going to have to go away for a short time until this clears up."

"What do you mean by clears up?"

"This is much more involved than just locating a couple of people as I was led to believe."

"Do you know who is behind this?"

"No, not exactly, I only know that we are all in grave danger. Did you have business in St. George?"

"My girlfriend lives there."

"Can you stay there for a few days?"

"Sure."

"I am going to give you a phone and will call when I think it's safe to come back to Vegas."

Jack took the number for the third phone and handed it to Bill Stanley.

"Bill, you need to go straight to St. George. One last thing, this program you developed is a giant leap forward, but if it is used by the wrong people, it will not be used for the right purpose."

"You're asking me to destroy it?"

"No, I am asking you to sit on this until we can sort everything out. If the wrong people get their hands on it, they will be the only ones using it and you will be silenced in the process."

"You mean killed?"

"Precisely. Let that phone ring four times before you answer it. That way I'll know you're safe. One last thing, is your personal cell phone off?"

"Yes, it is."

"Get rid of it before you drive out onto the highway."

Bill handed over the laptop, got into his car and started back north on I-15 toward St. George. The foursome started making their way back to Las Vegas knowing full well that attempting to get Special Agent Davidson to 'show his hand' now was a waste of their precious time.

Bill Stanley was about ten miles south of Mesquite when he was pulled over by an unmarked Highway Patrol cruiser. Before he had a chance to show his license to the officer, a 9mm slug tore through the side of his skull killing him instantly. His body was shoved to the passenger side and his car was driven out into the Nevada desert where it was searched for the laptop now in the possession of Jack Harding.

On the drive back to Las Vegas, Jack's cell phone rang,

"Damn, I forgot to turn this off. We've been had. It's a 202-area code. It has to be Davidson."

He switched the phone off and was lowering the window to toss the cell phone when Murray stopped him.

"Hold on to the phone. I have an idea, Lori, is your phone turned off?"

"Yes, for some time now."

"Good, let's head south through Vegas to Whiskey Pete's on the state line. Estelle, here's my phone. Please shut both of ours off in about ten minutes. There's enough traffic on the road that they won't be able to connect Jack and Lori with us."

Jack seemed to know what was about to happen.

"What are you planning Murray?"

"When we get to the state line, we go to the truck stop first. Jack and Lori, you have to stay out of sight. Estelle, you are going to go into the station and buy a roll of duct tape."

Forty-five minutes later, Murray was taping Jack and Lori's cell phones under the rear bumper of a car. They heard the driver say he wanted to be in San Diego by 7:00 in the morning.

Jack was concerned about Bill Stanley's safety, even though he had innocently involved him in the investigation.

"Murray, I'm going to give Bill a call to make sure he got to Mesquite."

He called the third burner phone, it answered on the first ring.

"Jack is that you?"

It wasn't the voice of Bill Stanley. Jack knew he was dead.

It was time to head to the Waxman's and settle things up. Even though Jack was pleased that they had diverted Davidsons efforts for the time being, he was terribly concerned about their long-term prospects. No one said so much as a word all the way back to Murray and Estelle's until they had closed the garage door. Jack wasn't able to contain himself.

"Murray, you were right all along, but what are we going to do now? We can't hide here for the rest of our lives."

"Jack, we're all safe for the time being. Let's go inside where we can talk."

The four of them filed into the house and sat at the dining room table. The stress of being the hunted was starting to take its toll on Jack and Lori Harding. It was more evident to Estelle and she motioned to Murray with her hands.

"It's late and I know this whole thing is weighing very heavily on both of you. All I can tell you right now is that we have a plan. After we have all had a good night's rest, over breakfast, lunch and dinner Estelle and I will give you a full briefing on what you will have to do. Now, the guest room is on the right at the end of the hall. Get some sleep."

After the Harding's had shut the guest room door Murray and Estelle went to the opposite end of the house so they could talk.

"Estelle, I have something I have to take care of tonight."

"Murray, it's 1:00 a.m."

"I know but this has to be done to make the whole plan viable."

"Murray, you're not thirty-five anymore."

"I'll be fine. I'll be back as quickly as I can."

When Murray was sure their guests were settled in, he opened the garage door and drove off into the night. He had gotten Jack and Lori's address when they exchanged information for golf. He used a Las Vegas street map deciding not to take any chances with an internet connection and when he was close he parked several blocks from their house and walked up. He was dressed in dark sweats and looked like a local out for a late-night walk. As Murray rounded the corner, he spotted the same dark SUV that was at the bar earlier. The driver's window was open and there was a plume of smoke trailing out.

He put on nitrile gloves as he walked and when he was directly alongside and mere feet away, he pulled a knife from under his shirt, a gift from an old Marine veteran when he was leaving for his first tour and put the tip to the neck of Special Agent Vincent Davidson. So as not to have his voice recorded if Davidson was using any special equipment Murray whispered, "Do you have any connection to the two men I killed thirty-five years ago at my home in Darnestown?"

Vincent Davidson's expression was that of 'a deer in the headlights'? John Golden, former Army Ranger and combat veteran did what he was trained to do. He pushed the corpse to the side laying it over the console, wiped the blood off on the deceased's jacket and started the walk back to his car. As he walked, he put the knife back into the sheath, took off the gloves and put them in his pocket. One half hour later, Murray Waxman was pulling into his garage. Estelle was waiting up for him.

"Murray what happened?"

"I had to get Davidson out of the picture if there was any way for Jack and Lori to have any chance. He was watching their house on the off chance they would try to get home to put some things together to run."

"Do you think anyone may have seen you?"

"No, I was very careful."

"What do you think will happen now?"

"I'm guessing the same that happened before. No names, no publicity and a new assassin will be assigned to look for them and us, but it will buy them valuable time."

Murray felt no remorse for what he had done. These were the people who had destroyed their lives and would have killed them had they been given the chance. They all slept in as they should have after their previous day's excitement. When Jack and Lori woke at 8:00 a.m., it was to the smell of bacon cooking and coffee brewing. The four of them sat down to have breakfast.

"When Estelle and I ran, I bought two sets of identities as insurance in case we were ever found. Over the years, through our business, we showed salaries and paid into Social Security for both."

Jack and Lori were stunned by the announcement.

"You will both have to change your appearance, accents and mannerisms. Some very minor plastic surgery is a major plus and we can help with some of the funding."

Jack felt a certain amount of relief knowing it would be years before anyone would ever develop recognition software that even came close to what they had in their possession.

"We have a motorhome and think it would be a good idea if we all took a road trip. One, to get out of town for a few days, but more importantly, to find a suitable place for the two of you to settle. There're paper and pencils on the table. While we are having breakfast, please write down your sizes to include shoes, so we can get

new outfits for you. Remember, going forward, you must avoid any resemblance to your past. It won't be quite as simple as it was in 1975, but with modest and consistent effort you will be ok.
Today you start your new lives as Jim and Jill Gillette."

The EXIT

On Saturday evening October 15th, at precisely 7:00 p.m., the queue line for the buffet at the Sun Burst Casino in Las Vegas snaked well beyond its roped off confines. At one point, reaching half way around the casino floor. Standing in line was Fred Bockholt with his newly minted fifth 'wife', Layette. Married three hours earlier at the Chapel of Love; ceremony officiated by Leroy Burton, an Elvis tribute artist who for an extra fifty sang 'Can't help falling in love' with the aid of his well-used Karaoke machine.

The courtship began four days earlier at one of the casinos in old Las Vegas where the smell of old smoke and stale beer is so strong that you'll still taste it next Tuesday. Sixty-seven-year-old, Fred was completely love-struck when he laid eyes on Layette, a tall middle-aged bleached blond with enough red lipstick on to stripe a basketball court. In her overly revealing push up black mini dress, she passed by the Elvira slot machine, a favorite of Fred's because of the jiggling boobs, and in a low smooth sultry voice looking directly into Fred's eyes said,

"Cocktails?"

Fred, a slovenly overweight balding oaf whose trademark droplets of sweat dripping off the wrinkles in his thick brow gave the impression he suffered from a serious nervous disorder. He spent most of his time in the offices of the family business sorting through masses of internet porn traded back and forth with a small circle of perverse friends from childhood and acquaintance's he cultivated in chat rooms. Fred believed that anyone who invests in anything other than tangibles was an idiot which was why he had three quarters of his sizeable inheritance tied up in sports memorabilia. He stored his collection in a warehouse that was not secure and worse, not climate controlled. There were rumors within the family that Schuyler II, his father, had planned to name his youngest after himself until he became suspect of Fred being conceived by his mother and their butler. Oddly, whether the rumors were true or false, Fred shared many of the same contemptable traits displayed by his brothers.

By Fred and Layette's count, they were number fifteen to the cashier and four more to the hostess. It was just then that he noticed two faces from his past, faces he never thought he would ever see again, let alone in Las Vegas. They were being led past the anxious buffet goers into the dining area when in a very hurried voice he said,

"Layette move in front of me."

"Why Freddy?"

"Just move in front of me and stand still." The man glanced his way and smiled for just a split second causing him to turn away and try to duck behind his bride of four hours to avoid any further eye contact.

"Freddy, do you know that man and woman?"
Fred had a look of confusion and appeared to be talking to himself.

"It can't be them. That's what they looked like twenty-five years ago. She died from a drug overdose and he drank himself to death."

"Freddy, what's wrong? What are you talking about?"

"Nothing, nothing. I have to call my brothers right away. This can't be, as he repeated again and again. They're dead ringers."

"Dead ringers for who or what? Why are you talking to yourself?"

"It's nothing. I'll be right back I have to make a call."

Chicago Steel Fabricating, the largest specialty steel fabricating company in the Midwest in the fifties and sixties was rapidly fading into the sunset under the combined direction of the Bockholt brothers. Third generation management not even remotely possessing the talent of their grandfather and founder Schuyler Bockholt Sr.

The three brothers traveled to Las Vegas for their annual trip, a possible last hurrah, to the North American Steel Fabricators Show since they no longer had any salesmen to cheat out of their accounts. It was also the perfect time for Raymond and Howard, the two oldest, to swindle their younger brother of five years, Fred, out of his share of the business.

Raymond didn't answer so he frantically called his other brother knowing they would be together. He answered on the first ring.

"Howard, I need to talk to Raymond."

"Fred, he is with customers right now. Call back in an hour."

"Tell him I saw Phil Johnson and his wife."

"Fred, you are hallucinating. Phil Johnson and his wife are long dead."

"I saw them here at the Sun Burst."

"What are you doing at the Sun Burst? You didn't get married again did you?"

"As a matter of fact, I did, and if you recall, Raymond took care of my lodging."

"One of these days, Vera is going to find out."

"Only if one of you says something and besides, the marriages aren't legal anyway. Have Raymond call when he gets freed up."

"Have you been drinking?"

"No, I haven't. Just have him call."

Howard Bockholt, a witless dolt, lacking both talent and moral compass, driven only by greed and the relentless badgering of his social climbing shrew of a wife Constance. At one-point, Howard briefly struck out on his own and when he found out that he would have to actually work to make a living and came crawling back to the family business. Swallowed what little pride he possessed and was forced to beg his younger brother Raymond to take him back into the family business. As much as he wanted to, Howard couldn't leave without forfeiting the hefty monthly check from the family trust and the paltry salary dictated by his brother Raymond.

"Freddy, why did you have to leave me standing here in line to make that call. Was it more important than our first night as husband and wife?"

In Bockholt' world, lying is always easier than telling the truth.

"I had to call my brothers to let them know I won't be at a meeting they had planned for tonight. There won't be any more interruptions, I promise." At times the buffet lines in Vegas at seem like the wait will never end and just when it seemed like never ending was the order of the day, Fred and Layette found themselves next to be seated. The hostess approached them and asked for their receipt.

"Sir, would you like a table or booth?"

"Booth would be fine. Is that alright with you Layette?"

"Yes, it is Freddy."

"Then follow me please. You will be in that booth along the wall."
Fred Bockholt spotted the Johnsons and said,

"Do you have something in another part of the dining area?"

"I'm sorry. We are so full tonight, that is the best I can do for you."

"Layette honey, I know it will be a little tight, but can we both sit on the same side of the booth."

"Freddy, I didn't know you were such a romantic?"

"Sometimes, I surprise myself."

"Freddy, those people we saw being led in are two booths behind us."

"I know they are."

The guilty will generally go out of their way to avoid eye contact with someone they have wronged.

"They were looking at us and smiling when the hostess was showing us to our booth."

"I know Layette, I know."

The server approached the booth where Fred and Layette were seated.

"My name is Jean and I will be taking care of you this evening. What would you like to drink?"

Layette, not missing an opportunity to let anyone who would listen, took charge.

"Champagne please, we were just married."

"Well, congratulations."

And as relationships are sometimes in Las Vegas,

"Have you known each other long?"

"Oh, Freddy and I just met a few days ago, but it feels like we have known each other for years."

"That's so cute. Did you get the upgrade to include liquor?"

"Yes, we did. Freddy, can you show her the receipt?"

"Thank you, I'll get it for you right away."

"Layette, let's head up to the buffet,"

"Wait here Freddy. I'll get a plate of appetizers together for starters, ok?"

"Go ahead, I'll be right here."

While waiting for Layette, Fred was having a minor anxiety attack waiting for Raymond to call. When he felt what he knew was the firm grip of a man's hand on his shoulder, it instantly caused him to shudder as a chill ran down his spine. At the very moment the hand gripped him he could swear he heard the voice of Phil Johnson saying,

"I forgive you, Fred."

Fred sat motionless, eyes closed as a chill ran down his spine. Even though it only took a second it seemed like an eternity. He still felt the man's grip on his shoulder when he heard Layette's voice and opened his eyes.

"Well, how did I do?"

Fred spun around and saw no one behind him but Layette. The Johnsons' were seated at their booth eating and talking to one another. Layette noticed right away that there was something very wrong by the look on her new husband's face.

"Freddy, is there something wrong? You look like you have just seen a ghost."

"Layette, did you see a man standing next to me with his hand on my shoulder?"

"No Freddy, I didn't."

"Did you see anyone walking away? Specifically, that man in the booth over there, the one that smiled at me earlier."

"No, I didn't see him or anyone else. In fact, I have had my eyes on you since I left to go to the buffet line to make sure I wouldn't get lost and go to the wrong section."

In the short time Fred and Layette had known each other, Layette learned early on that the quickest way to calm Fred Bockholt down was to put a plate of food in front of him.

"Fred, look at all of the wonderful appetizers I put together for us. Let's enjoy these and then we can go up and get dinner."

Fred wasn't about to let a plate of food go to waste, but knew he had to call his brother.

"Layette, I have to run to the men's room and wash my hands. I'll be back in a minute."

"Alright Freddy, but don't take too long."

As Fred made his way through the casino he made the call to Raymond. The first call must have caused some alarm with his brothers because this one was answered on the first ring.

"Raymond, it's Fred. Did Howard tell you what I called about?

"Yes, and what you called about is impossible."

"Raymond, it's him. You need to see this."

Fred then went on to tell his brother the whole story about the hand on the shoulder and Phil

Johnson telling him he was forgiven. Raymond wasted no time telling his younger brother.

"You are hallucinating Fred. You're hysterical, you have to calm down. It can't be them the Johnson's are dead."

"Listen to me Fred. Do some checking and if you can find out what their names are and if it is them we will come over there right away."
Before setting out on his investigation, Fred and Layette sampled food from four different countries, six desserts, a bowl of ice cream and six champagne minis'.

"Freddy, can we gamble for a little while before we go back to our room?"

"Good idea, I need to let that meal settle a bit."
As they were getting up to leave, Layette saw the Johnsons.

"Freddy, those people you know, they are going out through that EXIT door in the corner."

"Let's follow them out Layette but let the door close first. I don't want to let them know we are following them."
As the door was closing, Fred noticed a soft golden glow around the door frame, not the usual harsh casino lighting.
Fred conveniently let Layette try to open the door.

"Freddy, the door seems to be locked."

"Here, let me try."
Fred pushed hard against the door even kicking it once for good measure.

"You're right it is. Layette, let me check with the hostess. Wait here and let me know if anyone else leaves through that door."
Luckily, the hostess was walking by from seating another table of guests.

"Miss, we tried to leave through the EXIT door back in the corner and it appears to be locked?"

"It is locked sir. The EXIT sign above the door isn't even lit."

"But we saw the two people who were in the booth next to the door go out that way and I would swear the light was lit."

"I don't see how that is possible. It's been locked as long as I've been working here."
And to placate a customer who more than likely had a little too much champagne with their dinner, the hostess said,

"I will check with the manager to see if the door is operational."

"By the way, do they come here often?"

"Oh yes, they come here every night for dinner right at 7:00 p.m."

"You wouldn't happen to know their names, would you?"

"Why yes I do. Their names are Phil and Leslie Johnson."
Fred believing, he had just scored an investigative coup gave the hostess his Bockholt best,

"Thank you so much for your help." And no tip.

Just ahead of the start of the evening's festivities, Fred had to call his older brother with the news. One more small lie to Layette and she would have his undivided attention for the rest of the night.

"Raymond, it's Fred."
And in a most annoyed sounding voice on the other end of the call the response was,

"I know Fred. What do you want?"

"I checked with the hostess and she said their names are Phil and Leslie Johnson."

"What, are you absolutely sure?"

"Yes, I'm sure."

"She told me they come here every night for dinner at 7:00 p.m."
There was a pause almost to the point that Fred thought the call may have dropped when Raymond came back on.

"Here's what I want you to do. You make sure you and your new wife are there tomorrow night. If they are there, call me right away,"

"Are you going to come over here if they are?"

"Yes, we will, but make sure they are there first."

"Ok, I'll do that."

As was always the case with the Bockholt's annual trip to Las Vegas, Raymond and Howard booked rooms at the top hotel casinos on the strip while Fred, more interested in indulging his whims and avoiding any possibility of being seen with one of his convention wives or anything else that could possibly get back to his wife, was always booked at off Strip hotel casinos far from prying eyes.

"Howard, Fred just called and said the couple he saw at the Sun Burst Casino were Phil and Leslie Johnson."

"He must be kidding."

"Fred isn't that inventive. He's called twice tonight and says he checked with the hostess and she told him they come for dinner every night."

"What do you want to do?"

"Nothing yet. Let Fred see if they are there tomorrow, if they are we'll figure something out then."

Raymond Bockholt, possessing a certain rodent like charm with a personality so disingenuous that he leaves most everyone he meets with the distinct impression they will be busy the next time he calls on them. If Raymond was able, he would without hesitation break the family trust and leave his brothers penniless. Their late father, Schuyler II, acutely aware of the personality flaws his sons possessed and at the behest of his wife, set up a trust so well written and so iron clad that years of Raymond's efforts and the hundreds of thousands of the company's monies wasted on law firms who claimed they could break it, yielded nothing.

Over dinner at one of the pricier steakhouses on the Las Vegas Strip, Raymond and Howard requested a booth in a back corner where it would be difficult for anyone to overhear them discussing the day's events and justifying how they were going to cut their younger brother out of his share of the business.

"Raymond, at the show today, I was notified by American Racking that they plan to move most of their steel fabrication off shore next year. Bob Hiller's non-compete expired this month and they are working with him and the manufacturing agents he developed a relationship with while he couldn't do business with them."

"Is there any way we can sue to stop him?"

"No, there isn't, I called the lawyers after I spoke to American Racking and they said we would be wasting our time."

"How much business did we do with them last year Howard?"

"About twenty million."

"Do we have anything in the pipeline to replace it?"

"No, we don't."

"Raymond, there's more."

"What do you mean by more?"

"The accounts we took from Larry Greenbaum when we fired him are all gravitating back to him at the new company he started."

"Howard, have you looked at his non-compete?"

"Yes, I have, and it expired this week. Between the major retailers and the warehousing companies, he'll probably do about twenty-five million."

"Do you think we can get any of it back?"

"We can't even get an appointment."

"Look Howard, I'll call the CEO at North American and several vice presidents whose names I got at the show today, at companies Greenbaum deals with."

"You know Raymond, your track record going around people isn't very good. In fact, it never works."

"Mind your own business Howard I'll do as I please."

"Raymond, we need to talk about Fred. With half of our business going out the door and nobody bringing in anything new, there is no time better than the present to finally get rid of that dead weight."

"What do you suggest?"

"I say we tell him he's going into sales. He's been our production manager for years and knows all the customers. If he doesn't cut it, which I'm sure he won't, we can shove him out the door."

"Howard, I'm surprised and impressed. You really have put some thought into this."

"I have Raymond, I don't want the family to think we outright screwed him even if we have."

"He is supposed to look for this man and woman that resemble Phil and Leslie Johnson tomorrow. Let him check the 7:00 p.m. dinner crowd. According to the restaurant people, they come in every night. If they show, we will run over there."

"He won't want to be embarrassed in front of his Vegas wife, so he will agree to being 'promoted' to sales."

Even though they had only known each other for a few days, they were getting on as though they had been married for years.

"Freddy, do I have time to run to the salon to get my hair done before we go to dinner?"

"I don't think so, it's 6:15 p.m., and we must be in line by 6:45 p.m. to make sure we see the Johnsons."

"Freddy, why don't you just go up and talk to them?"

"I can't do that Layette. This has to do with old business and it's best if I keep my distance."

"I don't understand Freddy. He looked right at you last night and smiled. That isn't what someone does if they don't want to talk to you."

"Just let me handle this my way. It has to do with old business."

"Alright Freddy."

At 6:30 p.m. the happy honeymooners started down to the lobby at the Sun Burst Hotel Casino for dinner at the buffet. They made their way to the queue line and started their watch for Phil and Leslie Johnson. Promptly at 7:00 p.m., Phil and Leslie walked past Freddy and Layette with the hostess. Phil looked directly at Freddy and smiled broadly as they were led back to the same booth they had occupied the night before. When it was their turn to be escorted back, they asked the hostess if they could have the same booth they had before.

"Layette, would you please sit across from me tonight? I enjoy looking at you."

"Freddy, that's so sweet of you to say that." Fred as usual had an ulterior motive.

"Layette, please take my phone and see if you can get a picture of them when they aren't looking this way. I need to send it to my brothers, so they will have proof positive that I know what I am talking about."

"Is that why you had me sit across from you Fred?"

"No, it's not. It just dawned on me that Raymond wants a picture."
Reluctantly Layette took the phone, waited for just the right moment, zoomed in slightly and got the shot Freddy requested.

"Here it is Freddy. I hope it is what you want." And handed him the phone.
At first Fred looked at the picture Layette had just taken and thought 'this dummy can't even get the right people'. then he took a second and looked over at the Johnsons, then a third look at the phone.

"Layette, they look older in the picture than they do sitting in the booth. They look like they did when they finally lost the last of the court fights with us."

"Could it be the lighting Freddy, and what do you mean by court fights?"
Fred handed the phone back to his Vegas wife.

"Layette look at the phone. It's not the lighting."
She was startled at how sad and broken they looked.
At that, Fred burst forth with an excuse trying to distance himself from the whole mess.

"I'm just in charge of production. I had nothing to do with destroying the Johnsons lives. I don't want anything more to do with this. Raymond and Howard are going to have to sort this out themselves."

"Fred, explain to me what this is all about. These aren't just two people your family had business dealings with that turned sour."

"I can't talk about it. I must send this over to Raymond and Howard right now."

Fred Bockholt sent the picture over to his brother Raymond, sat back in the booth and started to formulate a plan in his mind of how he was going to terminate his involvement and not anger his two brothers.

"Fred, what are we going to do?"

"Since we are already here, let's get something to eat and wait to hear from my brothers. Then, I think I may just tell them the truth that I don't want anything to do with this."

Raymond and Howard were in the middle of a meeting with the buyers from American Racking, attempting to offer them a bribe to get the business back, when Raymond's cell buzzed indicating that he had a text message. Holding the phone halfway under the table, he saw the image of Phil Johnson and his wife. Raymond gasped while simultaneously being told not only he, but all representatives from his company would never be welcome at American Racking again. As the buyers were leaving the meeting, Raymond handed his cell phone to Howard who was equally stunned by the image on the small screen.

"Raymond, what are we going to do?"

"I'm going to text Fred and let him know we will be there tomorrow night. I have to confirm this, and we can decide what we will do after that."

"I don't get it; this picture looks like Phil and Leslie at the last court appearance. Fred said he and his wife looked much younger at the Casino."

"I am texting him that we will be there tomorrow evening. We have to see if it's them." On their way to the buffet line, the text from Raymond came through.

"Layette, I just got a text back from Raymond. He and Howard are going to be here tomorrow night for dinner."

"Freddy, will I get to meet your brothers then?"

"I hope so."

"Aren't they going to have dinner with us?"

"I would think so, but I have to see what their plans are."

"Freddy, it seems awfully strange that they wouldn't want to meet your new wife."

"I'll talk to them tonight. I'm sure they will want to meet you."

Raymond looked at the picture a second, third and then fourth time. Each time, he felt little twinges of a feeling he had never experienced before, guilt. Howard did the same and was also struck with a similar feeling. Since they had not really adjusted to the time change and the events of the day had left the brothers stressed, they decided to turn in early. Neither Raymond or Howard was able to get a decent night's rest and at first, they thought it may have been something they ate; however, pangs of conscience have never been considered a food ingredient. Both were, for lack of a better term, being haunted by the images of the man and woman whose lives they had ruined.

Phil and Leslie Johnson owned a small specialty welding company that contracted with Chicago Steel Fabricating to manufacture welded parts. Raymond Bockholt had them sign a contract that he knew they would never be able to fulfill as written and subsequently ruined them. The Johnsons along with a long list of suppliers to the fabricator lost everything and ended up living in a broken-down old car. They did not have the resources to fight the brothers in court and it eventually led to a very sad ending for two very nice, decent people.

Howards cell rang at 3:00 a.m.,

"Raymond, do you have any idea what time it is?"

"Yes, I do, it's 3:00 in the morning."

"Are you having trouble sleeping?"

"Yes, I'm just trying to sit quietly and hopefully, that will be enough so I won't be falling asleep at the show tomorrow."

Raymond and Howard had an early breakfast and caught the monorail to the convention center. They arrived at their booth as the convention visitors were starting to fill the hall. The Bockholt brothers would take turns walking the show floor to see how much traffic the other fabricating companies' booths were getting. Everyone seemed to be busy except them, for some reason. They literally had no traffic all day.

Midway through the afternoon, with a steady stream of people passing their booth, Raymond spotted a couple that had a striking resemblance to Phil and Leslie Johnson before he ruined them. He told Howard he was going to run out for a minute and made his way through the crowd to get a better look at them. Almost as soon as Raymond disappeared into the crowd of convention goers, a young couple walked past the Chicago Steel Fabricating booth in the same direction his brother had just gone. The young man looked Howard's way and smiled. Howard turned as though he was shying away and didn't want any further eye contact. As quickly as they passed, they seemed to vanish leaving a rattled Howard Bockholt in their wake. Raymond returned after several minutes and told Howard what he had seen and that he could not find them. Howard told him about his sighting and couldn't understand why Raymond hadn't run into them on his way back. He should have walked right into them.

One would think that the Bockholt brothers had sprayed their booth with customer repellent. It appeared Raymond and Howard couldn't even pay anyone to come into their space that day, so they decided to close early and head out to the Sun Burst Casino to meet with Fred.

The drive from the convention center to the Sun Burst Casino gave the two brothers forty-five minutes to talk about their sightings of the Johnson lookalikes.

"Howard, I was in court a couple of years before Phil Johnson died and he looked bad, really bad. The alcohol and the stress of the court appearances had taken its toll. The last time I saw him, he looked like a feeble old man. I was told his wife looked equally bad. She died shortly after the suit was thrown out of court for the last time, from an overdose."

Raymond made a quick call to Fred and told him that he and his new 'wife' should get in line for the buffet and save places for them. They were on their way

Raymond and Howard Bockholt pulled up in front of one of the most glamorous shrines to gambling in all of Las Vegas, handed their car over to the valet and made their way into the casino looking for the buffet. They passed by row after row of slot machines, gaming tables and virtually every other gambling attraction known to mankind until finally arriving at the world-famous Sun Burst buffet with no sign of Fred and company.

"Howard it is still a little early. Let's look around and see if Fred is anywhere close by." At 6:00 p.m. Raymond and Howard spotted their younger brother Fred and his new bride at a roulette table.

"Howard let's hold back for a while, I don't want to be forced to carry on a conversation with them any longer than I have to. Let's head over to the other side of the casino and catch up to them when we spot them in line."

At 6:15 p.m., Fred and Layette started to walk to the buffet line knowing full well that they had a forty-five-minute wait ahead of them and Fred did not want to incur his brother Raymond's wrath if he was late.

"Freddy, when are your brothers going to be here? I'm already getting tired of waiting in line."

"They are very punctual. They will probably show up close to 7:00 p.m. when the Johnsons are supposed to be here."

"But that's forty-five minutes from now."

"Layette it is very important that we wait in line, I promise I'll make it up to you."

Raymond and Howard were playing slots in one of the far corners of the casino when they saw a couple that looked like the Johnsons walking past several rows of slot machines. The couple appeared to be smiling and looking directly at them.

"Howard is that who you saw at the show?"

"Yes, it is."

"Raymond are they the same ones you saw?"

"Yes, they are."

"Howard, we have to follow them. Don't let them see us, but don't let them get away."

The brothers cashed out and started making their way to the row they had observed the couple turning into. When they got there no one was playing on any of the machines in the entire row.

"I don't see how they covered that distance. We all but ran here."

At precisely 7:00 p.m., Raymond and Howard Bockholt were passing the line to the buffet when they both spotted Phil and Leslie Johnson being led into the dining area. Fred saw the Johnsons at the same time, looked over the crowd, saw his brothers and waved to them to join them in the line. The two brothers pushed and poked their way in typical Bockholt fashion treating everyone in line as though they were plantation help, who should have been clearing a path for their betters', until they reached Fred and Layette making them fourth from the cashier. Fred immediately made his introduction.

"Raymond, Howard, I would like to introduce you to my new wife, Layette."
And then the ever-courteous Raymond turned on the 'charm.'

"It's so nice to meet you. I apologize for not coming sooner, but we write the bulk of our business here each year and it was impossible to break away sooner."
Layette, having been around the block more times than she would care to admit, handled the insincere greeting with an equally phony smile and replied,

"It's so nice to finally meet you both. Freddy has told me so much about you."

So much for pleasantries. Fred pointed out the Johnsons to his brothers. Raymond was struck at their resemblance to Phil and Leslie Johnson but thought they were just lookalikes that coincidently had the same names. It would be impossible for it to be them. After all, they had both died. Howard was equally taken aback by the uncanny resemblance and proceeded to move close enough to whisper in Raymond's ear.

"It's impossible for it to be them, furthermore we concluded our business with them years ago. Why are we wasting our time here?"

"Howard, do you know if they had any children?"

"To the best of my knowledge, they didn't."

"I suggest we only play along with this until they finish dinner. I refuse to be intimidated and if this is some relatives of theirs who think they are going to get something from us, I am going to make sure they understand they are sorely mistaken."

It was the Bockholt's turn at the register. Fred and Layette presented their casino cards so the four of them could get 'the discount' and when the hostess came to guide them in, Raymond stepped forward.

"Miss, would you be able to find us a table near that couple in the booth along the wall?" Slipping her a ten-dollar bill as he talked.

"Oh, you mean the Johnsons. I think I can do that, wait here for just a minute while I make sure there is a table set up for you."

"Raymond, you don't need to pay for tables. They go out of their way to seat you where you like."

"Mind your own business Fred. I plan to get to the bottom of this tonight. We have other things to discuss after this issue has been dealt with."

"Like what?"

"We'll get to that when Howard and I are done."

When they had been shown to their table, Layette excused herself, so she could run to the women's restroom. After shaking hands with

Raymond and Howard, her first thought was to wash her hands before touching her dinner.
Layette was no longer in sight when Fred turned to his brother.

"Raymond, do you have to talk to me like I am one of your minions? You may get away with talking to our employees like that, but not to me. I'm a partner in the business."
As Raymond did on many occasions, he let his brothers know who was boss.

"I hold the majority stake in Chicago Steel Fabricators and neither you or Howard should ever lose sight of that."

"After dinner, Howard and I want to meet with you alone. Do you understand, alone?"

"Yes, I do, and what is this regarding?"

"We will discuss that when the three of us are alone. Here comes your new 'wife.' Here Layette, let me get your chair."
Howard was the first to notice the Johnsons returning from the buffet line with their dinner.

"Raymond, the Johnsons are on their way back. When do you want to confront them?"

"I think I will let them get comfortable first. Why don't we all go up to the buffet line."
Fred and Layette, without saying a word to each other, went to the opposite side that the brothers went toward so they could talk.

"Freddy is your brother going to make a scene with that nice looking young couple?"

"I don't know for sure. I think he wants to find out who they are and why they keep turning up at the same places as us."

"It is probably just coincidence. Las Vegas is a big town. They could be going to the same convention your company is at. You said they were in the same business you are."

"Yes, it probably is just that. The people they resemble were subcontractors of ours. Raymond and Howard had a contract written that they knew the Johnsons could never fulfill and when they were unable to, we didn't pay them and in effect put them out of business."

"Did they try to sue?"

"Yes, they did but my brothers' political contributions for a certain judges' re-election made sure they couldn't win."

From the tone of Fred's voice, it was simple to put two and two together.

"Fred, how many times has this happened over the years?"

Fred was totally consumed by the Johnsons at this point and just babbling to himself unable to answer.

"They look the same as they did twenty years ago. It is virtually impossible that they could look the same today. They were reported to have died miserable deaths."

"Fred, why didn't you tell me this before?"

"I had no part in this. I had nothing to do with ruining their lives. I don't want any part of this. Let's get dinner and get back to the table and don't let on that I have told you anything."

"Fred, what are you talking about?"

"When dinner is over, we need to get away from them."

"Alright Fred, but you are going to tell me everything when we are alone."

Fred being Fred knew he had said too much, but the break for dinner would give him a chance to come up with something that would pass for plausible.

Fred and Layette made their way back to their table and seated themselves with their backs to the Johnsons. They noticed on the way that they were already finishing their meal and looked like they were getting ready to leave. Raymond and Howard were on their way back when they first saw the exit sign in the corner flashing on and off. Then, they saw the Johnsons heading toward the exit. While working their way down the buffet, Raymond told his brother that he was going to openly confront these people to see what it was they were up to and he wanted to catch them before they disappeared again. When Raymond Bockholt saw them leaving, he turned to his brother,

"Just set our plates on the table, I don't want to let them get away."

They threw their dinners on the table, several items spilling off the plates almost landing in the laps of

Fred and Layette. Raymond, ordering them in his usual condescending way,

"Wait here until we get back. This will only take a few minutes."

In classic Bockholt style; Raymond led the charge across the dining room. Pushing and shoving anyone in their path out of the way, in a mad dash to catch the Johnsons as they exited. As they reached the exit, the light over the door was still flashing on and off and the door was about an inch from closing. Raymond hit the push bar on the door to make sure it did not close and lock. At the same instant he was forcing his way through he noticed a strange red glow coming from the open areas around the perimeter of the exit door. Fred and Layette looked on as it appeared that Raymond and Howard were being pulled through the door. When the two brothers were out of sight, the door slammed so hard that it briefly got the attention of all the guests from one end of the dining area to the other. The first thing Fred and Layette noticed was that the Exit light over the door was no longer lit.

The Johnsons were gone. Raymond and Howard were gone. Fred and Layette had been given instructions to stay put, so they decided to make the best of a tense situation. The 'newlyweds' made several trips to the buffet to include two to the dessert counter, at which point they were both full and bored stiff from waiting.

They were both becoming antsy when Fred made a command decision.

"Layette, I don't care what Raymond said. I'm tired of wasting my night sitting here. Let's go out to the casino and see if we can find them."

The sound produced by the door slamming was far more ominous on the other side than the banging noise in the dining area. In fact, it was the same as the clang or clunk produced by the door on a prison cell when slammed shut guaranteeing a positive lock.

The two brothers were not in the casino. They were in what appeared to be a very elegant busy hotel lobby similar to where they were staying on the Strip. A man in a perfectly fitted tailored business suit with jet black hair, dark piercing eyes, chiseled features and a penciled-on smile seemed to appear from nowhere and approached the Bockholt brothers.

"My name is Damon Bose. I am the concierge and I would like to personally welcome you."

Raymond interrupting as always took the lead.

"We are not guests. We're just trying to catch up with a couple of old friends, we followed them through that door behind us and it appears we lost sight of them. Their names are Phil and Leslie Johnson. Can you tell us what room they are in. We would like to give them a call."

Damon Bose appeared to be thinking for a few seconds when he answered,

"Mr. Bockholt, we have a Martha Johnson, Charles Johnson and Lyndon Johnson. We are anticipating the arrivals of George Johnson, Milton Johnson and Sarah Johnson sometime in the future, but, we have no guests here by the names of Phil and Leslie Johnson."

"They must be new. We followed them in here. Would you please check at the desk and how do you know our name is Bockholt?"

"It is my job to know everyone who checks in."

"But, we are not guests here. We're staying at the Grande Palacio on the Strip. Our suites are paid through the weekend."

At that, Damon Bose began to turn while waving them on.

"Please, follow me through the double doors on the other side of the lobby."
Raymond, finally sensing something very wrong, ran to the door they had come through, grabbed the handle, pulled it with all the strength he possessed, but the door would not budge. Mr. Bose called from across the lobby.

"Mr. Bockholt, that door cannot be opened. It is locked from the other side. Now please follow me."

Dutifully, Raymond and Howard followed Damon Bose through the double doors at the end of the lobby on into a large dimly lit room resembling a movie theater.

"Raymond take seat thirty-four and Howard take seat thirty-five in row H please."

As they made their way across the aisle to their seats, Howard noticed there was one empty at the end of the aisle next to the wall and began to wonder who would be occupying thirty-six. When they were seated, the theater seemed eerily quiet with the only exception being muffled cries and moans off in the distance, not loud enough to be distressing, but just enough to capture the brothers' attention. Howard had barely spoken a word to his brother since they had arrived in the theater when he finally in a very low voice almost a whisper said,

"Raymond, I have been giving this some thought since we got here. Don't you find it odd that the Johnsons Mr. Bose mentioned as guests here are all names of murderers, serial killers and one politician?"

It was approaching mid-night. Fred and Layette had been taking advantage of all the casino had to offer. Fred was on his fifth visit to the ATM machine when it dawned on him that he had exceeded the paltry verbal limit for withdrawals Raymond had given him on his company credit card. He swore to himself that was the last one for the night, made his way back to the roulette table and seated himself next to Layette. He had just bought another thousand dollars in chips from the croupier for himself and Layette when Phil and Leslie Johnson took two of the seats opposite them at the table. They purchased a modest two hundred dollars in chips, smiled at the newlyweds and proceeded to win every bet they made letting them all ride for the next hour. There was a crowd assembled to witness a winning streak unlike any other seen in the history of gaming at the Sun Burst.

Fred and Layette finally decided to call it a night and started back to their room. They had not seen his brothers since dinner and as far as he was concerned, if they wanted to talk to him, they would have to call. By the time they left, Fred had gone to the ATM three more times making his total withdrawals and losses for the evening somewhere just north of twenty-five thousand dollars.

The following morning, Fred woke to one of the worst hangovers of his life. A smoke-filled casino, bar liquor, gambling losses and age had all caught up with him at once. There was one other thing looming on the horizon for Fred Bockholt that day, it was time to head back to Chicago, alone. From the outset, he had told Layette he worked for Cleveland Metal Stamping, lived in Shaker Heights, and as far as she knew, his last name was Randall. Raymond and Howard were well aware of the charade and had gone along with it for years.

Fred had made an appointment at the Sun Burst Spa at 10:00 a.m. for Layette; hair, nails, body treatment and massage. In the four hours she would be there, Fred would pack up, drop his rental car at the airport and be half way back to Chicago, leaving not so much as a trace of who he really was or where he was from.

Fred hadn't heard from his brothers since the night before and began calling just after he had skipped out on Layette. He called Raymond first and got a, 'This number is no longer in service' response. He called a second time and then tried Howard's. The recorded message was the same. He took a call from the convention center and instructed them to have a crew take their booth down and crate it for the return trip to the storage facility in Chicago. Fred called the Grande Palacio Hotel & Casino, but there was no answer at either room. Since he did not want to chance being caught by Layette anywhere in Las Vegas, he left for home. On the flight, he wondered how many more times he could get away with the Vegas wife scam. This may have been the last, but a year is a long time and he had thought the same in the past.

Monday morning came and Fred was back in his office sorting first through some business-related emails and then on to a week's worth of internet porn. The Bockholts' may have been a lot of things, but one thing they never were, was late. It was so odd when neither of his brothers were in their offices promptly at 8:00 a.m. They so enjoyed watching to see if any of the staff were so much as a minute late, so they could descend upon

them like plantation bosses. This was the first time
Fred became concerned. He called their homes
and neither of their wives had heard from them.
Next he called the Grande Palacio and they hadn't
spent the night there and hadn't checked out. He
called the airline and they were not logged as
passengers on their scheduled return flight. Fred
called the Las Vegas Police to see if they had any
information, there was none. They had
disappeared so cleanly that there was no trace of
them. He filed a missing person report, so they
would at the very least check the security cameras
at the Sun Burst to get a possible time when they
were last seen. This would also prove to be
fruitless. The Bockholts' hired a private
investigator to look into the disappearance and
after a month finally gave up.

   None of the Bockholt children were
interested in taking over the business, since they
had all done nothing more than live off the 'Fat of
the Land' leaving all of them eminently
unqualified to run anything. Fred, owning a third
of the business, was given unanimous approval as
the new CEO. He proceeded, as the old saying
goes, 'To drive the bus into the river.'

   Layette for her part was more hurt than
heartbroken by Fred's sudden departure. He did
pay for the spa treatment, but she was still
determined to get her revenge. It was obvious that
her 'marriage' to Fred was a sham and if there was
any chance to get even, Layette had to start at the

very beginning at The Chapel of Love. Leroy Burton acted like he was taken aback when Layette showed up on his doorstep. Layette then set about explaining to Leroy what she was going to do to him in very graphic terms and that he had very little time to come clean. He told her everything including the names of the four other 'Mrs. Randall's.' Layette warned him that no harm would come to him as long as he did not tip Fred off about their meeting. She contacted the others, all aging cocktail waitresses, scattered from Las Vegas to Reno to Pahrump to Mesquite. To the last one, they admitted he wasn't their dream catch by any means, that they had some fun while it lasted, but were still very angry that they had been used and payback was in order. One of the 'girls' was friendly with a retired detective who with little effort provided the quintet with all of Fred's vital information. After that, it didn't take long before Layette contacted Vera Bockholt, Fred's real-life wife.

Vera Austin grew up in the same wealthy North Shore suburb of Chicago as Fred. Her parents were decent moral people and raised their daughter that way. They attended the same grammar and high schools although several years apart. The families knew each other, but never socialized, since the Austin's did not move in the same social circles. Fred began to pursue Vera during her junior year in college and they were married by the Archbishop himself shortly after

79

she graduated. At her bachelorette party, her maid of honor, Mary Jensen handed her keys to her family's summer home located on an island in northern Wisconsin. She begged her not to marry Fred and that she could stay in the summer home until everything settled down.

Fred and Vera had three children in rapid succession, killing any chance of her leaving. Once, she brought it up to Fred, but the threats and intimidation were so great that she never brought it up again. She stayed with Fred out of fear and consideration for their children. When they were all raised and on their own, she was in her mid-fifties and the prospect of starting over was less than appealing. The only way that could happen would be to catch him in an act that would produce a sizeable divorce settlement. She would have to bide her time. Vera was practical that way.

After the conversation with Layette, the two made plans for a showdown. The five fake wives booked cheap round-trip fares to Chicago and showed up on Fred's doorstep at 10:00 a.m. for coffee with Vera. After coffee, cookies and a little salacious conversation they all piled into her car and made their way to the offices of Chicago Specialty Steel.

Promptly at 12:00 p.m., as he did every day, Fred sat down to lunch at his desk. Two cans of Hormel chili with beans heated in the lunchroom microwave, leaving a mess for the employees to clean up that resembled the aftermath of a small explosive device. Vera parked in Howard's reserved spot, since Fred had taken Raymond's after the promotion. The six women walked into the lobby and Vera told the receptionist she was there to see Fred. Fred had just scooped up his first mouthful of chili and oyster crackers when he heard the receptionist say,

"Come right in Mrs. Bockholt. Mr. Bockholt is in his office having lunch."

His first thought was, 'I hope she makes it quick. I don't want my lunch to get cold'. Vera walked into the office first, followed by the five fake wives. The shock of being found out caused him to inhale with such force that he began choking on the mouthful of chili culminating in a massive heart attack. No amount of help would have done any good. As he lost consciousness he fell forward on to his desk, his face landing squarely in the oversize bowl of Hormel chili with beans. To add insult to injury, playing on Fred's chili splattered computer screen was pornography even the five fake wives had never seen or heard of in all their combined years around Las Vegas.

Layette, Candy, Misty, Charmaine and Tawny gave their deepest condolences to Vera for her loss and among themselves were satisfied with the payback. Vera was informed by the company's lawyer that there was a five-million-dollar life policy that Raymond and Howard had taken out on Fred with her as the third beneficiary after them. Six weeks after the 'Vegas' wives were back in their respective locals, they each received a thank you note for coming forward, an apology for the late Fred Bockholt's deception and a check for two-hundred-thousand dollars for their pain and suffering.

"Raymond, how long do you think we have been here?"

"I don't know for sure, maybe a few hours." Howard kept noticing the people in the rows around them filing out as soon as all the seats were filled.

"Raymond, I think the reason we have not moved is that we have this empty seat in our row. I wonder who it's for?"

What seemed like a moment later, they heard Mr. Damon Bose speaking to a new arrival.

"Please take seat thirty-six in row H please." To the brothers' amazement the new occupant pushing his way to the end of the aisle was Fred. As he always did, Raymond spoke first. "Fred, what is that mess all over the front of your shirt and what are you doing here?"

"Raymond, Howard, I don't know what I'm doing here. The last thing I remember is Vera and my five fake wives coming into my office and the mess is from the chili I have for lunch every day."

"Fred, what are you talking about, came into your office? We just left you last night at the Sun Burst?"

"Raymond, you and Howard don't know?"

"Don't know what?"

82

"You and Howard disappeared one year ago today. I was named CEO and have been presiding over the liquidation of the company's assets for the last three months."

Damon Bose literally appeared at the opposite end of aisle H.

"All souls in Aisle H, please rise and follow me single file toward the door marked EXIT."

As they approached the door, it began to open slowly. The screaming, crying and moans became louder and louder as the door opened wider. When the last soul had passed through the doorway, it slowly closed, and the EXIT light went out.

There was never a trace of Raymond or Howard found. The Las Vegas police scoured the desert around the valley to no avail. Vera had Fred cremated. She picked up the urn at the mortuary, took it home, opened it and dumped half of his ashes under the bird feeder in front of the large bay window in the kitchen. Then had the Doggie Doo contractor cap off the urn with fresh droppings from Claude, the family's English Bulldog. Who Fred despised and occasionally booted around because of the inferences that they bore a striking resemblance to one another. Vera resealed the urn and personally delivered it to the Bockholt family crypt at the Lord of Heaven cemetery on River Road in Des Plaines, Illinois for eternal interment.

The Waiter

"Can you move a little faster, please?"

"This is a delicate procedure, if the cuts are too deep, the tire will fail earlier than I have planned. If the cuts are too shallow, we have wasted our time."

"Why is this one so important that we must risk being caught in this busy hospital parking lot doing this in broad daylight?"

"Because you refuse to let up, I am going to relate a story from when I was in the seventh grade and hopefully, you will understand why this one is so important. We were at a local park for a school function when a friend of mine saw a girl who was probably five years older than us and very attractive as most teenage girls are. From the second he saw her he was smitten. I thought it would pass in a day or so, but it didn't. He obsessed over her throughout the rest of that school year and through the next.

This went on through high school. He would constantly bring up his dream girl to the point of it being almost nauseous. I heard he eventually took his own life and can only guess that this was the cause. From the time I spotted this woman, like my late friend, I have become more obsessed each day. Although, I highly doubt I would take my life and I will not be deprived of my pleasures. As a matter of fact, I plan on keeping her, part of her, for a while anyway."

At the offices of Colorado Western Construction in Rock Falls.

"Guys, Etta and I were in Chicago over the weekend and looked at several homes in a suburb called Arlington Heights. She grew up in that area and says we're a perfect fit for it."

Dave Weld, Ramon Hernandez, DeAndre Gleason and Ellen O'Hara, the soon to be new owner/partners of Colorado Western Construction, broke into hysterical laughter. Dave Weld the new CEO said, "Etta, maybe?"

"Ok, you're probably right, but I intend to give it my best effort."

Eliciting even more laughter from his co-workers.

"It's been a great ten years out here in the mountains even though it took seven for me and Etta to be accepted into small town America. The four of you helped make this business through hard work, showing up, providing the best quality workmanship and finishing the jobs on time. The partnership papers along with the five-year buyout agreement we talked about are at the lawyer's office.

I would like to push things ahead a little and surprise Etta. As far as she knows, I'm just thinking about retirement. I have a realtor coming out in the morning to list the house and already called the movers to come at the end of the week. I called the realtors in Arlington and my offer on the home she was crazy about was accepted."

While Joe was making the announcement, Etta Rox was making a call on the way to her retirement party.

"Karen, I'm on Hwy 84 just south of town and I should be there in about fifteen minutes. I got held up at the hospital. I think I said goodbye to everyone from the CEO to the greeters at the front entrance."

"That's ok Etta, take your time. The reservation is for twelve-thirty so there's plenty of time and we are all planning to be here for a few hours anyway."

"Alright, see you in a, oh my God, I've just had a blowout."

"Etta, are you alright? What's all that noise? Are you there?"

As the rumbling from the blowout subsided, she was able to answer.

"Yes, I'm here. I managed to stop and pull off on the shoulder, I am going to get out and look at the tire then call Joe and have him run out to help. I'm too damn tired to do it today and he still has fits if I do these things myself, old school."

"That's her truck. It's almost exactly where I told you it would be when I slit the tires."

"I don't see anyone. We must get there quickly to make sure she hasn't left and gone for help."

"Look, there she is in the cab. Start slowing down."

"Alright, alright, I'm going to slow down, so we can get a good look at her and stop treating me like an amateur this is the thirty seventh time we have done it this way!"

Etta Rox was unbuckling the seatbelt to get out and check the blown tire before calling when she noticed an older white SUV coming her way from the opposite direction. It appeared to be barely moving causing her to glance at it a second time, leaving her with an uneasy feeling. So much so that she opened the glove box and took out the 32-colt pocket pistol her grandfather had left her and slipped it into her purse, it was the one that she had told Joe a hundred times she didn't need.

It seemed like an eternity before the white SUV finally reached her. As their front bumpers were adjacent she noticed the driver's head starting to slowly turn to the left. There was an eerie, almost mechanical look to the way his head was turning at the same speed the SUV was moving and how it stopped as the SUV did. He was now looking directly at her through the open window. The stop was just long enough to make her uneasiness turn to outright fear. His half open predatory eyes and shark-like smile gave the distinct impression he was trying to peer into her soul. He was talking excitedly as he stopped the SUV, stuck his head partially out the window and appeared to sniff the air, followed with a long low echoing whisper, "Ahhhhh." It was though he had just captured the scent of his prey, then he started talking even faster to whoever or whatever was riding along.

The inventory process ended as fast as it had started. The white SUV accelerated rapidly heading north on Hwy 82.

"I'm going to get the other car."

"Don't do this, you're running the risk of being pulled over."

"Stop right there and don't start up again about my getting us caught. Must I remind you how many dozens of times we have done this and never left any loose ends. Besides, I need another look since I can't take her yet. Oh my God, she's absolutely perfect. How did we get so lucky?"

"We shouldn't be here. Your thinking that Aspen would be more cosmopolitan was completely off base. It's a world unto itself as is the surrounding area. Population has always been our cloak. We have always been able to blend in. Here being socially adept means nothing other than possibly getting a nice tip on a check."

"Enough of this. We're only going to be here for a short time. By the time these people catch on, we will be gone."

Etta started the call before the SUV had completely passed by keeping it in her rear-view mirror when he answered.

"Joe I just had a blowout on the truck and just as I was getting out to check it a white SUV pulled up alongside and the creepiest human I have ever seen was driving. He looked me over like I was going to be his dinner."

"Do not leave the cab of the truck. I will leave the office immediately and get there as fast as I can. Tell me exactly where you are."

"I am on Hwy 82 by the ranches on the southbound shoulder, five miles north of Carbondale."

"Stay in the truck, I'll be right there."

She made sure that the road behind her was clear, grabbed her purse and stepped out leaving the door open. She hugged the driver's side and made her way around the back. The right rear tire was shredded. She walked up the passenger side to see if there was any further damage, saw there wasn't, got back in the cab and locked the door. Maybe ten minutes or so had passed, but to her it seemed like hours with no traffic coming from either direction, when she caught a glimpse of movement and reflection in the rearview mirror. She saw what looked to be the distinctive front end of a black G Series Mercedes SUV coming up a small rise about fifteen hundred yards back.

For a second, she thought about trying to wave the Mercedes down, but Joe was on his way so asking for help wouldn't be necessary.

As the SUV was closing on her, she noticed that it appeared to be slowing down. When the vehicle arrived alongside, time came to a halt as she was engulfed in a cloud of stark terror. She looked through the open window on the passenger side of the Mercedes SUV into the eyes of the same driver that had passed her in the white SUV minutes before. His eyes appeared even more intense than the first passing and the smile more defined. His head moved quickly up and down as though affirming he had found what he was after and she could hear him rapidly repeating the word "Yes" over and over in a disturbing monotone voice. She grabbed a pen from the change tray and wrote down the plate number THNBRG on the palm of her hand as he began accelerating away. She dialed 911.

"I told you she's perfect."

"She's older."

"That means nothing, look at the way she carries herself."

"Then why don't you just take her now?"

"Because, I want to watch her for a few more days, I have preparations to make and there are others ahead of her. It's not open for any more discussion, so please stop nagging me!"

"We should get to the barn and cover this truck. The police will be looking for it very soon."

Her call went right through, "911, what is your emergency?"

"I have a flat on my truck and am on the southbound shoulder of Hwy 82, just south of Rock Falls."

"Have you been injured?"

"No, I haven't."

"Have you called a tow truck or anyone to help?"

"Yes, I have called for help,"

"Then ma'am, this doesn't sound like an emergency."

"I have just had a man pass by me twice talking to himself and staring at me like he would like to grab me."

"Has he made any advances toward you?"
"No, he hasn't."

"Well he may be a little strange but this still doesn't sound like an emergency."

"I do need to get some basic information from you though. Can I have your name?"

"Dr. Etta Rox that's spelled ROX."

"I'm sure everything will be just fine when your help arrives."

"Stop talking to me like I'm hysterical for just a second. This man pulled up first in an older white SUV and ten minutes later pulled up in a black G Series Mercedes license number THNBRG."

The operator asked, "Are you absolutely sure about the plate number?"

"Yes, I wrote it on the palm of my hand as it was pulling away and I can guarantee it was the same person who was driving the white SUV earlier."

There was a long pause and then. "Dr. Rox the police are on their way as we're talking. Lock the doors and do not leave the cab of your truck. Do not open the door for anyone other than a uniformed state patrol officer driving a marked vehicle. There will be three state police officers. I am not authorized to say anymore but can stay on the line with you until the police arrive if it would help?"

In a very courteous but curt voice, Etta Rox replied to her question, "Thank you, but it's not necessary." and ended the call.

Five minutes after the Mercedes SUV was no longer in sight, Joe Rox was pulling up behind his wife's disabled truck. He could see her sitting erect in the driver's seat and was relieved when their eyes met in the rearview mirror. He got out of his truck and walked up to the driver's door which she was opening when he got there. To break the tension as their eyes met, he said,

"Sweetie, you've always had a special way of attracting the real creepy ones."

She gave him a nervous smile.

"This one set a whole new standard on the creep scale Joe."

He knew this was serious business and all the joking was over. He walked to the back of the truck and started to remove the spare from under the bed. While lowering the tire, he noticed two thin parallel curved open slashes on the inside wall of the flat. He looked and there were similar slashes on the outside wall. He called his wife,

"Etta, come back here and look at this. This tire has been slashed on the inside and outside sidewalls with a tool of some kind. One of the slashes on the inside was where the tire blew. The other cuts are visible because of the flat these would not have been visible when the tire was inflated. It looks like you've been set up and singled out for something."

Etta gave her husband a brief rundown of the 911 call. Something didn't sound right.

"Let's see how this plays out when the police get here. Etta, stand by the side of the truck and look for anything that looks suspicious."

Joe was just getting the jack set under the truck frame when two Colorado Highway Patrol cruisers pulled up behind his truck. A third was arriving on the other side of the highway. All had their lights on. He was approached immediately by one of the patrolmen. "What is your business here sir?"

The second officer stood back several yards and off to the side giving him a clear view, both officers with the palms of their right hands squarely on the grips of their service pistols. In a very calm, but direct voice, Joe looked the police officer directly in the eyes and said,

"My business is with my wife who has had a blowout on her truck that needs to be changed." The third officer was exiting his vehicle with a pump shotgun in his right hand. Quickly crossing the highway, he quietly took up a position at the front of the disabled truck off on the passenger side which gave him a clear view of them and made sure the patrol officers were outside his field of fire.

The patrolman said in a mildly intimidating but polite tone, "Can I have your name sir, and do you have some identification?"

"My name is Joseph Rox."
At the same time slowly taking his wallet out of the left rear pocket of his work jeans. Sensing tension in the policeman's voice, he turned slightly toward the officer to make sure the patrolman knew he was only reaching for his wallet. He opened the wallet, slid his driver's license out of

the pocket by the edges and handed it to the patrol officer.

The patrolman then asked her name and if she had identification with her. "My name is Dr. Etta Rox and my license is in my purse on the seat in the truck."
She turned on her heel, walked back to the truck, got the license from her purse and brought it back to the officer intentionally leaving the purse with the gun in the cab. He took both of their licenses and as he turned to walk to his patrol car said,

"I'll be right back with your ID's."
Neither showed any emotion, but inside were aggravated by what they saw as a ridiculous low-key show of force. Within a few minutes, he came back and handed them their licenses and casually asked, "Where are you from?"

"Rock Falls."

"Before Rock Falls? Your accents give you away."

Joe quickly answered, "We're from the mid-west originally."

"Can you give me and my partner a description of the Mercedes you told the 911 operator about?"

"Yes, I can. It was a newer black G Series SUV. I know it's newer because it didn't have a mark on it. The license plate number was THNBRG. I wrote the letters on the palm of my left hand as it was driving off to the south,"

"Are you absolutely sure ma'am?"

"Yes, I am. Would you like to give me a breathalyzer or drug test me?"

"No ma'am. We just have to be very sure of the answers we get."

He continued his questioning. "What is your business out here today?"

"I am meeting a group of my friends at the Pour House in Carbondale for lunch to celebrate my retiring from Mountain View Hospital."

"Oh, you were a doctor at Mountain View? What department?"

"I was one of the ER doctors."

"I generally don't work this far north or I'm sure I would have met you before."

And then the second officer continued the questioning,

"Dr. Rox, it's very important that you come with us to Aspen to State Police Headquarters to look at some photos."

It didn't take a rocket scientist to figure out that there was way more to this state sponsored soap opera than the police were letting on to. Early on, Etta sensed that this was something very serious and decided to keep her answers as brief and benign as possible.

After the police failed to ask for a detailed description of the white SUV to see if there was any connection, not look at the blown tire and only show interest in the Mercedes SUV meant only one thing to Joseph Rox. Power players were involved and anyone outside of their realm would not receive the same treatment unless they had some value they were not being made aware of. Joe came to the immediate conclusion that no one was going to look out for them but themselves.

Without letting on as to how serious the situation was, the patrol officer made another request,

"Doctor, would you mind riding with one of us? That way, we can get you there while the image is still fresh in your mind?"

"I will never forget that face as long as I live, however, I would like to stay with my husband while he changes the tire, go to my retirement party and come in first thing in the morning. It's been a long day."

"I am sorry, but it is imperative that you come now. I'm not at liberty to discuss facts other than there may be lives at stake and finding this man or men is of the utmost importance."

Joe had been standing silently and took his que.

"Look, I'll finish changing the tire and we'll drop the other truck a couple miles up the road toward Aspen at a service station. It'll take about an hour for us to get there. We're both a little rattled and the ride will give us a few minutes to settle down a bit."

After a short conversation among the three state police officers and a call to their headquarters the decision was made not to press the issue any further, and asked,

"Can we help with the tire?"

"No, that's ok it will be done shortly."

"We are going to wait until you are rolling. Do you need directions to the police station?"

"No, we'll use the GPS and we'll be on our way directly."

On that hot Monday afternoon in August, the three state patrolmen, who had so strategically positioned themselves around the disabled truck didn't have so much as an inkling as to who they were really questioning. If they had their pistols would not have been holstered and the third man would not have been pointing his shotgun up in the air. But then again just three law enforcement officers wouldn't be nearly enough to handle the task of dealing with this man. Even Dr. Etta Rox, his wife, only knew him as Joseph Rox. Whose real name by birth was Guido Adami.

There was something unsettling about the directness of this man that set him apart from people the police normally encounter in similar tense situations. The lead patrolman thanked them for their cooperation and let them know everything would be ready to look at when they arrived at the state patrol headquarters. They excused themselves and began walking back to their cruisers. As the two patrolmen were walking to their cruisers, the lead officer asked,

"Did you get all their pertinent information?"

"Yes, I put in a request to run their names for anything that may connect them to the disappearance or any other criminal activity."

Disappearance, that is, of Mrs. Claire Thornburg, the owner of the black Mercedes AMG G65 SUV, heiress to the Thornburg copper mining fortune and one of Aspen's most prominent residents.

As soon as Joe had the tire changed, he called to Etta,

"Follow me to the service station up ahead. Don't call on your phone. If you have any problems with the truck, just flash your lights." It didn't require a lengthy explanation. They drove south on the big highway several miles to the service station on the west side of the road. Joe let the manager know they were leaving his truck and would be back in a few hours to pick it up. He got in the passenger side of her truck and said,

"There is something about this whole mess that isn't right. The police could have cared less about the white SUV. My guess is it belongs to another missing person, who I would bet is not listed in the social register. I don't know why this guy didn't try to grab you when he had the chance. Do you have that gun from your grandfather? I told you to keep in your truck?"

"Yes, I do. As a matter of fact, it's in my purse right now."

"We'll stick close together for the next few days. This isn't some local, this is something else. If it was a local, he would have done something like this before and the police would know him and had him right away."

"Joe, do you think the photo lineup will be a waste of time?"

"Yes, I do."

"Do you think we are suspects?"

"You better believe it, but hopefully cooperating now will get us cleared or at worst moved way down the list. Just remember, if whoever they are frantically looking for turns up dead and there isn't a ton of evidence, they will go out of their way to pin this on persons closest to it. I was in the office all day and you were at work until you started driving and had the flat. We have rock solid alibi's, but where something big is concerned they'll go out of their way to attach anyone they can to get a conviction."

While they were driving on a long sweeping right curve above the Roaring Forks River, Joe kept adjusting the rear-view mirror looking behind and above, then said,

"Etta, there is a police cruiser several hundred yards back and off to the right rear at about the same speed we are going and a helicopter about a thousand feet above the ground escorting us to Aspen. What does that tell you?"

As they were passing a big open pasture with a large white metal barn a few hundred yards off the road a white SUV sat just inside the entrance. A man was standing next to the SUV watching the truck drive south toward Aspen followed by the police cruiser followed by the police helicopter. Before the police reached the barn, the man laid the binoculars on the hood, walked casually to the sliding door and closed it eliminating any chance of being seen.

"We should have taken her when we had the chance."

"No, we are doing the right thing by waiting. Everything will settle down in a couple days. It doesn't matter that the woman we took today is very high profile out here."

"You're right moving around right now would get us caught and we need to see how the authorities set up their surveillance. Who knows if we are lucky, we may get a police officer or two before leaving town."

They arrived at the Aspen State Police facility within the one-hour window they had promised. In that time, the police had run their names and gathered their personal information. They even collected the vin numbers off both trucks, making sure they hadn't so much as an outstanding parking ticket.

Going over the information they had gotten the lead police officer was talking to his partner. "I was hoping we would have found something to hold them for. These people are about as clean as they come. She's been an ER doctor at Mountain

View in Rock Falls for the past ten years and was an ER doctor in the Dallas area before that. He started Colorado West Construction ten years ago and worked in the Dallas before that. Vietnam Vet, clean record from what we could gather, two grown children. We have nothing. I have requested an in-depth on both of them just to be sure."

Joe was politely asked to wait in one of their interrogation rooms while Etta was escorted to another where she was given a thick book of pictures to go over. The image of the driver was so etched in her mind that it only took about fifteen minutes to flip the pages, cover to cover.

When she had finished her exercise, Etta turned to the officer who was monitoring her progress,

"Officer, I have gone through all the pictures you gave me one by one and he is not here."

"Are you absolutely sure ma'am?"

"Yes, I am. There is not one picture in this book that resembles that man."

As Etta was leaving the interrogation room she was met by a state police captain.

"Mrs. Rox, I am Captain Cross. I apologize for any inconvenience, but we have to follow every lead we get and you have seen a man that is potentially a kidnapper and worse. We would appreciate it if you would call us if you ever see this man again. It is imperative that we speak to him. Here is my card with my personal cell number."

"I'll do that captain. It was nice meeting you."

While Joe was waiting two men entered his interrogation room. The first identified himself as Bruce Taylor, an agent with the Colorado Bureau of Investigation and the second as William Lampe, from the Denver office of the FBI. Joseph Rox was not a man to be rattled by much. Though he showed no emotion outwardly, inside he felt a strange uneasiness as he knew from his past, this investigation was moving to another level. The last person whose radar he wanted to show up on was an FBI agent's.

Upon their meeting, William Lampe sensed that there was more to Joseph Rox.

"Mr. Rox, I'm an old Chicago boy and if someone heard the two of us having a conversation, they would swear we were raised in the same neighborhood?"

"You're probably right. My dad was from Chicago and I was the one that managed to get the accent growing up. I was born in Chicago, but my family moved to Dallas when I very young."

"What was your father's name?"

"Joe, the same as mine and my son's."

"How old is your son?"

"He's thirty and before you ask, he lives in Chicago. He just started a new job with a large engineering firm there."

"Have you ever been in any trouble?"

"No, I haven't."

"How about military service?"

"Army, drafted in 68'."

"Did you make it to Vietnam?"

"Oh yes, twice as a matter of fact."

"What type of work did you do there?"

"Helicopter Pilot first tour, went to Ranger school when I got back, then Special Operations and was assigned to 5th Special Forces I got back in 72', spent two more years down south and was given an Honorable Discharge."

"Why did you and your wife come to Rock Falls of all places?"

"We wanted to try a little slower pace."

"And?"

"It's basically what we expected."

"What did you do in Dallas?"

"Ran a large construction company for some people."

"Can I get you a coffee, water?"

"No thanks. Are we almost done here?"

"Yes, but we may have to talk further. As I'm sure you can surmise this is a very serious situation."

"I understand."

"Your wife is in the lobby. You are free to go."

Bill Lampe looked at Bruce Taylor.

"This guy didn't have anything to do with this, but we need his wife to identify the guy and whether she likes it or not, use her for bait."

"Bill, why do you think he had nothing to do with it? You just talked to him for the first time."

"I have spoken to only one other man like him since I joined the Bureau. The tone of his voice, directness of his answers and the complete lack of fear tells me he didn't have anything to do with this. Here's some free advice, don't ever run into him in a dark alley."

When they were getting into the truck,

"Did you get a chance to call your girlfriends about being delayed?"

"Yes, I did. They asked if we could move it to Thursday evening for dinner. I said that would be fine."

"Good, then we are not rushed, so let's stop here in Aspen and get a five-dollar cup of coffee at one of their overpriced shops."

"Joe, you're not funny, but you are probably right. Look there's one on the corner."

They parked and started walking into the coffee shop.

"Who was talking to you in that interrogation room for so long?"

"An FBI Agent named William Lampe."

"What did he want?"

"Just asked one question after another trying to see if I had any connection to this case."

"When he was done, he said I was free to go. How about you and the pictures?"

"Nothing."

"Joe, why were you so quiet on the way here?"

"Because I think they are going to use you as bait for this guy and they want to be able to track your movement. I'm guessing we can find a GPS tracker if we take a good hard look when we get home. They may have even planted a listening device inside to monitor our conversations."

"Are you kidding?"

"No, I am not, there are orders being sent down to these people from high up. The FBI wouldn't be here this early in the investigation if that wasn't the case."

They finished their coffee and started driving back home, Joe seemed a little antsy.

"Joe, is there something else going on you seem distracted?"

"Yes, there is. I was going to surprise you, but with all that's going on, it's best that I tell you now. I need to concentrate on this nut job and whatever he is trying to pull off.

I signed all of the papers to sell the business to my guys this morning. I know we have talked retirement and moving."

Etta Rox was completely taken by surprise.

"Joe, that's great."

"There's more."

"What do you mean by more?"

"Well, I called the realtor in Arlington Heights, put an offer on that house you thought was perfect and it was accepted. Since it's going to be a cash deal and we're taking it as is. We can be in the house in a matter of weeks."

"Is that it Joe?"

"There's more. I also called the realtor in Rock Falls and they will be at the house in the morning to start the listing. We could have potentially kept it for a vacation home, but I have no real desire to come back here after we're gone. I'm looking at Colorado as been there done that. We had fun and did well."

"So, we can relax a little?"

"There's one last thing. I have the movers coming at the end of the week. Before you ask why I didn't talk to you first, well, I just made the decision to leave the company and now I want to get on my way as soon as possible."

"If it was anything else, I would probably throw a fit, but I'm as ready to go as you are. Let's get home and start packing."

Other than her life being in grave danger, Etta Rox was ecstatic about entering the next phase of their lives.

"When we followed her home before I slit her tire, I spotted a perfect location to observe her. Fate is on our side once again. She lives in an area that lends itself to taking another prize without disturbing any neighbors."

"Do you want to take her at her home?"

"Maybe but let's just observe for now. We will have to be very careful since there is no doubt the police will be watching too."

"Maybe we should hike in from behind tomorrow to see what the police are up to?"

"I think that's an excellent idea."

"We should take a drive out to Grand Junction tonight to get another vehicle. We have had these two long enough and need to get one that won't draw any attention to us."

"Then, go for a large very rare bar hamburger."

Agent Lampe appeared to be showing a particular interest in the investigation.

"Bruce, has the Highway Patrol checked every barn and out building along Hwy 84 from Rock Falls to Aspen?"

"Yes Bill, they have. They are also checking secondary roads now and will work their way to the dirt roads by sometime tomorrow. This area out here is vast and will end up taking resources from the state and local to cover it."

"I can't help that. My orders are coming from the top and this has to be carried out or heads will roll, personally I don't have a beef with Colorado it's a great place, but I don't know where they will send me next if this blows up in our faces. Bruce, I have to step outside and take this call, I'll be right back."

"Bill, this is Director DaCosta. Do any of the law enforcement agencies there have any knowledge of what this is really about?"

"No sir, they don't. As far as they know, this is about the abduction of the Thornburg woman and possibly one other person."

"I saw the report about some woman who he appears to be playing cat and mouse with?"

"That's true sir."

"What is your take on this whole thing?"

"Sir, we are in at the beginning of a cycle for the first time. I think there will be another victim tonight, but because of the small population out here he may travel some distance to do it. I'm against not saying anything, but if we alert the police in every locale he may bolt and we may never have an opportunity like this again."

"The woman, is she rattled? Is there any indication she knows what we are doing or any chance she may run?"

"Not that I can tell. Her husband could possibly pose a problem though."

"What about him?"

"Army, Vietnam two tours, Special Forces."

"He's an old man."

"But not the kind of old you might think."

"We ran his name. Did an in-depth. I interviewed him personally and he has all the right answers. He shouldn't."

"Do you think he has anything to do with the disappearance?"

"Absolutely not."

"Well, keep him under surveillance along with his wife and let me know if you find anything else about either of them that may shed some light on this investigation."

"Yes sir, I will."

One hour after dark, the white SUV pulled into a gravel parking lot on the west side of Grand Junction, Colorado. "Right there. 'The Roundup Bar,' that looks like a good-old redneck joint." "We should be able to slog up something in there,"

"It would be nice if we could get something we can drive for several days without it being reported missing or stolen, something we can use if we are forced to leave early."

"I think I have an old ball cap, tee shirt and jeans in the bag in the back that belonged to a truck driver in Boston that are a perfect fit. I'll look just like a local."

Edward Malcolm Calvert Jr. the only son of The Honorable Edward M. Calvert Sr., a man that treated any beneath his station who came before his bench with such scorn, as he handed down the maximum sentence allowed by Federal law, that those who assisted in his courtroom looked upon the convicted souls as victims themselves. His mother, Cynthia Winslow Calvert was one of the few remaining heirs to the Winslow petroleum and coal mining fortune. An attractive and decent woman of fine upbringing, she brought social standing, money and connections to the pairing. Edward was extremely bright and reputed to have an IQ in excess of 180, he was affectionately known as Ned by his family and his only two friends Charles Edwin Wittington and J. Robert Parker.

Ned was committed to the St. Dymphna Hospital on Long Island at the age of seventeen, a facility where families with vast resources and social status could be assured that their loved ones would be cared for in the most humane and gentile fashion. Taken into custody one warm August evening shortly after the beginning of his senior year at the prestigious Buckley Preparatory Academy. His only crime was that of turning in his father for the years of abuse he suffered at the hands of that predator.

Edward senior used his tremendous influence as a Federal Judge to quickly have his son declared legally insane, a danger to society as well as himself and had him placed in a locked ward. Unbeknownst to the Calvert family this confinement was the trigger for something more singularly evil than they could have ever imagined. Young Edward as it turned out, was a true Psychopath. On a bright note, two hours before the 'men in the white coats' arrived to wrap Ned in a sheet for transport to his new home, he gave the family a glimpse into who he really was. When he rendered the perverted jurist a veritable vegetable by bashing his skull in with a new five iron from the judge's own golf bag.

In his twelve years of residence at St. Dymphna, Edward studied theater, took voice lessons, obtained his bachelor's in finance and went on to complete the requirements for a law degree. Took industrial arts training in auto mechanics and an online course in Locksmithing of all things while maintaining a fitness regimen an Olympic athlete would envy. At the age of thirty, after cheeking his medication for days returned him to full strength and alertness, he strangled an orderly during his evening walk-through of the hospital gardens and disappeared into the night.

The following morning, his mother took a call on her personal line.

"Mother, it's Ned. Have you heard I left the home last night?"

"Yes dear, we were notified late last night."

"I am going to dictate my terms before you waste time trying to convince me I should return. The terms are not negotiable.

You will set up a special trust that will be administered by your own accountant, the one you have been carrying on an affair with for years. I will periodically give you account numbers and he will make deposits into those accounts. I am acutely aware of your obsession about being discrete, so I can assume you have already started the cover-up process for last night. Am I correct?"

"Yes, you are dear."

"Complete the process. I wish to become invisible. If you do not agree to these terms, I will slaughter what is left of the Calvert family. Your demise, in particular, will be very painful and slow. If you understand and agree to my terms, say yes Ned?"

"Yes Ned."

"Then, I suggest you move along quickly I will have an account number for you and Mr. Jamison shortly."

After their 'coffee break' in Aspen the Rox's went directly home. The dogs had been locked up in the house all day and needed to be let out for a run. The ride home gave them additional time to sort things out.

"Etta, I have been thinking and there are certain things we are going to have to do without exception."

"What are you talking about?"

"First off and most obviously, you cannot leave the house alone."

"That's obvious."

"I know, but we can't leave anything unsaid."

"Ok."

"I don't know how much they're going to try to hinder our movement and right now, they have no idea about the movers coming."

"How do you think they'll interpret that?"

"Whoever this is, he has shown that he is very patient, so us moving shouldn't have a lot of bearing on how fast they think he will make a move,"

"Do you think they may try to force us to stay here?"

"I don't know if they can actually do that and restricting our movement would scare him off for sure. But there is no doubt they will have us under surveillance twenty-four hours a day."

"Do you think they will want to place someone in the house with us?"

"No, it would be impossible to keep them hidden. They will have people off at a distance surveilling any movement. This is a very dangerous predator. He does not play with his prey. If I were to bet on whether this missing person or persons are alive or dead, I would bet the farm on dead. I have a strange feeling that the FED's have been after him for a long time. This is part of a pattern and the authorities think they have a real chance to solve this, at your expense."

"Well then, let's just go about the business of living our lives."

"There's an old friend I served with who may be able to shed some light on what's going on here. His name is Jim Nowicki. He was with the FBI and several other agencies. Even though he's probably retired, he might be able to help."

Joseph Rox went on an old military unit site, found his friend's contact information and made his call. "Jim Nowicki, who's calling please?"

"Jim, it's Joe Rox."

"Joe, my God it's great to hear your voice. How long it has been?"

"Too long my friend, too long."

"How have you been? Are you married? Do you have any children?"

"Etta and I have been married for thirty-five years. We live in Rock Falls Colorado. She is an ER doctor and have two children, boy and girl both great kids grown and on their own, how about you?"

"The same, married thirty-five years with two grown great children. You know sometimes I don't think I deserve the life I have for all we did way back."

"I know. I have felt the same way over the years."

"Jim, you can probably guess this isn't just a social call to catch up on old times."

"What can I do for you Joe?"

"Jim, let me tell you a little story and see if maybe you can shed a little light on things? Etta's truck was intentionally sabotaged."

"In what way?"

"Slit one of the rear tires with a tool of some kind that appears to have caused a timed blowout."

"She's alright?"

"Yes, she is. When she pulled off the road some guy passed by her twice in two different vehicles one was an older SUV and the other a new Mercedes SUV, but for some strange reason, didn't try to grab her."

"That's very odd and probably a first."

"You mean not grabbing her?"

"Yes, exactly."

"Are you familiar with this at all?"

"Yes, I am Joe. Are there any FBI agents working the case yet?"

"Yes. There is one so far."

"Do you know his name?"

"I was questioned by a William Lampe."

"I know him well, a fine agent."

"What can you tell me about this?"

"It appears to be a serial killer who is smart enough to have eluded us for ten years, kills in cycles. With DNA technology what it is today, we have plenty of that, but has never left so much as a partial fingerprint. Disguises himself like a stage performer. We have never gotten a clear look at him. We've had several suspects over the years, but nothing ever panned out. I have always thought he was being supported in some way by a well-heeled family, because he doesn't bother with the victim's cash or credit cards. Our profilers believe he does work though, occasionally, as a waiter in high end restaurants, but not necessarily on a regular basis. Possibly even exotic or luxury auto sales or repair. They think the only reason he works is to choose his victims."

"Where did he start and how many cycles has he had?"

"East coast and up to now, big towns from Boston to Miami, Atlanta and as far west as Dallas, eleven cycles. I wonder what he's doing out there? Your population is so thin. He's always worked urban areas. What are the authorities doing to protect your wife?"

"Nothing, just surveillance."

"I bet they are using her as bait although I can understand why. This guy has slipped through their nets eleven times as far as I know. How many people so far Joe?"

"Two from what I can guess."

"That's why the FBI. It's the beginning of a new cycle. You should be very careful."

"Jim, we are moving to the Chicago area. We had an offer accepted on a house there yesterday. I have a mover coming at the end of the week, we were going to stay at a hotel until the closing in a couple weeks."

"If you can get away without the police or FBI stopping you do so. It will force the killer to move, if he has some special interest in your wife. Be extremely cautious, this man if very smart.

When this is all over, why don't you two come out here for a visit. We have plenty of room and I have spent countless hours telling Mariel about our lives and times in another life. She would finally get to meet the man that saved her husband's life, so he could marry the love of his life."

"Jim, it's a promise as soon as this is over."

"Joe, if you meet him, do what you do best."

"You can rest assured I will."

When the call ended, he turned to his wife and said, "Etta, I am getting old."

"What do you mean?"

"It's pretty much what I thought, only worse. This has been going on for ten years or more and no one seems to be able to get a handle on it. In the past I would have gone right to worst case scenario. I apologize for not doing so right off. I put you at terrible risk."

"Joe, it's ok. You have been away from this kind of violence since your days in the Army."

"Close."

"What do you mean by close?"

"Well Jim and I worked for several government agencies after we were discharged up until just before we met."

"I have a vivid imagination, so I won't even bother to guess."

"Thanks."

"So, what do we do now Joe?"

"We prepare for whatever comes our way. When the moving truck pulls away at the end of the week, we will be right behind it. Let him chase us, it will be easier to get a look at him that way, same face different surroundings. Oh, and one more thing, if the FBI was not aware of the call I made to my old friend, he is likely on the phone with them right now. Jim was funneling some basic information to us and even though he is 'retired,' he still maintains some ties."

Everyone was about to be in the loop. Joe Rox had been given just enough information to allow him to protect himself and his wife.

"Bill, this is Jim Nowicki."

"Yes sir, what can I do for you?"

"I just finished a call with Joseph Rox, first time we have spoken in over thirty-five years."

"How would he know to call you?"

"We go way back. He knows I was FBI after we served together."

"How did the call go?"

"Couldn't have gone better. Let me bring you up to speed. I gave him a basic briefing on the case history. He has a mover coming at the end of the week. They are buying a home in the Chicago area. I advised him to leave if he can avoid being stopped by the police or FBI, which he will not. He knows this will give him a chance to pick out a face somewhere on the trip.

Bill, do you know Chief Inspector Hassman from the DC office?"

"Yes, good guy."

"Well, he's being sent to take over the Chicago office temporarily to cover the sudden retirement of their director. Make sure you contact him when Mr. & Mrs. Rox start their trip to Chicago and you will be going too. Follow them, but keep your distance and you will be the lead on the case when you get there."

"Does he suspect anything?"

"Bill, do you have any idea what you are dealing with here?"

"He's an old man."

"Bill, take it from this old man, Joe Rox has degrees of mental toughness, discipline and resolve unlike anyone I ever served with."

"Those are all admirable traits and I don't mean to sharp shoot, but can he protect himself and his wife if things go south?"

"Will it be enough if I tell you a lot of people to include me, are alive today because of the lethal skills he possesses. He has an uncanny ability to blend into the shadows like a ghost."

"You don't need to say anymore."

"We kept loose tabs on him for a number of years. That woman being targeted by this serial killer, she's the only thing he's ever loved in his life. She made him whole. Bill, if anyone crowds these people, our man will run and we may never get him."

"I understand maybe better than anyone."

"I'm having breakfast with the director in the morning. I think everything's going to work out just fine".

That she is the only thing he ever loved in his life is a pale understatement. Born in 1954 and named after the great Etta James, she grew up in the sixties during all the turmoil taking place throughout American society. The product of a broken home determined not to repeat the mistakes her mother made. Her choice of men would be the opposite of what she had been exposed to as a child. Left home at sixteen when her mother brought home another less than desirable. Started working doing odd jobs. Lied about her age at eighteen so she could work as a barmaid in one of the nightclubs on Rush Street in Chicago. One thing Etta couldn't escape though was inheriting the gene that didn't allow her to drink socially.

A friend asked her to go to an AA meeting one evening at a location she normally didn't attend. That night, a young man named Joe Rox was there to say goodbye to some friends. He was doing the exact opposite of what he should have been doing with his life, taking a mercenary job or as he put it, going back in the business. He spotted her in the doorway as they were all preparing to leave. She looked to be about twenty maybe twenty-one at best, blue flip-flops, tight faded jeans, a form fitting white tee shirt, short dark brunette hair, about five eight and a shape that wouldn't quit. When she finally looked his way, he peered into the darkest, kindest eyes he had ever seen. If it was possible that time could come to a screeching halt that night, it did.

When his call with Jim Nowicki was done, Agent Lampe wanted to make sure that everyone knew he was in charge. "Bruce, this is Bill Lampe. You need to get in touch with Captain Cross at the State Police and let him know there is to be no surveillance on the Rox home in Rock Falls. Make sure he lets the Rock Falls police know they are to stay away. He also needs to contact the Sheriffs of both McKinley and Pitkin counties and tell them absolutely no press conferences or leaks of any kind. Let them know if they do, we will resurrect the public relations nightmare that runs all the way back to the Ted Bundy escapes in 1977. They should continue their investigations, but do not interfere in their daily lives and before you ask, these are my orders."

"I'll take care of it right away Bill, thanks."

Agent William Lampe was a Yale graduate with a degree in political science, who the FBI recruited upon graduation. After several postings, he was transferred to the Washington office and assigned as one of the agents working on an investigation tagged 'The Waiter.' The waiter was profiled as a white male, highly intelligent, sophisticated, well-educated, able to blend into virtually any social environment and a meticulous planner. He started his killing spree with no special pattern starting in Boston, then New York, New Orleans, Memphis, Miami, Philadelphia, Richmond, Houston, Pittsburgh, Atlanta, Dallas and now Aspen. Because of the sporadic choice of locations and the speed at which he would sometimes take his victims, it was almost impossible to be present at the beginning of a killing cycle.

In the five years Bill Lampe worked the case, he almost made contact three times, three more times than anyone else, but it ultimately led to his demotion and transfer to the Denver office of the FBI working as a field agent. The move was purely political, done as usual to save the lackluster career of a very connected director who strangely was now unable to exert any influence.

One of Edward 'Ned' Calvert's greatest assets was that he never had to concern himself with the whereabouts of an accomplice.

"That was a good choice tonight. Her husband is an over the road truck driver who won't be home for at least a week. He doesn't bother calling, their marriage is all but over."

"Well, now it is."

"No relatives locally and if she is missed at the bar, it's not very likely that anyone will go looking for her."

"If someone does come looking, there won't be any smell coming from the house."

"Turning the temperature control on the refrigerator to coldest, when we stuffed the body inside, will insure that."

"We should get plenty of use out of this truck for the next few days."

"Good hamburgers out here in Grand Junction."

Before anyone could put surveillance in place, the state police were calling to make sure it didn't happen. "Rock Falls police department, how may I direct your call?"

"I would like to speak to the Chief. This is Captain Cross Colorado State Police."

"I'll transfer you right away Captain Cross."

"This is Chief Barlow, how can I help you?"

"Chief Barlow, this is Captain Cross, Colorado State Police."

"Yes Captain, what can I do for you today?"

"I'm sure you are aware of the Thornburg disappearance yesterday?"

"Yes, I have my people checking leads and possible locations where she may be."

"I have a request from my office. Your familiar with Joe and Etta Rox and the possible abduction of Mrs. Rox yesterday?"

"Yes, big construction company owner and she is an ER doctor here."

"Well, we don't want any surveillance operations run around or near their property."

"But, that's one of the most obvious places an abduction might take place."

"That's correct. The subject from all appearances is very smart and if he even thinks anyone is there he may run."

"Captain, my people are very well trained and I can guarantee they won't be seen."

"Chief Barlow, no one is to be on or around the property. I hope I have made myself clear?"

"You have Captain."

His next call was forty miles to the south.

"Pitkin County Sheriff, how can I direct your call?"

"I would like to speak to Sheriff Traxler, please. This is Captain Cross, Colorado State Police."

"Captain Cross, Sheriff Traxler here."

"Sheriff, you're aware of the investigation into the Thornburg disappearance yesterday?"

"Yes, my people are working the case here in Pitkin County."

"Sheriff, I'm calling to let you know there are to be no press conferences or leaks of any kind."

"But what if we find her or her abductor?"

"The likelihood of that is not good and any publicity will only hinder the efforts of a large group of law enforcement agencies involved in this."

"I'm the duly elected sheriff of this county and have an obligation to keep the people of Pitkin county informed."

"Sheriff, do we need to resurrect the public relations disasters of the past, all the way back to the escape of a certain serial killer back in 1977?"

"No, I get the message."

"I don't know how far up this goes, but I will warn you its way above the state level."

Last call of the morning. "McKinley County Sheriff, how can I direct your call?"

"Sheriff Lyman please. This is Captain Cross, Colorado State Police calling."

The operator asked him to hold while she located the sheriff before transferring the call.

"Captain Cross, what can I do for you today?"

"Sheriff, I'm calling about the Thornburg disappearance yesterday."

"Yes Captain, my people are working all of McKinley county following leads and locations."

"Sheriff, I'm calling to let you know there is to be no surveillance of either Mr. or Mrs. Rox, their property or in their general vicinity by you or your people."

"Captain, I already have the county tactical team in position at strategic locations around the

Rox property. If anyone even attempts to get close, my people will get them."

"That's just the point Sheriff. We believe this man is very smart and if he even thinks you have anyone out there, he will run and we may never find the Thornburg woman. You need to recall your team and anyone else out there immediately."

"Captain, I have a duty to the people of this county."

"And you will be doing them a far greater service by following our instructions."

"Alright, I'll order them off right away."

"Sheriff, there can be no press conferences or leaks either. If there are and it impacts this investigation, the famous serial killer escape will be one of the first issues revisited."

They decided they would ignore the two men in the tree line up on the hillside above their home.

"Etta, the movers will be here in a couple hours to give us a quote. I told them we want full service. Remember, we swore when we came out here we would never move ourselves again."

"So, you are saying its ok not to feel guilty about having someone pack for us?"

"That's right. Just don't leave anything incriminating lying around."

"Very funny."

"All we need to pack is whatever is necessary to get us by until we move into the house in Arlington Heights. I'll get the bags out of the locker in the garage."

As he was half way through the door to the garage,

"Joe, how much danger are we in here at the house?"

"Not a lot because of the dog. They will let us know if there is anyone out there, friend or foe, and they surely won't let anyone in the house unless we invite them in."

"How do you think the dogs will fare at the new house?"

"Just fine. They won't have the free run they had here but we're lucky we have a large yard and fenced gangways on both sides of the house. The basement windows are glass block, so anyone trying to enter will make a great deal of noise. The floor plan being open gives the dogs full run of the house, so if this guy is still around when we get there, I think we will be ok."

"I'm holding you to that."

"If anything happened to you I would only have the dogs to argue with."

Further up in the tree line and not visible to anyone down below, "Look they have dogs."

"Stay back here and don't move any closer."

"They don't look like we can do much with them. Who has a pair of giant Schnauzers anyway.'

"We would never be able to see them in the dark. We can't risk a confrontation with them and a dog bite would potentially be the end."

"Let's get back over the hillside. I don't want to leave the truck parked long enough to attract attention."

"Stop, I see two men in camouflage. Both are armed and sitting talking to each other like a couple of idiots. Why aren't they looking for someone?"

"Should we take them?"

"No, not right now. We will come back later when we look in on Mrs. Rox, her husband and their two dogs."

"Look, there's a car pulling into their drive with stick on door signs. Let's move a little higher above the police to our other viewing spot. I want to see what those signs say."

The sheriff decided he would remove the team he had in place on his timetable and with a little luck, might just get credit for catching the kidnapper. "Sheriff Lyman, there hasn't been any activity up here. We have to keep our distance because of their dogs."

"Are you set up to take someone down?"

"Yes sir, we are."

"Do you have your night vision gear with you?"

"Yes sir, operational run through tests will be conducted as soon as it's practical."

"Stay alert it's very important to get this guy if he shows, report anything you notice that looks suspicious, we have the rest of the team here ready to move out."

"Yes sir."

"Those are good watchdogs they won't let strangers approach the house unescorted when they are loose."

"Look at the signs on the car door, Mountain View Realty."

"I'll bet they are going to sell their home. I wonder why?"

"Let's see how long she stays, then get back to the truck and follow her."

"If everything goes our way tonight, we may get a realtor and a police surveillance team."

The dogs let Joe and Etta know that they had a visitor. They were both waiting outside as she got out of her car. "Mr. and Mrs. Rox, I'm Morgan Stevens from Mountain View Realty. It's so nice to meet you."

"You come highly recommended. Dave Weld at our company couldn't say enough nice things about you."

"Well, I appreciate that. I really do."

"I have brought some comps along today and they should give you a good idea of what your home is worth in today's market. Fortunately, the real estate market has come back quite well since 2008 and I believe we can get close to asking and possibly a little more."

"That sounds good. When do you think you can have it listed?"

"We have a pre-listing for one week to give local realtors a chance to see the property and then it goes into the multiple listing."

"We would like to have the house listed as soon as possible. When do you think you can have the contract ready to sign?"

"Normal lead time is a couple days."

"We would like to have everything here in the morning. You see, we have movers coming on Friday morning. We are buying a home in a suburb of Chicago."

"Oh, which one, I am originally from Park Ridge."

"Right next door, Arlington Heights."

"Great area, why Arlington if I may ask?"

"Etta is from that area and we decided to give it a try. Our son and daughter are also both going to be living close-by."

"We will be leaving when the movers are finished loading the trucks, so I hope you can understand why we are rushing a bit."

Then Etta said, "Our travel schedule may make it very difficult to reach us for a few days, but you can leave messages for either of us and one of us will get back to you."

"I can go back to the office, have everything drawn up tonight and be back here in the morning, say nine?"

"Will you be bringing the papers yourself?"

"Oh yes. I want to make sure you are comfortable with all the terms."

"We'll see you then."

"Joe, do you think we are being watched?"

"There's no doubt we're being watched. I just don't know by whom?"

"What do you mean?"

"I spotted two men up on the hill a while back, but don't know who they are with. The only thing I know is that they are not kidnappers."

"Why do you say that?"

"I think it's only one person and he's way to good at what he does to allow himself to be spotted. Also, I don't think the FBI is going to put a team out. They want this guy so bad they can taste it. He's been giving them fits for years and this is the closest they have ever gotten to him, so they will take extraordinary measures not to not to scare him off. The locals on the other hand think they have an abduction and they know about you, so they may put some of their people out there. It won't accomplish anything but putting their lives at risk. Keep that Colt with you even here in the house. I'll do the same. Regardless, we have the dogs, we're safe."

Morgan Stevens contacted several potential buyers on her way back to her office. She was even contemplating buying it for herself which was added motivation to get a signed contract from Joe and Etta Rox first thing in the morning. She was midway through filling out the papers when a truck pulled up in front of the building. 'What's that man getting out of that truck for. Can't he see the closed sign? I'll never get this contract done tonight if I have any interruptions.' "Sir, we are closed. There is no one here to help you right now."

"I can't hear you. What is it you're saying? Can you please speak up?"

"Ok, hold on. Let me open the door."

"I hate to bother you after hours, but I was held up by an accident on my way here from Denver. I just got into town. My name is Edward Harkness. I would like to purchase a residence here in Rock Falls as a weekend home. I will only be here through tomorrow morning and then I must get back to my ranch in Springfield, out in the southeast part of the state."

Like any good real estate sales person, always in pursuit of another potential sale. "Come in Mr. Harkness. Can I get you a bottle of water, coffee?"

Morgan Stevens should have adhered to company policy with regards to opening up shop after closing time. "We have a busy night ahead of us."

"She gave up information so easily. Let's dump the body in the river on our way to visit the lookouts up at the Rox property."

"Three in one day. When was the last time we did that?"

"I'll be famished by the time we're through. We should stop at that wonderful steakhouse along the river in town."

"Let's order the largest steak on the menu, au gratin potatoes, sautéed mushrooms and a chocolate sundae for dessert."

It was just before dark and the Sheriff still had his surveillance team in place.

"Base, negative activity up here. A couple bear, a half dozen elk and a moose moving through the property is all. We'll report back in thirty minutes, out."

"Quiet, over there on the hillside, I see them. They haven't moved since we left."

As he scanned the area around the house from his vantage point.

"Oh look, they have their luggage out. They will probably start packing in the morning. There's Mr. Rox already in his pajamas. Now, where's my Etta?"

"Look, look, she's in a nightgown. Oh my God, I think I am going to have her wear a beautiful red satin gown when I finally take her."

"We had better leave now. When the two lookouts don't report in, there will be police everywhere."

Thirty minutes later, there was no call from the team.

"Lookout, this is base come in. Lookout this is base come in."

"Sir, lookout is ten minutes overdue reporting."

"Let me try?" Lookout, this is Sheriff Lyman come in Sargent Harris, Sargent Tyler come in."

There was no response and that could only mean one thing.

"Get the team out there right away. There is something wrong."

As the Rox' were about to call it a night, they saw lights bobbing up and down in the night sky moving up their drive.

"Joe look, there are emergency vehicles coming up the drive."

"I'll get the dogs. They are going to be coming to the door in a few seconds."

A black SUV pulled up in front of their house, lights flashing, an officer in full tactical gear exited the vehicle and briskly walked to the front door.

"I'm lieutenant Wilcox, McKinley County Tactical Response Team. Have you heard or seen anything suspicious going on up here tonight?"

"No, we haven't. It's been very quiet. The dogs haven't even barked all night."

Another officer came to the door also in full response gear. "Excuse me for just a second sir, is there any access up on the hillside?"

"Yes, there is a rocky cattle path behind the barn. You'll need a four-wheel drive truck with plenty of clearance. There's also an old logging road that you can access from the highway and hike down from there. Why are you asking?"

"We have two personnel up there and we can't reach them."

"You know they're dead, don't you?"

"What makes you think they are dead?"

"You should not have put people out there."

"You're coming with us Mr. Rox. You apparently know something we don't, and we are going to get to the bottom of this now."

The call came over the radio.

"They found them sir. They have both had their throats slit, it's a mess."

"Get the Sheriff on the radio, now!"

Knowing the investigation was heading in the wrong direction, Lieutenant Wilcox of the special response team used his personal cell phone to contact Capt. Cross at the state police to brief him on the disaster. Following that call, Cross made his call to Agent Taylor, his contact.

"Agent Taylor, this is Captain Cross. McKinley County had two Tactical Response Team officers killed tonight on the Rox property. Sheriff Lyman has taken both Mr. and Mrs. Rox into custody. He even had animal control take their two dogs that moron could not have made a bigger mess of this investigation."

"Captain, I will call agent Lampe right away. You get over to Rock Falls and stop them in their tracks. We'll be there as soon as we can and if you must tell him, the FBI is on the way."

Agent Taylor was running to his car and calling Agent Lampe at the same time.

"Bill, this is Bruce Taylor. We have a real problem on our hands tonight. The McKinley County Sheriff put two men on the Rox property and they were both murdered. He took Mr. and Mrs. Rox into custody."

"I'm in Aspen and I'll leave right away. How soon can you get to Glenwood?"

"I'm in Eagle I can be there in less than thirty minutes."

"If you get there before me, get this under control. Do not let those idiots interrogate those people. Get them out of there."

"He even grabbed their dogs."

"Get them released with them. I'm moving now!"

At the Riverside Steakhouse.

"This is one of the best steaks I have ever had, and the sautéed mushrooms are to die for."

"The au gratin potatoes are a disappointment and only rate about three and a half stars."

"I can hardly wait for dessert."

"Look at all those emergency vehicles heading out over the bridge."

"They won't find the real estate lady until tomorrow morning at best."

"After desert, we should get back to the motel and pack I think it's best to leave tonight."

"There is a truck stop with a motel overlooking I-76 out near Julesburg, we can spot them and anyone else following behind them."

"No more talk about work, let's enjoy our dinner."

Joe and Etta Rox were brought to the sheriff's department and put into separate interrogation rooms. Sheriff Lyman planned to interrogate Joe first.

"Mr. Rox, you are going to tell me what you know about the murders of my two men."

"Where are you holding my wife Sheriff?"

"Your wife is being held in this building and that is all you need to know."

"No Sheriff, I want to see my wife and I want to see her now."

"Do you know who you are talking to Mr. Rox?"

"Yes Sheriff, I do. You are the man who has made the biggest mistake in his career."

"Are going to tell me what you know about this?"

A Sheriff's deputy entered the interrogation area and said, "Sheriff, there is an FBI agent in your office and he is demanding to see you immediately. There was also a call from Agent Taylor of the CBI and he will be here momentarily."

"Mr. Rox, you will give me what I want and you have my guarantee that I will get it."

"Sheriff Lyman you are a fool and you are responsible for the death of those two young men."

Wynton Lyman a politician using the office of Sheriff as a stepping stone to further his ambitious agenda and known for his huge ego and short temper, flew into a frenzy not for being told he was responsible for the men's deaths, but for being called a fool. The Sheriff's first blow glanced off the side of Joe Rox' head and the second connected with his cheek just below his right eye. Joseph Rox slid back in the chair hooking the heel of his left foot around the ankle of the Sheriff's left leg raising his right leg while turning his toe out, cross kicked and broke the Sheriff's knee.

The Sheriff fell to the floor letting out an agonizing yell. Joe lunged forward rotating his body to fall backside first, hands cuffed behind him, and landed squarely on top of the Sheriff. He grabbed the Sheriff's crotch in his right hand using his legs and right hand to push and drag the Sheriff across the floor of the interrogation room until he jammed his head against the wall, rendering him temporarily unconscious, while not releasing any pressure on his grip.

While the beating was being administered, FBI Agent William Lampe was making his way through the sheriff's department to the interrogation rooms.

"I'm Special Agent William Lampe of the FBI. I am taking charge of this investigation immediately. Get into that room and separate those two men now! Where is the Sheriff?"

"On the floor in the interrogation room sir."

"Let me in there. Mr. Rox are you alright?"

"Yes, I am, Agent Lampe."

"Would you please release the Sheriff, so I can help you up?"

"Lieutenant, what is he saying?"

"He thinks his knee is broken and appears to have sustained additional trauma."

"Get the handcuffs off this man and then call EMS. Was the camera on when this happened?"

"I don't believe so sir."

"Who gave the order to turn the camera off?"

"The Sheriff sir."

"This man is not a suspect in this investigation and never has been."

It was time for Joe to pipe in.

"They have my wife locked up somewhere in this building and God only knows what they did with my dogs."

"Get his wife right now. Call animal control and get his dogs over here immediately."

"Mr. Rox, would you please wait in the other room for just a minute? You three come in here and close the door."

With the Sheriff lying on the floor awaiting medical attention, Agent Lampe sat in the same chair Joe Rox had been seated on and looked directly at the sheriff.

"Sheriff, I know you are in a great deal of pain, so I will make this brief. The papers are going to report your handcuffing and beating an innocent man and since the three of you were witnesses to that beating, you will give testimony to that. You will then resign as Sheriff of McKinley County. Should any of you not agree to this, you will all be prosecuted to the maximum extent of the law. Am I understood?"

"Yes sir."

"Agent Lampe, agent Taylor from the CBI is here."

"Have him come down here."

It took Bruce Taylor less than a minute.

"Bruce, would you oversee this mess? I have to make a call and then I will bring you up to speed."

"Alright Bill."

It was after midnight in DC when the phone at his bedside rang. "This better be important Bill. It's the middle of the night here."

"It is Jim. The Sheriff here in McKinley county put two men on a surveillance detail at Joe Rox' place and they were both murdered. I'm presuming by our man. Then he took Rox, his wife and even his dogs into custody. While he was questioning him, he lost his temper and started beating him while his hands were handcuffed behind him."

"He what?"

"It appears Rox then broke his knee, spun around, dropped on top of the Sheriff, grabbed him and inflicted some serious trauma."

"Too bad he didn't finish the job. He must be getting soft in his old age."

"I have him on his way home with wife and dogs in tow."

"What about the Sheriff?"

"He's on his way to the hospital for a stay. I told him this was going to make the papers and his men have agreed to testify to the beating. I also told him he was going to resign as Sheriff."

"Good job Bill I have a couple contacts who will help ensure that this goof resigns, and that his political career is over."

"When do they move out?"

"Tomorrow, after the movers have them packed up."

"Keep me posted on any developments. I told you he possessed some unique skills."

"I'll keep you updated and sorry to bother you. I just wanted to make sure you were informed before your meeting with the director."

Joe and Etta were united within minutes.

"Joe what happened to your face?"

"It's nothing an ice pack won't help sweetheart."

"Who did that to you?"

"The Sheriff lost his temper. I guess he didn't care for my answers to his questions."

"Joe, did you get smart with him?"

"No, I told him the truth."

"Mr. Rox animal control is outside. They have your dogs."

"They'd better not have mishandled them?"

"No sir, but they are a little difficult."

" They are supposed to be. I'll come with you and get them."

"Thanks."

"You don't have to move. They will be fine, Sergeant, Pepper heel. Good dogs."

"Their names are Sergeant and Pepper?"

"I may not come across this way, but I do have a sense of humor."

Bill Lampe decided it was time to bring Bruce Taylor into the investigation to help ensure that there were no more foul-ups. "Bruce, I think you can see this is much bigger than a local problem."

"I can. What are you able tell me?"

"We have been chasing this guy for a long time. He is very smart and managed to stay one step ahead of every law enforcement agency in every jurisdiction he has ever operated in."

"How long has he been out there?"

"Over ten years, he's left DNA, but never so much as a print. This is the first time we have ever been at the beginning of his cycle. He has apparently targeted Dr. Rox and we believe he is just waiting for the right opportunity to grab her."

"What about Mr. Rox?"

"You saw what he did to the Sheriff with his hands cuffed?"

"But, he's an old man. He just got lucky."

"I said the same thing to a gentleman he worked with years ago. He's proving us wrong. He and his wife will be leaving Colorado sometime tomorrow and we need to make sure that no agencies associated with this state are anywhere near them."

"We can take care of that. I'll get on it right away. Bill, thanks for letting me know what's going on."

Agent Taylor chased down Captain Cross from the state police and asked him if he could make sure there were no more 'foul ups' in the handling of Joe and Etta Rox. "Mr. Rox, the state police are at your home right now. The locals searched the property after they took you into custody. We have all the items they confiscated."

"Thank you, Captain. For your own information, we had no idea what was going on outside. We were spending our time getting ready for the movers to arrive in the morning. If someone was in any proximity to the house, the dogs would have let us know. Could we get a ride home and then have a couple officers stick around long enough for me to check the property and make sure my vehicles haven't been tampered with while we were gone?"

"That won't be a problem."

"Thanks. I'll get my wife and the dogs."

On the ride home in a state police cruiser Joe and Etta were able to make some small talk.

"Etta, we need to get some rest. We have to be ready when the realtor and the movers get here in the morning."

"Is it safe to get back into my nightgown?"

"Only as long the Sheriff isn't released from the hospital."

"Joe, you're not funny. Did you have to do that to him?"

"I should have done worse."

After only several hours of sleep, they resumed packing for their move to the Chicago area. "Joe, it's 9:15. That realtor didn't seem like she has ever been late for anything in her life."

"I'll give her office a call right now."

"Mountain View Realty, how can we help you?"

"My name is Joe Rox. Morgan Stevens was supposed to be here with a contract at 9:00 a.m. can you tell me when we might expect her?"

"Mr. Rox, we just opened. Morgan's car was parked in front and the office door was unlocked. Your contract is on her computer screen and we're trying to locate her."

"You need to call the police right away."

"Pardon me?"

"You need to call the police right now. Ms. Stevens is more than likely dead. They need to initiate a search for her as soon as possible."

Joe abruptly ended the call. "Etta, he knows when we are leaving and where we are going. I'm calling Agent Lampe."

Bill Lampe was already following up with all of the local agencies to see if there was any more activity during the night when the call from Joseph Rox came in.

"Agent Lampe, I just spoke to the realtor's office in Rock Falls and was told the realtor who was coming to deliver our contract at 9:00 a.m. was missing. Her car is at the office and the door was unlocked all night."

"I'm on my way to Rock Falls right now. What is your schedule for leaving?"

"As soon as the movers finish packing."

"Keep me informed on your movement."

Bill Lampe arrived in Rock Falls forty-five minutes after his call with Joe Rox ended. He turned off I-70 and went directly to the sheriff's department looking for the acting Sheriff, he walked into the lobby area and went to the bullet proof glass covered desk, held his badge to the glass and announced to the desk officer that he wanted to see the acting Sheriff. His wait was less than a minute when a man opened a side door wearing captains bars and walked up to the FBI agent. "Agent Lampe, I am Don Caldwell, acting Sheriff,"

"Captain Caldwell, I want to make sure you are fully aware that the FBI has taken over the investigation regarding the disappearance of Mrs. Thornburg, your two deceased officers, the attempted abduction of Mrs. Rox and what looks to be the abduction and probable murder of a local realtor named Morgan Stevens?"

"Yes sir, we are."

"I want to be notified immediately of any developments. I will be out at the Rox home and then back here this afternoon. There will be four agents from the Denver office of the FBI here within the hour. I would appreciate your making some space for them. They will only be here for the day."

At 10:00 a.m., a pickup truck with New World Movers markings pulled up to Joe and Etta's home. The driver got out of the truck and walked to the door and rang the bell. He heard the dogs bark once, then silence and the door opened.

"Good morning, I'm looking for Mr. Rox?"

"That's me. You're the movers?"

"Yes, we are. I'm Cal Hammond from New World Movers."

"Tell me something, do you have anyone working with you today who is new?"

"No sir this is a crew we use whenever we do moves in this area."

"When will your truck be here with your crew?"

"They are on their way and should be here in just a few minutes."

"Thanks, come on in. It's all yours."

As the mover walked into the house he quickly noticed the two dogs sitting quietly behind the door. When he had walked by them, the dogs followed Joe outside. Joe took the dogs and made a quick pass around the house and out buildings before going back inside. Etta caught him as he was coming back inside.

"Joe, the movers want to know if you have anything that you don't want them to pack?"

"No, I have everything I need for the trip."

"I only have a couple things left to pack then we can put our bags in the truck."

"I made a point of asking if he had any new people working with him today and he said no, they are all familiar faces."

"It would be nice if we didn't have any more excitement at least for today."

Bill Lampe was just getting into his car for the trip out to the Rox residence when his cell rang. "Agent Lampe, this is Captain Caldwell. We found the Stevens woman just west of town floating in the river."

"I'm sorry to hear that."

"Have you had a chance to look at the body?"

"Yes, she appears to have been strangled and there are no indications of sexual assault."

"Do you have any idea how long the body has been in the water?"

"If I was to guess, I would say at least twelve hours."

"Thanks."

He ended the call and immediately put a call into Joe Rox. "Hello, this is Joe Rox."

"Mr. Rox this is agent Lampe."

"Yes sir."

"The McKinley County Sheriff's department found the Stevens woman in the river just west of town, she had been strangled and no indications of anything else. They said it looks like she had been in the water for at least twelve hours."

"Then he has a twelve-hour jump on us?"

"Yes, he does."

"We anticipate being packed up here around 4:00 p.m. and leaving shortly after the movers pull out. We will stay in Denver tonight and get on the road about 10:00 a.m. tomorrow. Right now, we're planning on staying in Kearney, Nebraska Saturday night. There's a Best Western and a great steakhouse just off I-80. We'll be calling ahead tomorrow to reserve a first-floor room. I don't want to rush. I would like to get a good look at this guy along the way."

"So would we."

"The realtor said they were planning on leaving today when the movers were through packing."

"That means they will probably stay in Denver overnight. Why don't we run back to Sterling tonight and create some chaos?"

"We should easily be able to get two and if we're lucky, we might get three."

"Whoever is shadowing them will have to drive ahead and show themselves because they will know who killed them."

"We'll place the bodies, so we can watch everything unfold."

When his call ended with Joe Rox, Bill Lampe had to place another call to DC.

"Jim Nowicki."

"Jim, its Bill Lampe."

"Yes Bill, more bad news?"

"Yes, he killed another person last night and it throws another wrench into the works."

"How so?"

"A realtor who was supposed to deliver a seller's contract to the Rox' at 9:00 a.m. today. Her car was found parked in front of her office the contract still on the computer screen and they estimate the body was in the river for at least twelve hours. Without a doubt, he now knows when and where they are going. I'm sure he has himself positioned somewhere along the highway between here and Chicago."

"What are you doing about surveillance?"

"I have four agents coming here from Denver to shadow them along their route. Any more than that and I'm afraid he will spot them and run. It could be years before we get another chance like this."

"Follow your instincts Bill and keep me informed."

"Yes sir."

At 4:30, the movers were finished, and the truck was pulling out of the drive when a car pulled up with Mountain View Realty signs on the doors. The person introduced himself as Mark Hogan, told them Morgan Stevens murder was a great loss and proceeded to present them with a sales contract for their home. Since they had intended to go with Mountain View, they signed the contract, shook hands with the realtor, gave him keys to the property and he was on his way. They took one last walk around the property with their dogs and headed back to their truck. "Etta, take your last look. It's been home for the last five years. A great place, but time to move on."

"Joe, are you glad to be going?"

"Yes, I am. It's a little slow for my liking and I would like to get back to a big town again."

"Do you think we will like it there?"

"I don't know. I hope we do."

"What if it doesn't work out?"

"Then, we move again and if necessary again until we land in the right place. More than anything, I want you to be happy."

"Thanks Joe."

"Bags in, dogs in, we got everything. Let's head for Denver. I let Tim and Dianne Wright know we were coming through tonight a while ago and they insisted we stay with them. We had better call Agent Lampe and let him know our plans. His number is on my favorites list Etta. Would you call him?"

It was as though Bill Lampe was waiting for their call, because he picked up on the first ring.

"Agent Lampe speaking."

"Yes sir, this is Etta and Joe Rox. We're on the road and want to let you know our itinerary."

"Go ahead Dr. Rox. We are on our way to Denver. We will be staying with an old army buddy of Joe's and his wife. He has garage space for us, so the car will not be on the street. We should be there around 8:30 this evening. Do you want the name and address?"

"Yes, I do. Go ahead."

"Tim Wright, 1212 36th St, Denver. This phone will be on while we are there and Joe or I will call when we are ready to leave in the morning."

"Thanks."

The trip to Denver was uneventful. Joe and Etta parked in the Wright's garage and the two couples had dinner in. The team of agents following them, along with Bill Lampe, all went to their respective homes for the night confident that they had not been followed by Edward Calvert. At 4:00 a.m. a call was placed to the cell phone of Bill Lampe.

"This better be important it's 4:00 a.m."

"Bill, this is Jack Mitchell from the detail. We have three people murdered in Sterling."

"How were they killed."

"All three strangled, two women and one man."

"Call Art Kay and Danny Urban. Have them get out there right away and work with the local police. Hopefully, there aren't any more. You and Rob Stuebner pick up the Rox' when they leave in the morning. Tell our people to stay in the background. He could very well be there looking the police presence over, since we're easy to spot."

The following morning at 10:00 a.m. Joe and Etta were packed up and getting ready to leave Denver.

"Tim, Dianne, Etta and I can't thank you enough for putting us up for the night. It was great seeing you again."

"Same here Joe. Be careful if there's anything I can help you with just call."

"Will do Tim. Let's get going before the dogs think this is their new home."

As they were starting the drive to Kearney, Etta called the FBI agent.

"Agent Lampe, this is Etta Rox. We are back on the road again."

"Dr. Rox, would it be possible to speak to your husband?"

"I'll put him on the speaker."

"Agent Lampe, what do you need?"

"Joe, there were three murders in Sterling last night. We believe it was our man and that he did it to get a look at whoever is tailing you. I don't want to put you at risk, but if we stay close, he is going to run or just kill in numbers that will force us to back away."

"It's alright. You have our itinerary. If you go on ahead you can probably get rooms on either side of us for tonight. We have our dogs and we are prepared for just about anything."

"Good luck, we'll see you there this evening."

When the call ended, Bill Lampe made his first call in of the day.

"Nowicki?"

"Jim, it's Bill Lampe. We had three more murders last night. This time in Sterling a small town in far eastern Colorado, two women and one man all strangled."

"Where is Joe and his wife?"

"They are just getting underway they stayed with old friends Tim and Dianne Wright in Denver last night."

"If we give close cover, I think this guy will up the ante."

"By that you mean?"

"He will kill in even larger numbers than last night. Rox says he's safe with his dogs as backup."

"If he says he's safe, take his word for it."

"Where is your next meeting?"

"Kearney, Nebraska at the Best Western. We will try to get adjoining rooms. I am sure he will be spotted on the road today and our man will want to stay close until an opportunity opens up for him."

"You're probably right. Be careful."

"Did you know his dogs names are Sergeant and Pepper?"

"I always used to say, hidden somewhere inside that dark personality was a sense of humor. Let me know as things develop?"

"I will sir."

Three and a half hours after leaving Denver, Joe, Etta and their dogs were driving past a motel overlooking I-76 on the outskirts of Julesburg, Colorado.

"An amateur could follow that truck with Colorado West Construction painted on the doors."

"Look, there she is barely visible through the tinted glass."

"There will probably be a tail close behind and a second ten to fifteen minutes behind. Let's wait for the second and then join in the chase."

"I'm getting tired being interfered with. I will not be deprived. If they keep this up, it's going to be difficult to take her before they reach Chicago."

"A large distraction may just give us an opening. When they stop for lunch we will need to get new transportation. How do you think we would look in a semi-truck?"

Three and a half hours into the drive to Kearney, it was time for a break. "Joe, can we stop for lunch there's a truck stop ahead and the dogs need a quick walk."

"Good idea, I should have said something earlier, but I've been preoccupied with this killer and forgot about you and the dogs. We need gas anyway. Let me park in front, so I can keep the restroom entrances in sight through the front window. You go in and when you are here with the dogs, I'll go."

Etta was back in minutes and then Joe went in while she waited in the truck. When Joe was back, they took the dogs for a quick walk before deciding on lunch. "Joe, let's have lunch here. I'd like to spend a few minutes sitting on something other than a truck seat all day, and the restaurant here actually looks like a decent one."

"Good idea. I'll move the truck over where we can keep an eye on it from the restaurant. I'll call now to let Agent Lampe know where and what we're doing."

"Agent Lampe, this is Joe Rox."

"Yes Joe."

"We are pulling off at a truck stop in Ogallala."

"One of our cars is about a mile behind you and will follow you in."

"We are going to stop for lunch. They have a decent looking sit-down place here and it may give us our first look."

"My men will stay out of sight, but will be close-by."

"I'll call if we see anything suspicious."

Edward Malcolm Calvert was enjoying the chaotic nature of this cycle. His normal method was to snatch up his victims, dispose of them as quickly as possible and when his hunger was satisfied, vanish until his desires moved him to start another cycle. He had made the two agents sent to Sterling, Colorado, so avoiding them was a

166

simple task. Not wanting to expose himself, he chose to pull into one truck stop after another until he spotted their truck parked in front of the restaurant in Ogallala. "That is their truck parked over there with the dogs in back. I can see him inside in the restaurant."

"She's not at the table, probably in the women's restroom."

"She should be back shortly. It's time to get rid of this pickup truck. Our next ride is one of those trucks idling out there in the parking lot."

"There was a bunch of highway wrecks off to the side as we were driving in. There are tools behind the seat. We can remove the license plates and use a screwdriver to pop the VIN number off the dash. That will slow identification by a couple days if they haven't found the woman in the refrigerator yet?"

It took him less than five minutes to park, remove the plates and VIN number. Dressed in the flannel shirt, jeans and a ball cap worn in Grand Junction, he fit right in as he walked over to the terminal. "Look, the tail cars are both filling up. They must have just finished their meal?"

"One of the FBI agents is coming this way. If he uses the men's restroom, he is going to become our next big distraction."

On her way back to the table, she stopped to buy a couple cold sodas for the drive. As Etta was walking to the checkout, she saw him. Left the drinks and went straight to the table where Joe was waiting,

"Etta, I paid the bill, what's wrong?"

"We have to leave Joe. He's here."

"What do you mean?"

"I saw a man walk out of the men's room and out the door. As he was rounding the corner he looked back. I caught a glimpse of his eyes, it's him."

"Come with me and don't leave my side. I'll call as we walk."

Bill Lampe's cell rang. "Agent Lampe, my wife says she spotted your man walk out the door less than a minute ago."

"We are coming as fast as we can. Stay on the line, I have another call."

"Lampe."

"This is Art Kay; Agent Urban is dead."

"What?"

"Agent Urban is dead. He is in the men's room here at the truck stop, his body is in a rear stall and it looks like he's been strangled."

"Art, get outside and get to the Rox' truck."

He immediately switched calls. "Mr. Rox, this is agent Lampe. One of our agents has been murdered in the men's restroom at the truck stop. Get into your truck. One of my men is on his way from inside the building."

Bill Lampe called Jack Mitchell in the fourth car on the radio.

"Jack, get the state police to the truck stop in Ogallala. This madman just murdered Danny Urban. They need to lockdown this facility. I want to match a driver with every car and truck in this lot."

With the body of his eleventh victim packed neatly away in the sleeper of the Semi truck he had just acquired, 'Ned' Calvert was heading east on I-80,

"Our five-minute head start is more than enough lead time. By the time they get enough law enforcement here to close this place down, we will be ten miles down the interstate."

"They will be there all-night questioning travelers and trying to find out who killed their agent."

"We need to get to the next truck stop and change trucks. I intend to do this at least two more times in the next hour."

"We're lucky there are so many of these along I-80 here in Nebraska."

"It appears that Kearney has the best lodging. I am going to guess that my Etta Rox and her husband will spend the night there."

"They won't risk driving after dark, not after what we just did. This makes me feel so alive."

A call was made to Jim Nowicki detailing the murder of Agent Danny Urban in the restroom of the truck stop. Agent Lampe let him know that the state police were there, that they had the exits blocked so no one could leave. They were checking video of all vehicles that left the stop before it closed. The Highway Patrol was checking up on them, but that could take all night.

"Bill, he will probably change vehicles at least one more time if not more and if he is using large trucks, there isn't enough manpower to catch him."

"What do you suggest?"

"I'll call Joe Rox myself. I believe I may be the only person who can get him to do what needs to be done."

"And that is?"

"Stop this massacre of innocent people and finish this once and for all. I will get in touch with him and get back to you."

They were driving along not saying a word, both of them needed some time to make some kind of sense of what was going on, when Joe's phone rang.

"This is Joe."

"Joe, it's Jim. Are you driving right now?"

"Of all people, you know exactly what I'm doing. We should be in Kearney in about an hour. What do you need?"

"We need to talk about this situation and we need to do it now. Can you pull off the road?"

"Yes, there's a sign for a truck stop just ahead."

"Please call as soon as you get there."

They found a parking space where they could watch both trucks and cars coming and going and when they were comfortable he called.

"Joe, this whole thing is getting out of hand."

"I know it is, but we are potential victims?"

"We have nine dead that we know of in the last three days including the FBI agent today. He is doing everything he can to draw attention away from you and Etta, so he can grab her."

"Stop right there. I know where this is going. I will not have my wife used like bait on a hook only to have her taken from under your noses. She doesn't deserve that and I don't deserve that either. She's all I have."

"Joe, please talk to her before making a final decision. God knows we can't force you to do this, but we cannot continue to let this maniac slaughter innocent people."

"I know Jim. I know."

"Is she close by?"

"Yes, she is in the truck with the dogs. I'll talk to her and call back when we're done."

"Thanks Joe."

He took a few minutes to gather up his thoughts before getting back into the truck to talk to his wife.

"Joe, what did your friend want. You look upset?"

"He made a request and we have to talk it over."

"What does he want?"

"He wants to use you as bait. Not like they meant when this started, but basically leave you in the open with minimal protection. At least nine people have died at the hands of this monster in the last three days and the FBI believes he is doing this almost like extortion. He won't stop until you are essentially handed over to him."

"That's insane. No one could be that vile?"

"I think that's exactly what he is doing."

"Joe, in your heart of hearts, can you let this continue to happen?"

"No, I can't."

"And neither can I."

"But putting you at risk is a decision I cannot make and the possibility of you coming to any harm is something I can't comprehend. You are my life."

"Joe, if you watch over me like you have since we met, everything will work out the way it is supposed to."

"I'll call Jim back."

Jim Nowicki was sitting in his office waiting for a return call trying to get a read on his old friend when his phone rang.

"Jim, we discussed your problem and we will work with you. However, I have to be directly involved or it won't happen. We have to be absolutely clear on that."

"We're very clear Joe."

"It is going to be done my way or no way."

"What is you plan?"

"I suggest you and your people keep your distance. If there are any parallel roads, use those, I will give regular status reports on short intervals if my wife spots him again. I will try to get an eye on him at the same time. We have reservations at the Best Western in Kearney tonight. I requested a first-floor room not adjoining. I suggest that you get someone there as soon as possible.

'We're already moving in that direction."

"You will need to have the desk change our reservation to an adjoining room. That way you can get my wife set up with a tracking device in the event something happens."

"We can do that Joe."

"Do not have any of your vehicles on the premises. I have no doubt he can spot them coming and going,"

"There won't be any."

"I'll call when we get to Kearney and we're in the room."

"Joe, you don't sound like you are taking any chances."

"Sweetheart, I'm not anywhere close to done. Make sure whenever we stop you scan the areas constantly in the event he shows. I need to get a look at him."

At another truck stop several more miles down the road. "Look at that woman pounding on the door of the truck we just left."

"From her appearance she's a prostitute I think they call them lot lizards?"

"Our first stroke of bad luck with these trucks. I will bet that truck driver was a regular customer of hers. I figured we would have at least a five-hour separation by just leaving it at idle and making it seem as though he was sleeping before driving on."

"I wonder if taking her would cause any alarm?"

"Let's swing around and take her. Prostitutes come and go so no one will call the authorities if one is not around."

"Look for a pimp. If she has one he will be close by. Over there another woman is handing cash to the man in that car. That has to be him."

"Do you think the authorities would show some gratitude if we were to eliminate that pariah?"

"You're such a bad boy."

"As soon as we are finished here, I think it's time we change our method of transportation. Omaha has an airport, Amtrak station and bus station. We can spend a couple days in Chicago, then go to take a look at the Rox' new residence."

"We will pick them up in a matter of a few days if we just sit and watch. We can get new supplies when we get there. Several days at a decent hotel would be nice for a change."

They followed all of Joe's instructions and had none of their vehicles parked in the hotel lot. One hour after their call ended, they were parking in front of the Best Western in Kearney. The FBI was already there and had the room assignment changed so they had an adjoining room.

They took the dogs for a quick walk and went to their room. The dogs automatically went to the door of the adjoining room and growled. There was a knock from the other side,

"Mr. Rox are you in there?"

"Yes we are. Come in."

The agent opened the door slowly having heard the two dogs and seemed relieved when they were both sitting on the other side of the room. He proceeded to introduce himself,

"I'm Agent Kay."

"Agent Kay, we were very sorry to hear about your agent being killed earlier today."

"Thank you. We had worked together for several years. He was a good man. We have the tracking device you requested for Dr. Rox. She can attach this to any part of her body and we can get an accurate fix on her indoors or out. The unit is switched on and we would suggest you wear it when you leave here in the morning. It has a four-week battery life and we are leaving you with a box of adhesive applicators. Mr. Rox, agent Lampe requested we provide a locator for you as well."

"Please tell agent Lampe I appreciate his concern, but that won't be necessary. Tell him I won't be far from my wife."

"It's remarkable those dogs don't move or make a sound."

"They do if they are told to. We will be leaving after breakfast in the morning, they start serving at 6:00 a.m. we expect to be driving by 7:30 a.m."

"Yes sir."

Edward Malcolm Calvert strayed from large metropolitan areas for the first time. After initiating the current cycle, he knew the only way to avoid being caught was to leave a trail of human destruction, creating the opening he needed to reach the safety of a big city. As the night wore on, the police were continuing their search of truck stops and rest areas when Bill Lampe's cell rang.

"Agent Lampe, this is Jack Mitchell. We just received a report that two prostitutes and what we think is their pimp were found in a car at a truck stop this side of North Platte."

"Is there any indication as to how they were killed and how long they have been dead?"

"It looks like they were strangled and they appear to have been dead four to six hours."

"Jack, call in and make sure they are checking videos and all of the trucks in the lot. If they are idling, knock on the door until you get a response. He bought himself a bunch of time. That's what he did."

He ended the call and went right to another of his agents.

"Agent Stuebner."

"Rob, this is Bill Lampe."

"Yes sir."

"Start checking the airlines out of Omaha as well as trains and buses to Chicago. He may be changing his mode of transportation again. He must show an ID to get on a flight but not necessarily for trains and buses. He's not quitting and heading back east. When you check with the airlines, if there is a passenger bound for Chicago with an eastern U.S. ID, he could be our man."

"I'll get on it right away."

It was approaching midnight. Everyone involved in the chase was spent and needed at least a few hours sleep if they were going to be able to match wits with their serial killer. At 5:00 a.m. central time, Bill Lampe's cell rang, he answered and before he could speak,

"Bill, it's Jim Nowicki, how is the investigation going?"

"The Rox' are at the hotel in Kearney and have met with our team in the adjoining room. There were three more killed last night, two prostitutes and their pimp east of North Platte. It fits his MO and was done to buy more time. I have all available forms of commercial transportation being checked."

"Bill, do you think he is on one?"

"I don't know for sure, but it's imperative that we check every method of transportation he can use. He made a huge mistake leaving the big cities and I think he is making a course correction as we speak."

"Bill, our people were safe last night."

"But when they reach Chicago, they are in his world."

"So he thinks, that's where we are finally going to end this."

"I am going to leave for Omaha now and should be in Chicago early in the afternoon. I will check in with Rick Hassman when we are through and bring him up to speed so we can be ready when I get there."

"Familiarize yourself with Arlington Heights as soon as you get there. It's upscale but very urban with lots of places to hide and observe."

Joe and Etta were up at 5:30 a.m., cleaned up, walked the dogs and were finishing breakfast at 7:00 a.m. "Decent breakfast, let's go back to the room, feed the dogs and be on our way I see no reason why we can't drive all the way into Chicago tonight."

Joe, I'll call the realtor while we're driving. I'm sure she will have numbers for several nice pet friendly motels right near the new house. Besides, I want to thank her for working so hard on our behalf. Do you think he's following us?"

"Hard to say. There was an article in the Omaha paper this morning about two prostitutes and their pimp being murdered at a truck stop just west of here and there was also a truck driver found dead in his truck. I say they are all related and that your guy did it."

"Please don't refer to him as my guy. I feel so bad that so many innocent people have died because of me."

"Etta, this man is insane. You have no fault in this. If it wasn't you, it would be someone else. Remember, very few if any would allow themselves to be put in the position you are in."

"Joe, do you think he's close-by?"

"No, I think he may have gone directly to Chicago and is going to wait for us there. That's why everything was so quiet last night."

"After I talk to the realtor, I will see what I can reserve for about ten days. I would have suggested staying at Joe Jr.'s, but he can't come near us and vice versa until this is over."

"We will have a phone conversation with him when we get into town."

Edward Calvert walked onto the 5:41 Amtrak with a group traveling to Chicago to ensure he raised no suspicion. He took a seat in coach, clipped his ticket on the seat back, leaned back and put his feet up. Roughly ten hours after the Amtrak train pulled out of the station in Omaha, it arrived at Union Station in Chicago. Edward made his way through the crowd to a waiting area where he found a semi secluded spot on one of the long wooden benches. 'I don't think I have any living relatives here. I know there were a few in the eighties, but I'm sure they are all dead by now. Besides, mother would have mentioned them over the years if there were any.'

"I think I will call the Four Seasons and see what they have available. Three or four days should lull everyone into a false sense of security and then we can get back to work."

"It was a wise move to follow my advice for a change and buy the carryon bag and the jacket,"

"You're right. No bag would have made spotting us easier if they were looking, Omaha was smaller than I expected. It would be easy to look out of place."

"We need a map of the area. There should be some in one of the shops."

While looking for a Chicago area map, Edward was putting his plan into action.

"Four Seasons Chicago, how can I help you?"

"I would like to reserve a room please."

"For how many nights sir?"

"Four, and do you have something with a lake view?"

"Yes, as a matter fact, we do. We have a superior one-bedroom suite available and it has wonderful lake and city views looking north along the shoreline."

"That will be perfect."

"And your name sir?"

"Edward C. Winslow."

"And, when do you anticipate arriving?"

"I'm on my way there from the airport right now."

"Then, we look forward to seeing you shortly."

"By the way, how is the shopping in the area?"

"The best in all of Chicago."

"Thank you."

Etta Rox talked to the realtor and then called to make reservations at an Extended Stay in Rolling Meadows, IL for ten days which would take them to closing and move in. Then she called their daughter who was vacationing in Florida for two weeks. Much to their relief. They told her nothing other than to keep them posted on her travel plans.

Agent Jack Mitchell reported his findings to Agent Lampe on the airlines, trains and buses, another dead-end. Bill Lampe called Agent Hassman in Chicago to let him know he would be there in the afternoon and asked if they would be able to meet to brief him on what had transpired.

There was not going to be a good time to contact their son, so Joe thought it best to get it over with when they were about a half hour out of town.

"McFarlin Engineering, how can I direct your call?"

"Joe Rox please"

"Transferring your call."

"Joe Rox how can I help you?"

"Hey Joe, how's the new job?"

"Great dad, where are you and mom?"

"We're about thirty miles out."

"Are you going to be staying at my place? I can't wait to see you and the dogs?"

"There's been a little glitch and we are going to have to postpone seeing you for a few days."

"What do you mean glitch?"

"I can't go into it right now other than to say we are alright."

"At least tell me where you are staying so I can run out there?"

"You can't do that either. You just have to sit tight and we'll see you in a few days I promise."

"This doesn't have anything to do with all of those people being killed from Colorado to Nebraska, does it?"

"No, nothing like that. Your phone isn't listed is it?"

"What do you mean by that. Am I in some kind of danger?"

"No, it just an academic question."

"I expect an explanation when we see each other?"

"You'll get the whole thing. We will call later this evening when we're settled in."

"Ok."

As fast as the call with his son ended, he put a call into Bill Lampe.

"Agent Lampe, I just got off the phone with my son. I don't need to recap the conversation because I am sure your people were listening. I'll just get to the point. That kid is not me. If there is any chance that this psycho extracted information from the realtor he murdered regarding our relocation and our children living in Chicago, then he needs to be put into protective custody right away. If you can't or won't, we are out."

"We will get someone over to his office right away."

"What is the name of the agent you will be sending to get him?"

"Jack Mitchell, he's been on this since Rock Falls."

"Good, I would like to have my son call when he has him."

"We will do that."

"Do you have children agent Lampe?"

"Yes, two."

"Then you know how important this is."

Having virtually left everything behind except for the clothes on his back, Edward Calvert had a great deal of shopping to do. First, the clothing and personal items he would need so he could move without attracting attention and second, the items he would need to live out his fantasies when he had Etta Rox. Water Tower Place looked to be the perfect place to start. He found head to toe men's wear befitting his social status. Though he would have preferred custom tailoring, he bought two off-the-rack suits, with the promise they would have the alterations done by the end of the day. After stopping in housewares at one of the department stores for the cutlery he would require he moved on to ladies lingerie.

"Good afternoon sir is there something I can help you with?"

"Yes, there is as a matter of fact. I'm looking for a red satin nightgown."

"In what size?"

"I'm not sure?"

"Do you know her approximate height and weight?"

"Why yes, about five eight and one hundred forty pounds."

I think I have something that will be perfect. Please wait here."

The clerk went into the back of the shop and a minute later came out carrying a very expensive-looking low cut, open back, floor length, deep red satin nightgown. "Will this do?"

"It's exactly what I had in mind, Can you gift wrap it?"

After a long day's drive, they arrived in Rolling Meadows at the Extended Stay.

"Joe, let's get checked in and go for dinner close to where we're moving. There's a Greek place called The Dunton House. I was told nothing fancy but very good."

"The realtor said there were some great restaurants in the downtown area and I'd like to start trying them. She said Gabrielle', in particular, is excellent, but very expensive."

"Let's see if we can get a reservation for tomorrow night?"

"Good idea."

"I'd like to get cleaned up first. Will you take the dogs out for a walk?"

"Sure, do you want to drive by the new place after dinner?"

"That's a good idea."

"Joe, will that make us visible enough?"

"More than enough. I'll be right back. I am going to run the dogs out now."

After outfitting himself properly, Edward Calvert decided a small celebration was in order. He called down to the concierge and asked to have a reservation made at the finest French restaurant in the city. After a most enjoyable evening, he looked forward to a well-deserved peaceful night's rest before he started planning the final phase of this cycle.

The following morning, he ordered breakfast in his room and went online researching fine dining when he found Gabrielle', a name he had heard mentioned in New York as one of the nation's finest establishments. During his search, he noticed that there was commuter train service to Arlington Heights allowing him to travel back and forth anonymously. It was all coming together before his very eyes. He called Gabrielle' and scheduled an appoint at 2:00 p.m. to apply for a position as a waiter, using the name Harris Hubert, one he used when he was employed at Leonard's in New York.

"You are exactly what we look for in our wait staff. Your knowledge of fine dining and how to treat our clientele is right in line with our philosophy here at Gabrielle'. When would you be able to start?"

"Would it be possible to shadow this evening and start as soon as you have me in the schedule?"

"That would be tomorrow, Charles will get a uniform for you before you leave, we can finish filling out the application tomorrow before we open, we'll see you at 6:00 p.m. Harris."

Bill Lampe was getting running reports, regardless of how trivial, as either Joe or Etta Rox made phone calls, he then reported them directly to his immediate supervisor, Rick Hassman, in the Chicago office. "Rick, they have reservations at a restaurant called Gabrielle' in Arlington Heights at 8:30 p.m. this evening."

"I'm familiar with it, food is supposed to be spectacular and very expensive."

"We have to be very careful with any surveillance operation. This guy has been doing this for so long he's developed an uncanny knack for spotting law enforcement. We cannot afford to lose him again."

"Bill, alert Mr. Rox that he will be pretty much on his own. If he see's something that isn't right, tell him to call. We will be close by, but completely hidden."

"Will do."

His next call was to Joe Rox.

"Mr. Rox, this is agent Lampe. I want to let you know we will not have active surveillance when you and your wife are out. If you or your wife see anything that looks suspicious or if your wife spots the killer, call us immediately. We will be completely out of sight but very close-by."

"We will check in with you when we leave for dinner. We are planning on running by the new house after dinner, then back to the motel."

Edward decided not to go back to his hotel and instead spent the afternoon watching the horses run at Arlington Park. Not that he was such a gambler, but it made the likelihood of being recognized remote at best. By 6:00 p.m., he was on the floor observing the staff. As the evening wore on, he decided he would let them know he had familiarized himself with the operation and would be ready for the following evening. Then he spotted a very familiar face.

"Should we call this good fortune?"

"Can we stay out of the way and keep from being identified?"

"I don't know. This just shifted our timetable into fast forward."

"Don't let her see your face. Don't take any chances. If she sees your face, we are through."

"Stop panicking, I want to listen to their conversation with their waiter. They are getting ready to leave."

"The dinner was everything we expected and more, Thomas. We have been living out west for the last ten years and I must say, the service here tonight made us feel like royalty."

"Thank you, Dr. Rox. When will we have the pleasure of serving you again?"

"Could you see if there is a reservation available for two on Saturday at 8:00 p.m.?"

"I'll check right away."

"Thank you. The doctor thing always plays well, Joe."

Their waiter, Thomas, was back in a minute.

"Dr. Rox, your reservation for Saturday at 8:00 p.m. is set, we look forward to seeing you then,"

"Thank you. Thomas, will you be waiting on us?"

"Absolutely, I'll see you then, good evening."

The news was exactly what Edward Calvert wanted to hear. Mr. and Mrs. Rox were helping bring his plan to fruition. Edward took his cue as they were getting up to leave. He walked to the manager's office knocking lightly on the door frame and asked. "Ms. Hamilton, do you have a minute?"

"Yes, Harris, come in."

He slowly closed the door to stay out of sight.

"I have to tell you, Gabrielle' is easily on a par with Leonard's in New York."

"Really, your serious?"

"I'm dead serious. I never thought there would be a restaurant that could come close to Leonard's, let alone equal."

"Oh, my goodness, I'm so glad you let me know."

"I am looking forward to starting tomorrow evening. I'll be here at 4:30 for setup."

"We'll see you then and thank you for the assessment."

Edward changed into street clothes and left to catch an evening train to downtown Chicago. The forty-five-minute commute would give him a chance to refine his plan.

"On a par with Leonard's, not even close."

"The conversation kept us out of sight, so we wouldn't be seen, didn't it?"

"Saturday night it is. We are going to take them both."

"Isn't that a little ambitious?"

"Not in the least, we have a great deal of planning to do over the next two days and then on to a new destination."

"Their new house is several blocks from here, let's wander by and get a look. We can easily catch the next train to the city and we need to check the layout."

"What if they are there doing the same thing?"

"We will stay out of the way. We're not ready."

The downtown areas in many suburban towns are often described as upscale and after gentrification and much redevelopment, the description fit. Joe and Etta were amply impressed at how the downtown area looked and decided to do some window shopping before driving back to the motel.

"Joe, are we going to take a drive by the house again tonight?"

"If you want to, yes."

"Just drive by, we don't have to stop. I think cars pulling into the driveway rattles the neighbors."

"They would be more than rattled if they knew what was going on in their neighborhood."

Their walk took them to the public garage on the west end of the renovated downtown area where they had parked earlier in the evening. The drive to their new home was only a few city blocks away. When they reached 3330 Webster Ct., Joe stopped.

"Look, it's beautiful isn't it?"

"Yes sweetheart, it really is."

Crawling alongside the darkened house behind a thick well-groomed hedge.

"That's them. They've stopped to look the place over. I wonder how many times a day they do that?"

"The landscaping on this property is going to make us almost invisible when we walk her in. Once we leave the sidewalk, the closest neighbors won't even be able to see us."

"Let's check the doors and windows, there has to be something we can open easily. I want to look around inside while we are here tonight."

"We have to do this quickly, the last commuter train back to Chicago leaves at 10:00 p.m."

"Mr. Rox has made taking her difficult. I am going to take him when I am finished with her."

Over the course of several days, more bad news came to Bill Lampe from out west, though not unexpected. The Thornburg woman's body was found by fly fisherman in the Roaring Forks River just outside of Rock Falls. The old white SUV Etta described belonged to a Mary Kay McNeil, a barmaid at a 'gentleman's club' called The Saddle Up Lounge just off I-70 west of Rifle, Colorado. Her whereabouts were still unknown and the authorities were assuming she was also deceased. The last report was regarding the abandoned truck just west of Ogallala. It was registered to a Kitty Smith in Grand Junction. Grand Junction Police forced entry the same night they were notified and found her body packed neatly into her refrigerator. The victims all appeared to have been strangled.

Agent Lampe had his team in place and could do nothing but wait. When and where was solely up to 'Ned' Calvert. The authorities had never been this close to their man and as frustrating as it was, they had to maintain a low profile. Even more frustrating was that they were forced to essentially put control in the hands of

Joseph Rox, an outsider. There was one additional reason it was imperative they end this serial murderer's killing spree. Because of the numbers of people involved in the investigation, there would eventually be a leak, at which point it was going to become a public relations nightmare of monumental proportions.

Edward Calvert walked out of the Four Seasons Hotel at 8:00 a.m., dressed in smart business casual carrying a black backpack. He walked south on Michigan Ave to Wacker Drive, then west until he found a coffee shop. He ordered a medium salted caramel coffee, while waiting, he used the men's restroom to change into work clothes he had purchased at a Salvation Army Thrift store the day before. He paid for his drink walked out to the street and hailed a cab. While climbing into the back seat he gave the driver an address eight blocks from a small specialty chemical distributor in Rosemont. When he arrived, Edward paid cash and a modest tip. Two hours later he was driving back to Chicago.

"One of the great things about money, it will get you just about anything you want if you have enough of it."

"That chemical distributor charged us ten times what that quart of chloroform was worth.

Then had the nerve to think he could extort more from us to keep from calling the police because he had, so called, doubts about the man he sold it to."

"We will only need his car until tomorrow when we leave Chicago, he can stay in the trunk."

"I understand that in the old days, mobsters would leave bodies in the trunks of cars in long term parking at the airport."

"That will help add to the general confusion."

At 11:30 a.m., Edward was driving through the intersection of Wilson and Broadway on the northside of Chicago. When he spotted the perfect subject. The negotiation with the addict took less than a minute. The young man got in the car and they drove west on Wilson Ave to the first clinic he saw.

"You are being paid five-hundred-dollars so repeat exactly what I have written for you until you have it memorized."

"Doctor, I have very bad insomnia and have great difficulty falling asleep. Doctors have prescribed several different medications without any real effect. Would it be possible to get a prescription for a fast-acting sleep aid?"

"If the doctor asks why you want this particular type of drug what are you going to tell him?"

"One of my uncles has the same problems I do falling asleep. His doctor prescribed it for him and it has worked very well."

"That should sooth his conscience when he writes the scrip."

"Study your lines. If we do not have to go to more than one doctor's office in this area I will give you a two-hundred-dollar bonus."

While waiting for the young man, outside of the clinic.

"That dope fiend will be looking for a reward from Crime Stoppers when this is over, when he makes the connection."

"Did you ever hear me say he wasn't going to join his fellow accomplice in the trunk?"

Timing is everything. The prescription was issued by the pharmacy at the clinic and Edward was able to drive to O'Hare Airport, and park the car, with the two bodies in the trunk, in long-term parking. He changed back into his business casual wear in a men's restroom on the lower level of the concourse, wrapped his purchases in the work clothes and carefully placed them in his backpack. He walked outside, hailed a cab and had the driver drop him four blocks from Gabrielle' by 4:00 p.m. Friday night would give him the opportunity for a practice run of what he was going to execute the following evening.

Saturday morning found Edward Calvert sitting on the couch awaiting breakfast delivery. His feet up on the ottoman and looking north along the shoreline of Lake Michigan through the picture window of his thirty fifth floor room.

"All of the preparations are complete. We will conduct this the same way we have in the past."

"We will create our own opening this evening."

At the same time, in Rolling Meadows at the Extended Stay, the Rox' were getting their day underway.

"Joe, after dinner tonight, let's run by the house one more time."

"You can't get enough of that place, can you?"

"I can hardly wait to move in."

"Then another ride by after dinner it is!"

The rest of their day was spent car shopping, a convertible for her and a mid-size SUV for him. Joe and Etta were determined to give living in the Midwest a real try. At the end of the day, they had made one purchase, a red Mustang convertible for her.

"Etta, we better get a move on or we will miss our reservation. I get the feeling Gabrielle' is packed on Saturday night."

8:40 p.m. Saturday, Joe and Etta Rox were seated in one of the three dining areas, each with fifteen tables positioned in and around dividers to give a degree of intimacy. At their request, Thomas would be waiting on them this evening. In another dining room, Edward was assigned three tables, each with two people, all had cocktails. Two of his tables ordered dinner after cocktails and the third additional drinks.

"They are on their third Martini and will be getting the scrip mixed into their dinner. At the rate they are drinking, they won't be able to taste their food anyway."

"This is supposed to be very fast acting, so a 20 mg dose should get us the result we are after."

Midway through dinner, there was something of a commotion in one of the other dining rooms. Their waiter Thomas calmly came to their table and quietly spoke to Etta.

"Dr. Rox, we have just had a woman collapse in one of the other dining rooms."

Without Thomas even asking her for assistance, Etta responded.

"I'll come right away and look at her. In the meantime, make sure someone calls for an ambulance."

The woman had passed out. Her face had fallen into her plate and she was not moving. Joe had come with his wife and helped to lay the woman on the floor next to their table. Etta checked immediately for a pulse, while the woman's very worried looking husband stood by.

"Will she be alright doctor?"

"I don't know. She needs to be moved to a hospital immediately. Her breathing is very shallow."

Thomas walked to where Etta was checking the woman. "The ambulance is on the way. It should be here momentarily; the fire station is just around the corner."

"Thank you, Thomas."

Everything about this was wrong and both Joe and Etta knew it.

"Etta, do you have any idea what this is?"

"No Joe, I don't."

Etta turned to the woman's husband.

"Sir, is your wife taking any medication that would have a reaction with alcohol?"

"No, she isn't. She is not taking any medications."

"I can't tell for sure, but this appears to be drug induced. Make sure you tell them when you get to the hospital."

The paramedics arrived. Etta told them about possible drug reaction. When they had removed the woman, the dining room was quickly returning to normal.

"Joe, I have to run into the lady's room for a second. I want to wash my hands and clean up a little."

"I'll be right here waiting."

As Etta rounded the corner of the restaurant out of Joe's sight and entered the Ladies' restroom, she was followed immediately by Edward Calvert. He pushed her forward letting the door close.

"Hello Etta, remember me?"

Putting his left forearm across her throat from behind, while taking a plastic bag from his pocket with his right hand, he tore it open with his teeth.

"If you don't want to die right here, you will not fight me."

As he placed the rag soaked with chloroform over her mouth.

"See how a little chloroform helps just enough to make her compliant?"

He walked her, half-awake, out of the restroom and toward a side door that led to the alley next to the restaurant, being careful not to seen by anyone in the dining area.

"Now, let's go right out this door. We are going to take a little walk this evening over to your new home. I have a surprise waiting there for you."

They were halfway through the darkened alley when he stopped and shoved her up against the building.

"It should be on the side of your leg. Let me see? There it is. We'll just stick this little tracking device on this dumpster. Now quickly, let's get moving."

Joe waited less than a minute when he walked to the woman's restroom and opened the door slightly and called his wife's name. When there was no answer, he knew she had been taken. He immediately called Agent Lampe while he was racing out the front door of the restaurant.

"We were at Gabrielle' for dinner. He grabbed her, I'm moving and won't be able to call. Track her, I don't think they could have gone far. He's probably dressed as a waiter."

Joe switched his phone off as he left the restaurant and disappeared into the downtown area.

Agent Lampe did not even have time to respond to Joe Rox when he was cut off. He instantly called his team by radio,

"He took Dr. Rox at Gabrielle'. Have the police lockdown the downtown area as fast as they can. They have to stop all traffic and go car to car, we have to get on the street right away. Do you have a signal on her?"

"Yes, I do, but it's not moving and about two blocks from here."

"Get to that spot and stop anyone you see dressed like a waiter."

He moved her, dark alley by dark alley through the downtown area with remarkable speed. They crossed an intersection and walked onto Webster Ct leading her along looking like a spouse helping his wife who had a little too much to drink. He spoke softly in her ear,

"I can't tell you what a pleasure it is to finally get this close to you. I have a surprise waiting for you."

The chloroform was making it very difficult for Etta to gather her thoughts. When they arrived at the corner of 3330 Webster Ct, Edward steered her behind a tall hedgerow, through the yard, to the door on the side of the garage that he had unlocked during his earlier visit. He stopped in the garage before entering the house to administer more chloroform to ensure that she would continue to be fully compliant. He opened the door to the house, guided her past the washer and dryer in the laundry room and into the kitchen, where, through her slightly blurred vision, she saw a red foil covered box.

"What is that?"

"It's a gift. It's the way I have envisioned you since we first met."

He proceeded to open the box, take the gown by the shoulder straps and hold it up to her,

"Now strip down and put this on."

Even in her dazed state, Etta knew following his instructions would buy her more time than fighting. When she had changed into the gown, he handed her two pills and a paper cup of water.

"Take these, they will help put you at ease."

Too drowsy to object, she swallowed the pills. Within minutes, she felt herself drifting into unconsciousness. He caught her as she was falling, lifted her up and laid her on the granite counter top in the darkened kitchen.

"I know even in your current state, you can hear me, so listen to what I have to say. I wish I could have done this in a friendlier setting, but you made this so difficult that we will have to make do with you laid out on this countertop in your new home. Souvenirs have never interested me, however, I am so obsessed with you that I must take one, I want to keep your heart close to mine."

As he picked up the knife from counter with both hands, raising it over Etta Rox, and preparing to thrust the knife into her heart. He was momentarily distracted by a ghostly outline resembling a man in a darkened corner of the kitchen.

"Who are you and what are you doing interrupting my pleasure?"

In a low deliberate voice, the shadowy figure responded.

"Are you so presumptuous as to think you are so smart that no one could figure out what your next move would be? You have never been out of my sight since you left the restaurant."
A somewhat surprised but indignant Edward responded.

"Do you have any idea who I am, you nobody?"

"No, I don't, but I know what you are and what you have that belongs to me."

As the serial killer began his thrust, the first round made its distinctive popping sound as it left the barrel of the Ruger MKIII at 1,450 feet per second. It entered the neck approximately one inch above the jugular notch passing through the trachea, striking and shattering C6. Time stopped.

In the seconds before his body collapsed onto the floor, he saw what appeared to be an apparition float out of the shadows and around the counter. Joseph Rox placed the barrel of the MKIII on an upward angle just below the right ear and fired twice at opposite ends of a ten-degree arc. The knife tumbled off the table onto the remains of the very recently deceased Edward Malcolm Calvert.

As Joe whispered in the ear of the woman who had made him whole so long ago.

"I know you probably can't hear me right now, but I was never more than mere feet from you. I had to wait for the right moment. I told you I would never let any harm come to you."
He turned his phone on and made one call. "Agent Lampe, you can find your man at our new home in the kitchen. I am on the way to the hospital with my wife."

"Has she been harmed?"

"I hope not. He used chloroform and pills to sedate her. I will call after I see that she is admitted and I know there are no complications."

The body of Edward Malcolm Calvert was removed from the Rox' residence and taken to the coroner's office. Cause of death, two gunshots to the brain. His fingerprints and a sample of his DNA were taken. And as Agent Bill Lampe suspected, there was a match to every victim from beginning to end. In the end, they were finally able to put a name to the monster they had pursued for so long. One of his last duties as Director of the FBI, carried out personally by Director DaCosta, was meeting with Edward's very well-connected mother to let her know her son was dead. There was always speculation that he received some type of financial support to be able to carry out his murderous rampage for so long. To investigate whether she had financed his reign of terror would take years as the funds she had put in place would be virtually impossible to uncover. The Director made a point of telling her exactly how many people her son had murdered, how he had done it and how many lives were devastated by Edward Malcolm Calvert.

As a show of how little affection Mrs. Calvert had for her son, she didn't even ask that his remains be turned over for interment in the family crypt at Moravian Cemetery. She would have been denied regardless, as he was laid to rest in an unmarked grave in the potter's field located at the notorious, antiquated, maximum-security Pontiac Correctional Facility south of Chicago.

Bill Lampe was getting packed up for his trip back to Denver when his phone rang.

"Bill, Jim Nowicki."

"Yes Jim, what can I do for you today?"

"I wanted to bring you up to date on what has been transpiring with the Calvert case. It has been decided that there will be no publicity."

"Then, it's going to be buried?"

"Yes, for several reasons. The most important being we don't want this to spawn copycats."

"I understand."

"Rick Hassman is on his way back to DC to take over the Washington office. You will be taking over as Director of the Chicago office. Your old boss was removed this morning and has been offered two options, resign or stay-on as a field agent in Fairbanks, Alaska. By the way do you know RJ Schissell?"

"Yes, I met him on several occasions."

"Well he has just been named Director of the FBI. I think you will enjoy working together. Stop and see me whenever you get back into town."

"I will and thank you sir."

At the same time Bill Lampe was getting his good news, Etta was being released from the hospital.

"I took care of the closing last Monday and had everything moved into the house on the bet that you would still want to live there."

"You made a good bet. I will not be run off even by the likes of that monster."

"Wait till you see how everything looks. It's a great place."

"I can hardly wait to get home and see it."

"Your red convertible is sitting in the lot with the top down."

"Then, let's go home Joe."

"The kids are coming by for pizza tonight. I hope that's ok with you?"

"I can't wait to see them."

"Joe is this over?"

"Yes, it is sweetheart."

"Do you love me Joe?"

"More than life itself Etta. More than life itself."

Conversations with the Angel of Death

Have you ever been sitting quietly, possibly doing something as benign as watching television or reading a book, it could be indoors or out, when out of the corner of your eye, you are distracted by the shadow of what appears to be a human like form moving quickly out of view? I'm sure if you have, you've kept it to yourself.

Peter Stone had spent forty plus years doing a good job of distancing himself from his past. When Peter met Jill Hart, they both knew from the time their eyes first met that they were meant to be together. If there is such a thing as soul mates, they were.

On a cold dark overcast Saturday evening in late October, Peter Stone thought he was alone in his dimly lit living room.

"Peter?"

"Yes."

"You don't sound alarmed?"

"I'm not. I have been expecting you for the last forty years and in fact have seen you pass by from time to time."

"You never acknowledged my presence so much as once."

"There was no need to. I will admit the first few times were distressing. I thought I might be going insane, then, I finally accepted the premise that it may have been presumptuous of me to think our association was over."

"Then, you know why I am here."

Peter Stone had one goal in life, he wanted to be like everyone else, even though his experiences made that almost unattainable.

"I have been preoccupied attempting to redeem myself since I met my wife."

"And I have been watching Peter."

"What is it you want of me?"

"There are souls that must be gathered for disposition and you are needed to carry out the task."

"Are you aware of how many years it took me to put a life together after the last time?"

"Yes Peter, I am, and don't forget, because of our agreement, you came through it all unscathed while so many of your friends were killed and wounded in those battles."

"Pete is there a woman out there?"

"No sweetheart, I'm here alone."

"You're talking to yourself? Why are mimicking a low woman's voice?"

"It's nothing, I'm just working on a few things and verbalizing a bit. It must just be coming out a little strange. I'll keep my voice down. Please try to get some rest. Your next round of chemo starts in two days."

Whatever the outcome he could not subject his wife to what may soon be required of him.

"Jill, I have to run up to the corner store. We are out of half and half for our coffee. I'll be back in a few minutes. Will you be alright?"

"Pete, I'm going to be fine. You don't have to ask me if I'm alright every five minutes."

"Ok, will you be alright?"

"Peter, get out of here. It hurts when I laugh."

Peter Stone and the Angel of Death began their walk to the store giving them the opportunity to continue their conversation uninterrupted.

"You two are very close, aren't you Peter?"

"Yes."

"What does she mean to you?"

"Explain mean, to me?"

"How important is she?"

"More than life itself."

"So, you are deeply in love with her?"

"Yes, I have spent all these years seeking redemption in the hope I would have a life with her. Now, she is dying and accepts her fate and I am the one falling apart."

"You are not falling apart Peter. I have witnessed this sadness in humans' countless times."

"What is my life worth without her? She is why I am who I am today. How was she able to hear you?"

"She is near death Peter."

"Can anyone hear you talking as we walk to the store?"

"No, they can't."

One of the advantages of living in cities is that neighborhood convenience stores are within walking distance.

"Good evening Carl."

"How are you today Pete?"

"I'm good."

"And Jill?"

"Comfortable."

"We pray for her every night."

"Thanks Carl, we appreciate that very much."

"Pete was there someone walking up the street with you? When I saw you coming this way, it looked like you had two shadows."

"No, it's probably just an effect from the street lights."

"Just half and half tonight?"

"That's all."

"That will be three dollars."

"Thanks Carl."

"Pete, if there is anything we can help with, please let us know."

"I will, thank you."

He began the walk home and only had to wait mere seconds before the conversation resumed.

"You have made friends over the years Peter?"

"Not many, but the few I have are good friends."

"Do you find it difficult to make friends?"

"Yes, I do."

"Peter are you ever plagued with thoughts and images from your past?"

"Only on rare occasions, but they do not last long. I deal with them quickly."

"Have you ever sought any help?"

"One time, and I decided that I was doing much better following the path I have laid down. It may not be perfect, but I have managed to have a good life with Jill. The fact that I have her tells me I am doing something right."

Peter always felt that he had fulfilled the terms of their original agreement and therefore, he was under no obligation.

"When we parted ways, I continued to look in on you from time to time. I was watching when you were on your knees praying, trying to make a deal with Him that you would never take another life again, if you could only be with her for eternity. That you would do whatever it took to achieve that Peter is why I am having this conversation with you today. I have a new proposition for you."

"And that proposition is what?"

"If you will work, as you call it, for me one more time, everything will be alright."

"That's your offer?"

"That's it Peter. Think about it for a day. There isn't much time."

"You mean I have a choice?"

"In a manner of speaking."

"Will you tell me what it is I am supposed to do, or do I have to agree not knowing what is involved?"

"There are people who will have a profound effect on events far in the future that are currently at great risk."

"Why can't you just intervene? You know, call for some miracle to be performed if that's what it takes."

"Peter, we deal only in life, death, reward and punishment. Mankind was given free will and rules to live by however, because of free will, how mankind conducts itself is totally up to them."

"Then why are you getting involved if all you deal with is life and death?"

"Because, if this is not corrected, mankind will cease to exist."

"When?"

"In the future."

"How far in the future?"

"That is not for me to say."

"Am I going to die if I help you?"

"That is not for me to say."

"Then what can you say?"

"Everything will be alright Peter."

The last time Peter Stone entered into an agreement with this being it was under extreme duress. He needed several minutes to gather his thoughts and the bench along the boulevard on his way home was the perfect place.

"Why are you speaking to me in a low woman's voice?"

"Because it has a calming effect on you."

"Are you a woman?"

"I am neither man nor woman, I am an angel."

"How many of you are there?"

"Many, six million people die every day around the world."

"Are they all processed every day?"

"Processed is not the right description Peter. They are received and given their reward or passed on for further disposition, but to answer your question, yes."

"I'll ask once again; do I really have a choice?"

"No Peter, you don't have a choice. That is why I am here. I had hoped you would agree without coercion. If you recall, during our previous relationship, you were charged with delivering all the souls of those you killed in battle."

"Yes."

"How many did you kill?"

"I don't know exactly, I didn't keep count."

"You killed one hundred fifty-eight Peter, will you tell me why you didn't count?"

"I always thought that people who counted their kills derived some perverse pleasure from what they had done. They could revel in it and I did not."

"You do recall that you failed to pass on all of the souls and, in fact, held on to some for a number of years?"

"Yes, I am well aware of that."

"How many did you keep and for what reason?"

"Forty, I was curious as to what it would be like to possess souls, but I meant no malice."

"You violated our agreement."

"Yes, I did, over time, I realized that what I had done was wrong and released them all."

"I received them all Peter, but to make up for your indiscretion, you will have to serve me one last time."

"Then, I would like to be told what it is you want me to do and how many souls I am going to be required to deliver?"

"We will discuss that tomorrow. Tonight, you should be home attending to your wife."

"What if I were to say you must cure my wife of her cancer as the price for my services?"

"I cannot do that Peter. My purpose is to gather souls."

"Can you tell me how much longer she will live?"

"That is not for me to say."

"But you know?"

"Yes, I do."

"When she dies, what is to become of me?"

"I told you everything will be alright."

Early Monday morning, as Peter and Jill were finishing breakfast and preparing for the day ahead,

"Jill what time are you supposed to be at the doctor's office today?"

"At 1:00 p.m. Pete."

"We should get moving, I don't want you to be late."

"We're fine. Pete, it's only 8:00 a.m., can we stop for a minute and talk please? Peter you seem so stressed. How can I get you to calm down just a little?"

"We planned our lives together and this was never part of the plan."

"Peter, life doesn't always work out the way we plan it. We have always made the best of what it has handed us, and we have never been any worse for the wear, Will you try to settle down a little Peter?"

"I'll try my best."

At the end of her appointment, one of the nurses caught her as she was leaving her examination room.

"Mrs. Stone, Dr. Hassen would like to see you in his office. I'll show you the way."

"Mrs. Stone please come in and have a seat. I want to talk to you about the most recent tests we performed. I told you when we started this process that I would be completely honest with you every step of the way."

"You did."

"The latest round of tests does not look good."

"By that you mean?"

"I would advise not trying another round of chemotherapy. I think it will only make you ill and take away from the time you have left."

"How much time is that doctor Hassen?"

"My best estimate is six months. Five of which can be made relatively pain free and then hospice will be required."

"This won't set well with Peter. He is already on edge."

"Would it do any good if I spoke to both of you together?"

"Let me talk to him first."

"You seem at ease today?"

"I had a feeling about this last night."

"Can you explain that to me?"

"If you can keep this conversation completely in your confidence?"

"Yes, I can. I assure you it will never go further than this office."

"At home the other night, I heard a woman talking to Peter. When I asked him if there was anyone there, he said no, he was alone and just verbalizing some things. He didn't see me watching him from the other room."

"And was there someone there?"

"Not that I could see, but he was carrying on a conversation with someone and it was not possible to be just him talking to himself."

"And why is that?"

"Because, whoever or whatever it was would talk over him while he was talking. Peter said he had to run to the store for a minute and I think, more than anything, it was to finish his conversation, but while he was gone the oddest thing happened."

"And what was that Mrs. Stone?"

A feeling came over me that everything was going to be alright it was almost as though the same voice I heard in the living room was whispering in my ear."

"Had you taken any of your medication before this happened?"

"No, I hadn't taken anything at all Dr. Hassen."

"Dr. Hassen, I will talk to Peter. It's best if I do. I know I can make him understand."

"Mrs. Stone I will have someone from the office call you in the next few days to discuss keeping you comfortable and I would like to see you weekly going forward so I can monitor the progression."

"I'll see the nurse on the way out about scheduling appointments. Thank you for everything, I know you have done everything possible to deal with this."

Peter was waiting in the parking lot and in Jill's mind the drive home was the best time to talk to her husband.

"Peter, I spoke to Dr. Hassen and we have things we need to talk about right away."

"What did he say?"

"I'll go over everything with you on the way home."

Peter and Jill, though they never had children, could not have been better suited for one another. The relationship that blossomed from their first day and literally grew stronger every day of their lives was about to be tested to its fullest.

For most people, the drive home is the best place to talk, since it is a time when interruptions can be held to a minimum.

"Well, what did the doctor have to say?"

"Peter, I have six months. He said going through another round of chemo would ruin the quality of what life I have left."

"Then, we have to seek another opinion."

"No Peter, Dr. Hassen is considered to be the very best in his field. He specializes in this type of cancer. I trust his opinion and advice."

"Jill, tell me what you want to do?"

"Peter, I want to live my life with you that's all. I want to get a little rest when we get home, then let's go out to some nice quiet place for dinner."

After arriving home from dinner, Peter told Jill he was going to sit up for a while. He wanted to take a few minutes to absorb all that had happened during the day. Jill was completely worn out and went to bed.

"Peter?"

"Yes?"

"You seem depressed."

"I am. I have no reason to go on. I will do as you ask, my wife has six months to live, so there is really nothing left for me."

"Peter, I told you everything would be alright."

"How? She is dying as we speak."

"Peter, I am not here to argue. You have terms that must be met and we must move forward quickly"

"Explain what it is you want me to do."

"Do you remember the McConnel brothers?"

"How could I forget. After the war they started trafficking drugs."

"I'm well aware of that."

"They have asked me to come with them a dozen times over the years and each time, I have told them I want no part of their business."

"Michael McConnel will approach you again in the next five days. This time, you will accept. Their vetting process will take several months, they are very careful."

"Why are they so cautious?"

"They have involved themselves in activities far more nefarious than just drug trafficking."

"What actually?"

"Weapons and human trafficking. They must be stopped soon, thus our agreement."

"How much time do I have with my wife?"

Until the vetting is complete."

"What do you want me to do?"

"You will wait until you get them all together and then, deliver the souls to me as you have done in the past."

"And what happens to me?"

"Everything will be alright."

When a loved one is gravely ill time seems to 'speed up.

"Peter, I don't know if I can get out of bed on my own. I have gotten so weak?"

"Just rest sweetheart."

"No Peter, I want to see you as much as possible. Stay here with me please."

Over the next few weeks, Jill Stone's condition worsened to the point that one sunny morning, her breathing became very shallow and rapid. Her last words to Peter were,

"I will love you forever."

Jill was buried in a plot that Peter had purchased several months before she died. Both of their names were inscribed in the granite headstone with the epitaph, 'The Love of My Life' and awaiting only dates.

After the death of his wife, Peter Stone set about getting all his affairs in order. He arranged for the sale of his home and left complete instructions for the disposition of his assets. Everything was put in writing, placed in a safe deposit box and the key was given to his brother Robert. Then, the wait for a call from the McConnel's began.

"Pete, it's Mike. You checked out, are you ready?"

"Yes, when do we get together?"

"This Saturday 7:00 p.m., at the Hacienda restaurant eighty-seven miles east of El Paso on Hwy 10 in Sierra Blanca, and Pete, sorry to hear about your old lady."

Peter flew into El Paso on Saturday afternoon without any baggage and rented a car for the trip to Sierra Blanca. The drive gave him a chance to think about the time he had with Jill and to speculate on what he knew was ahead.

"Hey Pete, good to see you. Let's go on inside. What do you think of this place?"

"It's decent. Why meet out here though?"

"We own the place and everyone here works for us. It's the best cover we ever came up with. Jim, Ronny, Earl, you all remember Pete Stone?"

The most gregarious of the brothers, Jim, came forward,

"You bet we do. Good to have you on board with us finally Pete."

"I'm glad to be here Congressman."
"You know when Jim was elected to Congress, it was like getting a 'Stay Out of Jail Card.' We can do anything we want for the right price. When Jim heard you were joining us, he said he had to come. He's said for years you were the only person we ever knew that we could trust and the only time we would ever have to worry was if you were getting your orders from God himself."

"What do you think of that?"

"Well, I can say this with all honesty, I'm not talking to God."

Mike McConnel brought Peter Stone up to speed on how the operation worked and what was expected of him. "We have three trucks coming tonight, one with weapons and explosives. We have two groups that have paid a real premium for these goods."

"What kind of groups?"

"One's anti-government and the other is far left. All scum but we don't care as long as they have the money when the transfer takes place. The second truck is drugs, Mexican heroin and meth that will be broken down here in the El Paso area and distributed across the country. The last truck is people. We have established quite a following with traffickers. We'll check them out and send the truck on to Los Angeles."

"What time do you expect the trucks?"

"Weapons about 10:00 p.m., the rest should follow right behind. You should check weapons, since you will be involved in that transaction."

"Good."

"In the meantime, lets order dinner and catch up on old times."

When dinner was over and the McConnel's and their men went to the bar adjacent to the small dining room, almost to the minute, the first truck pulled in the lot and headed directly to the large metal barn building behind the restaurant. A call came from the driver, it was the drugs. Within minutes, the second truck pulled in the lot and also headed for the barn. A second call, it was the weapons.

"Pete, why don't you take a quick look."

"Sure Mike, I'll be right back."

On his way to the barn, the third truck drove in and went directly to the barn without stopping. Peter didn't have to guess what the cargo was. Peter Stone knew he had to project an image of authority if he was to succeed at his assignment.

"Driver, open the trailer I want to look over the load."

"Who are you?"

"I'm your new boss. My name is Pete Stone. What's your name?"

"Chuck Wilson."

"Chuck, I want to inspect the load. Open the trailer and give me the manifest."

When the doors were open, he saw the arms, ammunition and explosives all neatly stacked inside the trailer and he said to the driver, "Bring out a case of grenades, a case of Semtex, one box of 7.62X39, an AK, one box of 5.56, an M4, a case of detonators and a case of timers."

When he had all the requested items lined up as ordered the driver asked, "What do you think Pete?"

"It all looks good, should bring top dollar." While loading a magazine for the AK, Peter asked the driver. "How long have you been with these guys?"

"About ten years."

"You qualify."

"What do you mean?"

"Just stand over here by the back of the trailer."

He saw the drivers from the other two trucks talking to each other.

"You two drivers come on over here."

"Sure, what do you want?"

For the uneducated, there are few things that strike fear into a man's heart more than looking down the barrel of a loaded AK47.

"Here's what I want. Take the pistols out of your belts and lay them on the ground. Then lie down side by side right here in front of me. If you don't follow my instructions right now, I'm going to kill you right where you stand."

Peter had grabbed a roll of duct tape on the way into the barn earlier. He used it to bind the drivers' arms, then helped each one climb up into the trailer with the weapons and explosives. He moved the drivers to the center of the trailer and duct taped their mouths and ankles and then taped all three drivers together. He closed the doors on the trailer, locked them and set to loading several magazines for the M4 assault rifle.

Peter Stone could hear talking inside of one of the semi-trailers. He cut the lock off the door and pulled it open and said,

"Does anyone in here speak English?"

A man's voice answered,

"Yes, I do."

"You must do exactly what I tell you if you want to live. Come forward, so I can see you."

It was a very nervous looking young man of maybe twenty-one or two. Without asking his name, Peter said,

"Get everyone out of that trailer. Take them all out that door over there. Tell them not to make a sound and do not stop walking for an hour. Now move. You have very little time to get away from here."

When the human cargo was completely offloaded and had cleared the premises, Peter Stone set about the task of attaching the explosives and setting the timers on the three tractors and trailers. When he was done, he slung the two loaded assault rifles, filled his coat pockets with grenades, picked up the remaining Semtex and started toward the restaurant.

"I thought I'd bring some samples from the shipment. This is some really good stuff."

Peter set the materials down and walked back to the entrance.

"Pete what are you doing?"

"I'm locking the doors. What do you think I'm doing?"

"What's this about. Why are you locking the doors?"

"It's about disposition."

"What?"

"You know something, Jill got this fancy watch for me just before she died. I wondered why she got such a fine timepiece and the answer came to me while I was out in the barn. In roughly thirty seconds according to my new watch this whole place is going to go up like you can't believe."

"I'm a United States Congressman, do you have any idea what you are doing?"

"You should have all started praying by now and yes, I know what I am doing. Times up!"

It only took one brick of plastic explosive under the section of the trailer where the balance of the explosives and grenades were located. Peter Stone threw the rest of the case of explosives into the center of the banquet room with several grenades for good measure. The explosion was massive, vaporizing anyone within twenty feet and blowing the rest to pieces. When the smoke cleared, there was literally nothing left, but a hole in the ground. Everything was gone. The following Monday, a letter was received at the offices of the FBI detailing what had happened along with a somewhat modified explanation detailing why. After the identification process was complete his remains were buried alongside his wife Jill.

"Why is it so dark and what are those agonizing screams?"

"Disposition Peter."

"I'm dead, aren't I?"

"Yes Peter, but you knew that was going to happen. There was no other way to deliver the souls I required of you."

"What now?"

"The terms of our agreement have been met Peter. You will not remember me again, well, until next we meet in the far distant future. I told you everything would be alright."

"Linnie, we have new neighbors moving in."

"Oh, that's great Jack. This development is filling up with young families so fast it's hard to keep up with their names."

"I met them on the way in. They have a ten-year-old boy. His father said his name is Justin."

"Why not have Alicia run over and introduce herself?"

"Good idea."

Linnie Burke called to her daughter to break the good news about the new neighbors.

"Alicia there is a new boy next door. His name is Justin, he's the same age you are honey, would you mind going and welcoming him to the neighborhood?"

"Sure mom."

Like all young children living in a development where everyone is from somewhere else, Alicia was very excited to meet the new boy next door. Alicia rang the doorbell and within seconds, Meghan Dennis, Justin's mother, came to the door.

"Hi, I'm Alicia Burke from next door I came over to meet Justin."

"I'll get him Alicia. Would you like to come in while I get Justin?"

"Yes, thank you."

"Justin, you have a visitor, can you come down here?"

"Yes mom."

Justin Dennis came racing down the stairs to meet his new neighbor.

"Justin, this is Alicia Burke. She lives next door."

"Hi."

"Would it be alright if Justin went to the corner store? My mom lets me go for ice cream if we have a group."

"That's fine, will just the two of you be going?"

"There will be two more, Bobby and Sarah Angel. They're twins and the same age we are. They live down the block."

"Justin be back for dinner."

"I will mom."

"Justin let's wait at the park across the street for Bobby and Sarah, then we can all walk to the store together."

And while the two children sat on a tandem swing waiting for the twins, Alicia looked at Justin.

"I'm so glad you're finally here Peter."

"So am I Jill. Can I hold your hand while we walk to the store?"

"You can hold my hand forever Peter."

The twins met them at the park and they all started walking to the store.

"Jill, look at the trees on the other side of the park. Do you see that shadow?"

"Yes, I do. It looks like it's following us. Peter are you afraid?"

"No, I am not."

"Are we going to be alright Peter?"

"Yes, we are."

Third times a charm

Three thugs, like hyenas tearing a downed gazelle to pieces, and in the excitement, failing to see the approaching lion.

Monday morning, June 1,1970.

In an alleyway on the west side of Chicago, an all too often act of violence is taking place.

"Help please, oh God, please don't."

"Shut up, one of you shut her up now."

"No, please don't do this, please no!"

Across the busy street, backed into the alley almost out of sight, sits an unmarked dark brown four door sedan with two plainclothes tactical officers in the front seat.

"If we go in there now, they will be charged with nothing more than battery and maybe attempted robbery. The lawyers will deal it out and these three pieces of garbage will end up with no real jail time."

"I hate to let it happen to this poor woman, but we need everything we can get to put them away for a long time."

In an area where few people other than locals are ever seen walking the streets, an outsider sticks out like a sore thumb.

"Look at that guy. He's going in that alley. The big one is getting off of her and reaching for his belt. He's got a gun."

"He just hit him in the forehead with something he's dropping like a bag of dirty laundry, look at him beating on the other two while he's pulling them off the girl."

"Don't move and give us away. Just wait and let's see what happens. This guy might have just saved the court system a ton of money."

The two thugs were against the brick wall where they had been thrown when they were dragged off the woman. Their eyes were glued to their attacker as it was obvious they had never sustained a beating like the one they had just been given.

"I can see that your pal here has a gun. What about you two?"

"What did you do to my shoulder? I think you broke it."

"Shut up."

"My ribs, it feels like you broke a couple of my ribs."

"You shut up too. Take a good look at my right hand, that's a nine-millimeter automatic with twelve rounds in the magazine. I'll have no problem killing the two of you if you make a move."

He paused long enough for his words to sink into the heads of the two lowlife's.

"Now, I'm asking you one last time if you have guns?"

Speak up, before I do the same thing to you that I did to the big one."

They spoke almost in unison.

"We have guns!"

"One at a time, take the guns out with two fingers and set them on the ground. You with the sore shoulder first!"

"What did you do to Big Al?"

"Don't worry about Big Al. He's not going to give anyone trouble anymore."

He reached behind his back and slipped the 9mm into his belt, then proceeded to dish out some additional punishment.

"Here's a little piece of advice for you two, forget what I look like. You see me on the street you don't know me from nothin.' You got that?"

The last beating had left the duo dazed.

"Answer me you morons."

"We got it."

"Now drag Big Al here over by that dumpster then get out of my sight. Call an ambulance for your boy. If he gets to a hospital soon, he might make it. Even if he does, he will probably eat through a tube for what's left of his life anyway."

The two dragged their accomplice, crying in pain from their beating, dropped him next to the dumpster and scurried off like sewer rats.

The young woman had pushed herself up against the side of the old brick building on the other side of the alley when she was freed from her attackers. With a dazed look on her face, she looked over at the large attacker lying face up along the side of the dumpster.

"That man, he has a large purple colored dent in his forehead. What did you hit him with and what did you beat the other two with?"

"What do you mean, what did I hit him with?"

"What's that in your hand?"

"It's a blackjack."

"You may have fractured his skull. He could die?"

"Does it matter? Don't feel sorry for him. You saw their faces. That means they were going to do a lot worse to you."

The man who had just delivered a dose of vicious punishment to three men gently took the young woman by her hand.

"Let me help you up. Did they take any jewelry, wedding ring, watch, anything?"

"No, I'm not married. There's my watch over there. The band is broken,"

"Straighten your clothes up, I'll get your watch."

He handed her the broken watch and with his handkerchief,

"Here let me wipe that blood off your face. Rolex, nice watch."

"A graduation gift from my parents."

"Do they know you hang out in this part of town?"

"I am here on a sales call."

The young lady was starting to calm down a little from her ordeal.

"My knee, look its bleeding all over my leg. My hands and my knuckles are bleeding. How bad do I look?"

"Not bad, considering. Do you want me to take you to a hospital?"

"I don't know."

"Don't you have clean underwear on?"

"What does clean underwear have to do with that?"

"Didn't your mother ever tell you that you should wear clean underwear when you go out in case you have to go to a hospital?"

"No, she didn't and yes, I have clean underwear on."

It was time to move.

"Gather up your things. Use this handkerchief to pick up those guns and put them in your bag."

"Don't you want them?"

"No, those are Saturday night specials, nothing but junk. They were probably used in other crimes, so just bring them along. Let's get out of this alley."

"My ankle."

"Can you walk on it?"

"Yes, I think so."

"Here, I'll hold you by your arm."

Even though she was still half dazed, she was surprised at how soft his touch was while helping her.

"I looked you over and you appear to be mostly in one piece, but you should get checked out sometime today."

The two TAC officers were still in their car.

"Dennis, he's coming out of the alley with the woman, looks like she got a real beating."

"Let's get coffee then take a ride over to Wilson General. I'm guessing the two he beat will be there and then we can head over to the morgue and look at the big one."

"He doesn't look like he's from the neighborhood, and he's not that big a guy, maybe six feet?"

Those punks really stepped in one today. I wonder what he's doing here?"

"If he's still around later we can ask him."

Since there was only one semi-secure parking lot in the general vicinity he began walking her in that direction.

"Where did you park?"

"In the lot down the street."

"We'll go on over and see if you still have tires on your car."

"You're kidding?"

"How many times do I have to tell you, this is not a nice neighborhood?"

"I won't forget any time soon."

Each step down the street gave her a little more composure.

"What kind of business are you doing in this part of town?"

"I am on a sales call for my company."

"And just who do you work for that would send you to this part of town unescorted?"

"I work for North American Lithograph Company in Elk Grove Village."

"I can't understand why they would have you come here."

"I was given an account to call on off the company's account list."

"And what is the name of the account?"

"Chicago Gasket, why?"

"I'll bet they don't do any business with your company and no established salesman in your company would waste five minutes on them."

"You're probably right."

"Look at that, a mailbox right outside that diner. Use the handkerchief I gave you to pick up the guns and deposit them. Let the government take care of disposal."

Most of the bleeding had stopped and after looking her over again, the diner presented the most logical place to get her cleaned up a little.

"Let's stop here. We can get a cup of coffee."

"I don't drink coffee."

"Well today's a good day to try something new. Besides, you can use the restroom to get cleaned up a little before I walk you to your car."

"I have a sales call."

"Not today you don't."

"Who are you calling on at Chicago Gasket?"

"His name is Phil McCarthy."

Aside from the burglar bars on the windows and door, it appeared to be a nice little diner.

"I wonder how much those punks were holding them up for every week?"

Mugging victims must have been a regular sight, because no one seemed to be alarmed when the two of them walked in the door.

"Miss, would you happen to have a first aid kit, a couple aspirin and a clean cloth that she can use to get cleaned up a little?"

"Yes, we do. I'll go get everything. What happened to her?"

"My friend here slipped and took a nasty fall in the alley down the street."

It only took a few seconds for the waitress to return.

"Here you are."

"Thanks, two coffees please for here, one teaspoon of cream in each. You go ahead and cleanup, I'll be in the booth over there. Miss where's your payphone please?"

"At the end of the counter to the right."
"Thanks."

He didn't have much time for the call and was surprised to find a phonebook without half the pages missing. He was flipping through the pages, talking to himself,

"Let's see. Chicago Gasket, there it is."

He put a dime in the slot and dialed.

"Good morning, Chicago Gasket, how can I direct your call?"

"Phil McCarthy please."

"Hold on, I will transfer your call."

On the second ring, a rugged sounding male voice answered.

"McCarthy."

"Mr. McCarthy, you had a meeting scheduled with a young woman from North American Lithograph this morning?"

"Yes, if you want to call it that."

"What do you mean by that?"

"Well, she sounded nice, so I thought I'd give her a look see."

"What's the chance you would ever do business with her company?"

"That depends?"

"Depends on what?"

"You know?"

"No, I don't know. Explain it to me?"

"Who is this anyway?"

"You don't need to know, all you need to know is this, she was jumped by some of your local neighborhood talent on her way here this morning and won't be coming in today. You had an obligation to tell her to be careful and at worst, should have had her park right in front of your building."

"Now hold on, do you know who you're talking to?"

"Yes, I do, so shut up and listen to me. Here's what's going to happen Phil. I am going to keep an eye on her and she is going to come back with someone from her company. If you have work she will compete for it like anyone else. If you don't, you will tell her straight out. If you try anything with her, you and I will have a meeting of our own and I can guarantee, you'll be the one who ends up worse for the wear. If you think I'm lying, ask anyone in the neighborhood what happened to those punks today. Furthermore, if you say one thing to her about this call and it gets back to me, you will regret it in spades. Got it?"

There was no response on the other end.

"I said got it?"

"Yes!"

The call must have taken longer than he anticipated, he started back to his seat.

"I'm sorry, I didn't see you back in the booth."

"I wish you had told me how I really looked."

"Nothing's broken. In a few days, you won't look like anything ever happened."

"I hope you're right."

"Listen, I would like to walk you to your car when we're finished."

"You don't have to. I should be alright."

"You really don't have any idea where your company sent you, do you?"

"Can I ask why you helped me and why you are making sure I don't run into any more trouble?"

"I don't know. I would probably help just about anyone I guess, but for some reason, when I saw what was happening to you, I had to step in regardless of the risk. I just want to make sure you don't run into anyone else like those three today."

"I can't thank you enough. I must apologize, in all the excitement, I haven't asked what your name is and haven't offered mine. I'm Pat Ricketts."

"I'm Nick, Nick Slater. It's good to meet you Pat Ricketts."

He gently shook her bruised and cut hand.

"I don't know where I would be if you hadn't come along,"

"It's ok I'm glad I was able to help and that you only got knocked around a little."

Nick paid for the two coffees, gave the waitress five-dollars for the first aid supplies and a five-dollar tip. Nick and Pat left and began the half a block walk to her car and as they were walking up to the lot. "Let me guess that nice new yellow Mustang convertible is yours?"

"Ok, you don't have to rub it in."

"And look, it hasn't been touched."

By now, they were both laughing. Nick wanted to make sure she got out of the area safely.

"Turn right out of the lot and drive straight to the expressway west ramp. It's about a block and a half away. Stay in the right lane and don't get off until you reach the suburbs."

"You're a real smart guy Nick."

"You don't need any repeats of today. Do you feel ok to drive? I would be happy to drive you to your office."

"No, I'm ok. Just getting really sore."

"Take it easy for a couple days you're young and will heal fast."

"Thanks again Nick."

"I'll watch you as you head out."

"Will I see you again Nick?"

"Life's a funny thing. You never know."

"You're a good man Nick Slater. Thank you for saving my life."

"Get moving."

As he watched her pull off into the distance he thought. 'Nice, smart and what a looker I should have asked for her phone number, it'd never work.'

Nick Slater had one last task before getting back to his day.

"North American Lithograph, how can I direct your call?"

"I would like to speak to your sales manager please."

"That's Carl Spring, I will put you through."

"Carl Spring."

"Mr. Spring, one of your sales people was mugged out here on the west side this morning trying to make a sales call on Chicago Gasket."

"That would be our new rep Pat Ricketts. Is she alright?"

"What I would like to know is why would you send a young woman out here when she has no idea what the area is like?"

"Well, she chose the account."

"Stop right there. I understand the sales process and how salesmen and companies protect anything they think may produce, however remote that possibility. I also know that worthless garbage is what's normally handed to new inexperienced people."

"Who are you anyway? I didn't get your name."

"My name is Nick Slater. If that woman gets hurt calling on the dreck you call accounts in one of these neighborhoods, because you see this as an easy way to get her to quit, you and I will have another conversation and the outcome will not be good for you. Do you understand me?"

For the second time that day there was dead silence on the other end of the line.

"Answer my question Mr. Spring. Do you understand me?"

"Yes!"

"Goodbye Mr. Spring."

In all his years in sales, Carl Spring had dealt with tough individuals both in person and on the phone. This was different and left him sitting in his office shaken when over the intercom,

"Carl Spring, please come to the conference room."

When he got to the doorway, he was shocked to see his new badly beaten sales rep.

"Good lord Pat, what happened?"

"I ran into a little trouble on the way to my appointment."

"Pat, your face is cut and bruised and your clothes, they're all torn and filthy."

"I'm ok Carl."

Shirley Adams, longtime receptionist at North American Lithograph, let Carl know she was going to call Neil Moran, CEO of the company, to let him know Pat was in the conference room. Carl Spring didn't want to have to explain to his boss what had happened.

"It's alright Shirley. I can take care of this."

"No Carl, I know Mr. Moran and he does not like to be kept in the dark about something as serious as this. He will just be sick when he sees Pat."

As Shirley was going to call the boss, she turned back to Pat.

"Pat, can I get you some water?"

"Coffee would be fine."

"You don't drink coffee."

"After today I do, just a teaspoon of cream please."

Neil Moran, fit gray haired former star running back in college, literally ran from his office to the conference room only to be shocked to see what had happened to his new sales rep.

"Mr. Moran, you didn't need to race down here,"

"You're one of my employees. What the hell happened, my God who beat you like that?"

"Three men dragged me into an alley about a block from my 8:30 a.m. appointment at Chicago Gasket,"

"Chicago Gasket! Do you know what that area is like?"

"I do now. Anyway, one grabbed my bags and started going through them then they threw me on the ground and began punching and kicking me and tearing at my clothes."

"How did you manage to get away, who helped you?"

"There was this man who must have heard me screaming and he came into the alley. He hit the biggest of the three with something."

"Was he a thug like the men who attacked you?"

"Oh no, in his own way he was very kind. Anyway, when he hit the big one, it was so hard it may have fractured his skull and killed him. The man was unconscious. Then, he beat the other two unmercifully. He had a gun and told them he would have no problem killing them if they tried anything."

"Did anyone call the police?"

No, there were no police. Then he took their guns and we dropped them in a mailbox on the way to a diner to have coffee."

"Have coffee, after you've been beaten half to death? Does this man have a name?"

"Yes, Nick Slater."

"Who sent you to see Chicago Gasket?"

"I picked the name off the account list."

"Carl did you clear this?"

"No, he didn't. I researched the company, called and set the appointment myself."

"You are new to sales, everything you do is supposed to be cleared by management."

Carl Spring had the look of a man who wanted to crawl under the conference table and hide while Neil Moran continued his rant.

"There is no one in the printing industry in this part of the country that doesn't know Phil McCarthy is a slime bag. He's always had his hand out and has hit on every woman he has ever come in contact with. His nickname is three percent McCarthy, because he requires all vendors to tack that on to every order for him."

"Mr. Moran, I would like to reschedule that call, but I would like to go with one of the other salesmen. This time I will park right in front of their building."

"Carl does she know something I don't?"

"I don't know Neal. I will go with her when she reschedules. It will give me a chance to listen to her pitch and who knows, we may get something."

"Good, let me know what happens, but before you do another thing, you go over to North Suburban hospital and get checked out. Don't give me that look, this is an order."

At that, Neil Moran, CEO of North American Lithograph, stormed back to his office.

"Pat, thank you for not pushing me in front of the bus. Mr. Moran would have fired me on the spot. I'm sorry, I should have told you about McCarthy. No one from this company has been there in years. I had no idea that area had gotten that bad."

"Carl, I want to be in business. Let's just say my indoctrination into sales was a little rougher than usual."

"Get the appointment. They do huge catalog runs. A perfect fit for our equipment. Ms. Ricketts, you are about to get quite a raise when we sign Chicago Gasket the right way."

Two weeks later, the only real signs of being roughed up were the remnants of Pat Ricketts two black eyes. A little makeup helped to hide most of that. Nick Slater had gone back to his apartment on the northside of Chicago and was planning his next move when the phone rang.

"Nick Slater."

"Nick, it's Colonel Murray. How's life been treating you the last eight months?"

"Ok I guess. I met a nice girl a couple week's back, but other than that, it's civilian life."

"You'll have to tell me about her the next time I see you."

"Colonel, I can't imagine this is just a social call. I was discharged this past December and if I recall correctly, you were the one that advised me to go."

"Nick, you needed a rest and thirty days leave wasn't going to do the job. I can bring you back at your old rank and the time you have been off will still count toward your next promotion."

"Let me think about it for a few days."

"I don't have that kind of time Nick."

"Where would I be going?"

"South America and that's all I can say."

"For how long and what kind of a team would I have?"

"You'd be awhile, and you can pick from our list, there are a lot of your old guys on it."

"I need five days to clean things up here and get everything into storage."

"Then you're back?"

"Yes sir, I am."

"Lieutenant Slater there will be a boarding pass at the United counter next Monday morning at O'Hare for an 8:45 a.m. military charter to Miami. See you when you land."

"Yes sir."

At the same time Nick Slater was finalizing his arrangements to leave the country, Pat Ricketts was making arrangements to pick up her college roommate.

"Patty, I can't wait to see you."

"Jackie, we have so much to talk about. When do you get in?"

"We are supposed to land 8:00 a.m. Monday at the United Airlines terminal."

"I'll be in front waiting. Look for the yellow Mustang convertible."

"Really?"

"Yes, really."

"By the way, since you wouldn't say anything, your mother had to tell me about the mugging a few weeks back."

"I know. I just wanted to put it behind me."

"What about the guy?"

"What guy?"

"The one that saved your beautiful skin."

"Oh him."

"Come on Patty, it's me Jackie. What's his name? What does he look like? How many times have you gone out?"

"His name is Nick Slater. He's good looking and we have never gone out. I don't have his phone number and he didn't ask for mine."

"What's wrong with you. That's not the Patty Ricketts I know?"

"It all happened so fast and the next thing I knew he's watching me drive away."

"Did you try to look him up?"

"Yes, I did. I told several people I know about him, including the owner of my company. He said he had some friends in government that might be able to help."

"And what happened?"

"They said it was above their pay grade and couldn't get any information."

"So now what do you do?"

"Now, I wait and hope we run into each other someday before we are too damn old to enjoy each other's company."

"I hope so Pat. See you in the morning."

Monday morning, August 3, 1970.

The Checker Cab pulled up to the curb in front of the United terminal promptly at 8:15 a.m. with one occupant and no bags.

"That will be fifteen dollars and fifty cents sir."

"Here's twenty. Thanks for getting me here in time for my flight."

"Thank you, sir."

AT 8:30 a.m., Pat Ricketts friend Jackie Barret rode the escalator up from baggage claim and immediately spotted the yellow convertible parked at the opposite end of the concourse. She picked up her bag, began running and waving trying to attract her friend's attention, not looking or paying any attention to the other travelers making their way through the terminal. She ran into a young man wearing a dark shirt and sunglasses with a cup of coffee, knocking it from his hand and fortunately just to the floor. Jackie Barret apologized telling him she was in Chicago to meet her college roommate. She offered to pay for his drink, but he politely declined. He said he had to get to his flight, assured her that everything was alright and walked on.

Pat saw her friend coming out through the automatic doors, began to wave and got out of her car to greet her friend. "You sure stick out in the crowd with this Mustang."

"You know me, always trying to be noticed. How was your flight?"

"Smooth and on time."

"Jackie, look over there. Do you see that guy walking through the terminal?"

"Which one?"

"The one with the dark shirt, brown hair and sunglasses."

"Yes, I ran into him in the terminal and knocked his coffee out of his hand."

"That's Nick, Nick Slater."

"Are you sure?"

"Yes absolutely, I have to catch him. Please just stay here with the car. I can't let him get away."

She caught a glimpse of Nick as he was being handed his boarding pass and began to run to catch him. When she got to the gate, there was no one in the boarding area and the door was closed. She went directly to the counter.

"Miss was there a man at your counter a minute ago, brown shirt, brown hair and sunglasses?"

"Yes, I processed his boarding pass."

"Can you tell me where he went?"

"Yes, he's on that military charter starting to taxi out onto the runway."

"Can you tell me where he, it, is headed?"

"I'm sorry, I can't. We only processed boarding for that flight there was no published destination. Is there anything else I can help you with?"

"Yes, there is, have that plane turn around and come back to the terminal."

"I'm sorry, I wish I could."

Pat Ricketts started the long lonely walk back to her car and with each step, she wondered if she would ever see Nick Slater again.

"Why do you look so down, didn't you catch up to him?"

"No, he boarded a military charter flight before I could get there. They weren't given the destination. I don't know what I am going to do?"

"You're going to wait. If you are supposed to see him again, it will happen."

"I had no idea he was military. I wonder where he's going?"

"Patty, do you know what not in uniform, didn't have any baggage and gets on a flight with no published destination means? You don't want to know."

Monday morning, June 2, 1980.

Nick Slater had thought of Pat Ricketts often during the ten years since he had unknowingly left her standing in the boarding area at O'Hare International Airport.

"I'm on a five-hour layover here and I need a limo. What are your rates please?"

"Where will you be going sir?"

"I would like to be picked up at O'Hare. I'll be going to Elk Grove Village and possibly Chicago before going back to O'Hare."

"Our rate is eighty dollars per hour and we recommend a twenty percent tip for the driver."

"That sounds reasonable, when can you have someone here to pick me up?"

"We can have a car there in fifteen minutes. Can I have a name and airline?"

"Yes, Major Nick Slater and I am at United Airlines, lower level and I'm in uniform."

"Major our military rate is seventy-two dollars per hour and our driver is on his way."

" Thanks."

Fifteen minutes, almost to the second, the limo pulled up to the curb at passenger pickup.

"Major Slater?"

"Yes."

"You're easy to spot in uniform."

"We travel this way."

"I'm Gil Taylor, your driver. Where to sir?"

"2312 Green St Elk., Grove Village, North American Lithograph."

"You have business there?"

"No, just going to visit an old friend for a minute."

"I'll get you there as quick as I can."

With only three hours and fifteen minutes left before he had to catch a flight to parts unknown, Nick was going to have his reunion with the woman whose life he had saved and who he could not get out of his mind.

"Good morning sir, how can I help you?"

"I would like to see Ms. Pat Ricketts if she is available?"

"I'm sorry, she is out on a call with one of our salespeople."

"Can you tell me when she might be back?"

"Did she know you were coming?"

"No, we're just old friends and I'm on a five-hour layover here, and I thought I'd drop in and see if I could catch her."

"There's no way I can really get in touch with her right now and she could be gone for quite some time. They are signing a large contract this morning."

"I really wish I could have seen her. Would you please tell her Major Nick Slater was here and I am sorry I missed her."

"Nick Slater! Major could you please wait right here?"

"Sure."

After the beating that Pat Ricketts sustained way back in 1970, no one ever forgot the name of the man who saved her life. She went directly to Neal Moran's office, didn't knock and interrupted a call with one of their largest customers. In a very aggravated tone,

"What is it Shirley?"

I'm sorry to interrupt your call, but do you remember the name Nick Slater?"

"Of course, how could any of us forget."

"Well, he is standing in the lobby asking to see Pat."

"Don't leave him standing there. Let him in. I'm on my way there right now."

Neal Moran ran down the hall as fast as he had ten years earlier.

"Major Slater, my name is Neal Moran. I'm Pat's boss. You're the Nick Slater that saved Pat Ricketts' life ten years ago."

"I'm that Nick Slater sir."

"Oh my God Major, do you have a few minutes?"

"Yes, I do."

"Please come with me down the hall to my office. It's really something to have you here."

"Would you care for something to drink?"

"Coffee would be fine."

The hallway was filling with front office staff all wanting to get a look at Nick.

"Shirley."

"I already know. I'll be right there with it."

"Please sit down. I finally get to meet you. Pat told us all about you after she was attacked."

"I'm glad I was able to help her."

"She has been instrumental in the success of this company and I owe you a debt of gratitude."

"For what Mr. Moran?"

"I had a conversation with Carl Spring when he retired two years ago. You might remember him?"

"Yes vaguely."

"Well, he related a somewhat one-sided conversation the two of you had the day Pat was beat up."

"Yes."

"Well, that helped to set us on a new path. It took us from old line to the modern world, we made major changes in our approach to selling and the people who represent us."

"How is Mr. Spring?"

"He and his wife retired to Florida. He's doing fine."

"I'm happy to hear that."

"To this day, Pat doesn't know what you did and Carl swore me to secrecy. He also mentioned a conversation you had with that snake McCarthy at Chicago Gasket."

"How did he find out about that?"

"He and McCarthy were at a Blackhawks hockey game after we signed a contract with them. After a couple beers, he told him the whole story. McCarthy said he was never so scared in his life."

"Does she know about that?"

"Absolutely not."

"She put the business together herself and refused to get drawn into anything unless it was aboveboard."

"So, she is a stand-up act?"

"You better believe it."

Because it was Nick Slater, there was no such thing as 'talking out of school.'

"I might as well tell you this while you are here, Pat was married and divorced twice in the last ten years. I was at the first wedding and would have given her the keys to my summer home if she would have run away before the ceremony and had her stay there until that leach went away. The whole thing lasted for two years before she finally dumped him. He was just in it for what he could get out of her. Successful women, unfortunately, are sometimes easy marks. The second one was a Las Vegas wedding and didn't last much longer than the trip there and back, another ne'er-do-well."

"I'm sorry to hear that. I really am. No one deserves to be alone and unhappy. I kicked myself for not trying to contact her over the years, but one doesn't get into relationships in my line of work. Believe me Mr. Moran, it's not that I have not wanted to see her."

"I understand. Is there any way you can stay through tomorrow?"

"I wish there was, but when I leave here I am not at liberty to say what I will be doing or where I am going."

"I understand."

Time was starting to run short and Nick had obligations he could not and would not shirk.

"I do have to get back to the airport. It's important that I make that flight."

"I'll let her know you were here personally."

"Thank you, sir."

"It was a pleasure meeting you major. Come back for her as soon as you can."

"I'll do my best."

Moran called reception as Nick was leaving.

"Shirley, have Pat come to my office as soon as she gets back to the office."

"Yes sir."

Bad news is best delivered in person.

Nick was checking in for his flight when Pat was walking in the door of the office.

"Pat, Mr. Moran asked to have you come to his office as soon as you got back."

Pat could sense that there was something in the tone of Shirley's voice and went directly to Neal's office.

"Pat, have a seat."

"Is there a problem Neal?"

"You had a visitor this morning and I thought it best if I told you personally."

"It was Nick Slater wasn't it?"

"Yes, it was."

"How can a human being have such terrible luck. What have I done wrong? Ten years ago, I chased him, through the airport and before I could get to him he was gone. Then today it happens again."

"Pat, he'll be back. I guarantee it."

"But when? Do you know when he saved my life I asked him why he did it. He said, for some reason he didn't want me to get hurt anymore and didn't want anything bad to happen to me again. What do you call that?"

"Pat in his world that may just be love at first sight. You just have to be patient."

"That's what Jackie said ten years ago."

Monday morning June 4, 1990.

All good things must come to an end.

"Nick, you're really retiring?"

"Twenty-four years in countries run by despots, drug cartels, insurgent groups and corrupt dictators, I think I did my part."

"You know if you stay, you will probably get a star."

"O-6 is fine sir. There is another world out there and I'd like to experience it a little before I'm too old to appreciate it."

"Nick, we had a great run together. Your country will always be indebted to you for your efforts. What are your plans for retirement?"

"Well sir, I have several offers to do consulting with security firms and I have a brother who has a large farming operation in the Midwest. But first I'm going to take a trip to Chicago. I have some unfinished business there."

"Best of luck in your new life Nick."

Stopping at a newsstand in the United concourse at O'Hare Intl, on his way to catch a cab.

"That will be one dollar please."

"She made the front page of the business section."

The headline read, Patricia Ricketts named Executive Vice President of the North American Corporation. With corporate offices in Chicago and ten billion dollars in worldwide sales from combined operations of all divisions, it is one of the world's largest publication and catalog printers. Nick could hardly contain himself.

"Good job Pat."

For some strange reason the expressway traffic was light. The trip downtown took less than a half hour. Nick had the cab drop him at the corner of Ohio and Michigan, paid the twenty-five plus tip and started walking to Pat's office.

"Good morning sir, how can I help you?"

"I would like to know if Pat, I mean Ms. Ricketts might have a minute?"

"Do you have an appointment?"

"No, I don't."

"I'm sorry, but she doesn't see anyone without an appointment. If I may ask, how did you get through security to get up here?"

"I must have an honest face."

"Sir, that doesn't work with our security."

"Well, to tell you the truth, one of your security personnel served in one of my commands."

"You're military?"

"Recently retired. Can I leave my name?"

"Yes."

"Tell her Nick Slater stopped by and tell her congratulations on the promotion."

"Do you know her?"

"Yes, we're old friends. We go way back."

"I wish I could help, Mr. Slater but she is in meetings all day and gave strict orders not to be disturbed."

"I understand."

"Oh, there she is coming out of a meeting with all of those people."

"She hasn't changed bit."

"Pardon me?"

"Oh nothing, if you could just let her know I was here."

"I'll be happy to do that sir. May I ask what rank you were?"

"Colonel."

If Pat Ricketts learned only one thing from the beating she took years earlier, it was to always be aware of your surroundings.

"Carrie, that man walking toward the elevators looks familiar. Can you run over to reception and ask if he left his name? I'll be in my office getting ready for the next round with these union people."

"Right away Ms. Ricketts."

Pat's assistant could tell by the inflection in her boss' voice that she should actually run to reception and get the man's name.

"Bob did that man who just left leave a name?"

"Yes, he did. He said his name was Nick Slater, an old friend of Ms. Ricketts from way back. No appointment though and somehow got through security. Told me one of the guys there served under him. Said he was a Colonel. How is everything going in the meetings?"

"There's no doubt that she got to where she is by being the best. She's tough as nails. I don't think anyone in there has ever dealt with a negotiator like her and frankly, I think they hate her guts because she will get every concession she asked for."

"A big win for us?"

"You can call it that, but I feel sorry for her in a way. She doesn't have a life outside of this business."

"Bobby, I don't want to go through life alone like that."

"Neither do I Carrie. Are we still on for lunch?"

"You bet we are. I have to get to Ms. Ricketts office."

"Carrie what did you find out about that man?"

"He told Bobby he was an old friend from way back, his name is Nick."

"Slater!"

Pat Ricketts literally leapt out of her chair and began running for the door.

"Tell them I had to run out, something very important, an emergency. Tell them not to leave."

"Yes ma'am."

"I'll be back as soon as I can."

She was running out of the office past reception and stopped for mere seconds.

"Bob, did you see which elevator that man took?"

"Yes Ms. Ricketts, the center one,"

"Call down to the lobby. Have security stop that man and if he walked out, have them chase him down and stop him. Let them know I'm on my way down. Do it now!"

"Yes ma'am."

"Security, this is Bob Hartman up in reception, Ms. Ricketts wants you to stop the man coming out of the center elevator as soon as it gets there. She is on her way down. Don't let him get away."

"It already came."

"Do you see him in the lobby?"

"He went to the coffee shop. I'll check."

"Make it fast and if he's not there, have your people go looking for him."

Security was in the coffee shop in seconds.

"I saw a man come in here a minute ago."

"Yes, he ordered a coffee to go and asked to have one sent up to Ms. Ricketts, the same thing she gets every morning when she comes in, medium coffee with one teaspoon of cream. What's going on?"

"I don't know, but they want us to catch that guy."

The entire security staff from the lobby was looking for Nick Slater by the time Pat stepped off the elevator.

"Ms. Ricketts!"

"Did you manage to stop him?"

"No Ma'am. He was gone before the call came down to us. I have two security people going in opposite directions on the street looking for him."

"Have them check the exits at the closest parking garages and any shops a man might shop at. Nick, why can't you sit in one spot for longer than a minute?"

"Ms. Ricketts?"

"Oh, I was just talking to myself. Tell your people I appreciate everything they are doing."

"Yes ma'am."

"I'll be up in my office. Please call me right away if you find him."

She turned and made her way back to the elevators to start the long ride up to the top of the office tower alone. When she stepped off the elevator on the top floor of the North American Corporation office towers it was obvious she was devastated. Pat went straight to her office, sat in her chair and put her head in her hands.

"Bobby, we have to put lunch off today."

"But I thought we…?"

"Bobby, Ms. Ricketts is in her office sobbing like she just lost someone she loved more than anything in the world. She keeps repeating, Nick why do you keep leaving me? Nick please come back and take me away? I've been waiting twenty years for you to come back and when you do, you just leave me alone again. Nick please."

"I closed the blinds in her office and I will not let anyone near her. I let the union people know she had a family emergency come up and they are all to be back here in the morning. They were happy to hear that, because I'm sure they think they can work this in their favor. If anyone other than Nick Slater comes to see her today, send them packing."

"Done."

"Bobby, I want a life, and this just strengthened my resolve to have one."

"Well, I had plans for lunch that directly relates to that."

"I know that."

"How do you know what my plans are?"

"Do I look like I'm stupid?"

"No, you don't. Anything but."

"The answer is yes. We will go to lunch tomorrow, so you can do this the right way, then you can go ask my father and then take me out for a couple stiff drinks and dinner."

His expression went from dejected to elated.

"Bobby what are you so happy about?"

Pat's assistant wanted to make sure no one had access to her boss.

"Carrie, I apologize for falling apart in front of you and thank you for not letting anyone see me like that."

"That's ok Ms. Ricketts, at the risk of insulting you, I had doubts that you were even human."

"So, have I on occasion. Let's keep that joke between us. How long have you been working for me?"

"Five years."

"Are you aware how valuable you are to me and this company?"

"I've never thought about it?"

"No one ever does. What is your base salary?"

"Twenty-nine thousand dollars."

"You are underpaid. Why haven't you come to me?"

"I was always afraid I would be let go."

"Not on your life. You are not only key to my position, you may have saved this union negotiation. There will be a significant raise on your next paycheck."

"I don't know what to say."

"I'll say it. I'm sorry I didn't do this sooner. Now, what's the story between you and Bob in reception and before you ask, I'm also not blind?"

"He was going to ask me to marry him at lunch today."

"Oh boy, have I made a mess out of everyone's day."

"No ma'am, you haven't. We are going to lunch tomorrow and he's going to officially ask me then, although I did tell him yes earlier."

"So, you are going to have a life together?"

On that afternoon a friendship was formed between two business people.

"Carrie, please sit down and tell me a little about him."

"Well, Bobby had some problems early and managed to get beyond them. He works like a dog, is very smart and we both agree that we complement each other."

"Do you love him?"

"Like nothing else."

"How do you think he'll handle success?"

"What do you mean?"

"There is a whole new world about to open up for your Bobby."

"I will call the VP of sales this afternoon. He and I have worked together for years. I would like to have him meet Bob. I think he would be a great addition to our sales force."

"I don't know what to say?"

"You're supposed to say, I better contact Human resources and tell them they have to start looking for his replacement in reception."

Nick decided to give her a try again the next day and started walking to her office from the Marriott on Michigan Ave when he was approached by one very sorry looking down and out man.

"Sir, I hate to bother you, but would you have some loose change for a vet. I'm awful hungry?"

"You look about Vietnam age?"

"I am sir, 11th Armored Cav out of Pleiku 1969 through 1970."

"No kidding, what did you do?"

"Gunner."

"Dangerous job were you on an APC?"

"Most of the time sir."

"I did some work for you guys and got a chance to do an R&R to Bangkok with a couple of your Scout Pilots, shameful behavior."

"My life was never the same sir."

"I understand. I'm going to ask you a couple of questions and I would like honest answers"

"Alright sir."

"Have you been in jail?"

"Just for vagrancy and public intoxication."

"What do you want the money for?"

"Well sir, drugs and alcohol, mainly alcohol. It's the only way I can sleep and keep the thoughts from driving me crazy."

"Do you want help?"

"I've been through programs a couple times, I just can't seem to get hold of myself."

"I know a lot of water has run under the bridge over the years and I'm guessing your about fifty maybe fifty-five?"

"Fifty-two sir."

"What rank were you when you separated?"

"I was Sergeant first class, an E6."

"I'm sorry, I should have done this first, what is your name?"

"It's Leon Higgins."

"Well Sergeant Leon Higgins, my name is Nick Slater."

As Nick put his hand out,

"You don't mind shaking this dirty hand sir?"

"No, I don't. As a matter of fact, it's an honor Leon."

Nick had always felt he was one of the fortunate ones that had been able to deal with the effects of combat and go on to lead a relatively normal life. He also believed he had an obligation to help those who had a genuine desire to 'get better.'

"I have two more questions. Can you give me two honest answers?"

"Yes sir I can."

"Would you like to have a real life?"

"Yes sir, more than anything."

"Good."

"And would you be willing to give a treatment program one more try?"

"Yes sir."

"Both right answers. There's a program a couple old friends of mine run out in Colorado, no nonsense, no drinking, no drugs, very strict rules, hard work and it takes a minimum of a year."

"Sir, do you think this life is easy?"

"I know it's not Leon, are you interested?"

"Yes sir, I am, but Colorado is a long way from Chicago."

"Let me worry about that, when can you leave?"

"Sir, everything I own is on my back. I can go now if I have to."

"Let's do this then, I can't get you on a bus until tomorrow, can you make it one night without drinking or drugs?"

"Maybe just a little drink to take the edge off, but that's it."

"I have a room at the Marriott. You can get cleaned up there after we get you something to wear. Then, I think we will head to a diner I saw around the corner for something to eat."

"Can I ask why you're doing this for me sir?"

"Because I think you deserve better."

A cab ride to State Street for some new clothes and personal items, then back to the hotel. "Leon, you look almost human."

"I'll take that as a compliment sir."

"It is."

"Do you mind if I sit here by the window for a minute before we go?"

"No, not at all Leon, it's not a problem."

"I know it's your room sir, but could I have a minute here alone? I don't want you to see a grown man cry."

"I understand Leon. I'll meet you in the lobby, say fifteen minutes."

"Thank you, sir."

Leon was walking out of the elevator fifteen minutes later looking like any other guest staying at the hotel.

"Ready for lunch?"

"Yes, I am. If I may ask, what your rank was when you left the service?"

"I was a Colonel Leon."

"I started out as a grunt, a battlefield commission in 1967. You might say I have a real soft spot for the enlisted ranks."

A short walk later they were sitting in a downtown diner.

"Well, what's on the menu that catches your eye?"

"Would you mind if I had a real breakfast?"

"You can have whatever you want Leon."

Nick's charity only went so far. Leon slept on the couch in Nick's hotel room while Nick took the bed. The following morning, Nick took Leon to the Greyhound bus station on west Harrison Street and booked a seat on the 'Dog' for Leon's trip to Colorado.

"Leon, the bus trip is two days to where you are going. You'll be met by Sam Mathis and Bob Dance the two fellows I told you about. They are two tough old birds and will do everything necessary to help you succeed."

"How can I ever thank you for what you have done?"

"Help someone out someday. Goodbye and good luck Leon."

"Goodbye Colonel."

Once again, Nick had run out of time and had to leave to meet new commitments.

Monday morning, June 5, 2000.

While changing planes in Chicago on his way to another consulting assignment, Nick managed to grab a copy of The Chicago Tribune.

"That's a dollar fifty sir."

He wished he could just purchase the business section, since local Chicago news held little interest. When he opened the business section it was worth the dollar fifty he paid for the paper. Nick muttered to himself,

"Now that is really something. She conquered the corporate world. CEO of that communications conglomerate, you've done good. I wish I had time to stop and see you Pat, you're always on my mind."

Over on the other side of town in the executive offices of the North American

Corporation. CEO Pat Ricketts is having a conversation with her executive assistant.

"It's ten years and I have never gotten used to calling you Pat."

"I don't ever want it to go back the other way Carrie. How is Bob doing?"

"He's being promoted to Midwest sales manager this week."

"I'm sure he deserves it. I know the bosses. Nobody gets anything they don't deserve."

"With all of the outlets we have, why haven't you ever put his name out there?"

"I know he would be embarrassed beyond belief."

"I don't think so. I'll bet you he would be here so fast it would make your head spin."

"I just can't."

Monday morning June 6, 2005.

It was 4:00 a.m. when the cell rang at Nick Slater's new home in the Summerlin section of Las Vegas. His first thought was, 'That's a DC area code.' Only slightly annoyed, he picked up the phone.

"Nick Slater."

"Nick, it's Ron Murray."

"General Murray how are you sir. The last time we spoke, I was retiring."

"It was Nick, how's your golf game?"

"It could be better how about yours?"

"It would be better if I had more time."

"What can I do for you sir. I'm guessing there is more to this call than just talk about our golf games?"

"I wanted to run something by you Nick to see what your take is."

"Go ahead sir."

"We monitor chatter in various parts of the world and recently picked up some coming out of the Philippines. There was a call made from a union boss in Chicago named Charles Buntrik to one of your old team members in Manilla, a Thomas Petrone."

"Tommy Petrone, now there's a name I had hoped I would never hear again. I brought him up on charges for drug dealing. Caught him red-handed. He was court-martialed and dishonorably discharged along with three of his accomplices."

"From what we picked up, they are on their way to Chicago as we speak. It has something to do regarding union negotiations with the North American Corporation. Where are you right now Nick?"

"General you know exactly where I am if you are talking to me."

"Protocol Nick, you know how it is. Listen Nick, right now we have nothing to go on other than a benign conversation between a union boss attempting to solicit some undesirables in Manilla."

"General I'm sixty-five years old. I'm getting too old for this."

"Nick, I just wanted to run something by you, that's all."

"Sir, you know better."

"Alright, from our conversations over the years, you have more than a passing interest in someone at North American Corporation?"

"You might say that."

"Nick, what is your take on these four going to Chicago at the request of Buntrik?"

"If that slime bag Petrone is involved, it's nothing good. I'll look into it."

"How soon can you get started?"

"So, there is some real urgency?"

"Yes, there is."

"I can be in Chicago by the end of the day. Petrone will want to have familiar surroundings as a base of operations, so he will go back to his old neighborhood."

"Do you have any idea where that is?"

"Yes, I do, real close to where I grew up. I'm familiar with all the hangouts."

"General you and I both know the only reason people bring scum like Petrone to town is to handle their dirty work."

"We will arrange your travel from our end. There will be a credit card at the ticket counter when you get there."

"I'll need a few things I can't carry on the plane."

"Grab a pen Nick and write this down, Dick Burkowski, 4140 Green Tree Road, Des Plaines. He can take care of whatever you need. You can contact me at this number."

"Yes sir, I'll be in touch General."

Two hours later as Nick Slater was packing there was an early morning meeting taking place in the office of the CEO at North American Corporation.

"Carrie, this is the biggest union agreement we have ever negotiated. It's imperative that we are at the top of our game when we walk into the conference room next Friday morning, June 12th. I know Buntrik and his people are going to make demands we have never had to deal with before. They are still smarting from the negotiations in

1990, 1995 and 2000. This will be my last one. I want to make sure it's done right and in the best interest of this company and our employees. I'll be forced out by the time the next one comes around."

Nick arrived in Chicago late Monday evening, rented a car and drove to Evanston where he had made a room reservation at the Hilton Orrington. He knew without a doubt that Petrone and his men would not be staying there. Downtown Evanston was also a short ride to the northside where he grew up and where he would find Tommy Petrone. He waited for the morning rush to end and made his way to Des Plaines using a GPS to locate the address the general had provided. He rang the doorbell. A big man opened the door. Nick estimated six five maybe two forty or so, tattooed arms, gray black beard and shaved head.

"Can I help you?"

"I'm looking for Dick Burkowski, my name…"

"It's not necessary. Come in. I'll take care of getting what you need. What specifically do you want?"

"A non-traceable small 380 automatic, two boxes of Federal 380 90gr Hydra-Shok JHP ammo, a conceal holster, a blackjack and a good quality double-edge knife."

Will that do it?"

"Yes."

"I'll take care of everything. Can you come back at ten tomorrow morning?"

"I'll be here, thanks."

It appeared all the players were arriving in Chicago right about the same time. Tommy Petrone, as he liked to be called, and his three men cleared customs. His first order of business was to call Mr. Charles Buntrik using a prearranged alias.

"Mr. Buntrik's office."

"I would like to speak to Mr. Buntrik?"

"Who can I say is calling?"

"Thomas Chapman."

The call was transferred and Buntrik himself answered,

"Are you in Chicago?"

"Yes, we're in Chicago and we need to meet and finalize our arrangements."

"Do you have a place where we can meet and not draw any attention?"

"Come up to 6408 N. Broadway, The Double Shot Lounge. No one will have a clue who you are. We'll be waiting."

"Give me an hour."

Thomas 'Tommy' Petrone turned to his accomplices.

"He's on his way and he better have every cent he promised."

Then, from the other side of the dimly lit barroom came a familiar voice from the past. "Tommy, Tommy Petrone is that you?"

"Yes, it is. Slim, is that you? How you doin?"

"I'm doin' alright. How many years has it been?"

"I think about ten or twelve."

"Where have you been?"

"I've been here and there."

"I'm the only one from the old days that still comes here. Everyone else either died, moved away or is in prison."

"Well, it sure hasn't changed a bit since the last time I was here. The crowd's the same just different faces."

"Hey Tommy, could you cover me for a drink? I'm a little short today."

"Sure Slim, what happened to the foot?"

"Diabetes, the doctor said either stop drinking or they would have to remove the foot. I still have one and I get around ok on the crutches. These guys with you?"

294

"Yeah, friends of mine."

Charles Buntrik, President of the International Union, started at the bottom and over forty years clawed and beat his way to the top. His limo pulled up in front of the Double Shot. The driver opened the door and he stepped out with a briefcase full of cash in hand to meet the people who were going to give him the edge in his negotiations with the North American Corporation.

"This place is a dump."

"You wanted a place where you wouldn't be recognized?"

"But not mugged either."

"You have nothing to worry about. One of my men is out by your car with your driver and no one can get to you in here. I have two others over by the bar. Now, let's get on with our business."

"I have the one million dollars we agreed upon in this briefcase."

"Slide it under the table."

"Aren't you going to check it?"

"For what Mr. Buntrik, I have no doubt that it's all there."

"What do you plan to do with her?"

"That's our business. When do you need her gone?"

"Negotiations start Friday the 12th, anytime between now and then is fine. It'll all have the same net effect."

"We have to work out a few details and then we'll move."

"Just remember, it has to be done before the Friday meeting starts."

"It'll be done. Now, get out of my sight."

"Hey Tommy, do you think you could cover me for a couple more?"

"Yeah, here's ten bucks."

"How long are you going to be in town?"

"I'll be leaving on the 12th."

"Maybe I'll see you again before you go, huh?"

"Probably, see you Slim."

Nick had grown up on the northside and was intimately familiar with the various haunts and dumps the likes of Tommy Petrone hung out at. When Tommy was on one of his teams, before he got himself into trouble, Tommy had bragged about 'coming up' where he did. Nick parked up off Granville Ave and walked down Broadway toward The Double Shot Lounge. When he recognized one of them, he ducked into an alleyway across the street to watch. That's Sean Gleason by that car. He looks awful, ten years in

Manila hasn't been kind to him. That guy coming out of The Double Shot looks familiar. What is someone dressed in an expensive looking suit probably being driven around in that limo doing in that dump. At least I know where those lowlifes are hanging out. I think I'll wait until they leave and then go in.

Nick's patience paid off twenty minutes later. There's Tommy Petrone, that fancy briefcase can't be his. I'll bet it's stuffed with money. I know him well and his taste leans more to a paper sack. Jerome Johnson and Michael Hanks, that's the rest of the crew. Wow, they look as bad as Gleason. I might as well get a paper and kill some time before going in to see who we both might know.

He walked north toward Granville where he had parked the rental car. Under the 'L' tracks, there was a newsstand where he bought Chicago's other paper, The Chicago Sun Times. Nick turned to the business section There right on page one was a picture of Charles Buntrik, president of the International Union, and an article about the upcoming negotiations. I knew he looked familiar. Enough time had passed. Nick walked back to The Double Shot. There's a guy who looks like he's spent way too many days and nights in this place.

The rest of these bust-outs in training are way too young. He pushed his way through the crowd up to the bar where Slim was seated.

"Anybody sitting here?"

"You are."

"Bartender, let me have whatever you've got on draught."

"Bud or Bud light?"

"Make it a Bud."

"I haven't seen you in here before?"

"I haven't been here in better than ten years."

"Were you a regular?"

"No, just came occasionally I knew some guys from the neighborhood. My name is Bill O'Hara."

"I'm Steve Flanagan, but everyone calls me Slim."

"Well it's good to meet you Slim."

"Hey, do you think you could cover a drink for me? I'm a little short today."

"Not a problem, what would you like?"

"Bud and a shot, the bartender knows what I drink."

Nick motioned to the bartender,

"Can you get Slim, it's on me?"

"Hey, thanks Bill. Funny thing, there was one of the guys here about a half hour ago, haven't seen him in years."

"No kidding?"

"Yeah, Tommy Petrone, you know him?"

"No, I don't recall him. Maybe I would if I saw him."

"Tommy went into the Army, had to be at least twenty years ago. He would come back on leave once in a while and about ten or twelve years ago was the last time we ever saw him until today."

"Did he say how long he was going to be around? Maybe I could catch him here and might recognize him."

"Yeah, he said he's here until Friday the 12th."

"I'll see if I can get back. Here's twenty bucks. Hope this helps you out a little."

"It sure does, so long Bill."

Thomas Petrone and his team may have been lowlife's, but they were experts at surveilling from their days on the teams with Nick Slater. They took up positions along Pat Ricketts' route to and from work planning when and where they would grab her. Sean Gleason started reporting on his surveillance.

"Tommy, she walks from her condo to the office every day. Leaves precisely at 7:00 a.m. and gets to work 7:15 a.m. Stops at the coffee shop in the lobby, gets a medium coffee and tells them, one teaspoon of cream."

Thomas Petrone was thrown off for a second by the comment,

"Something wrong Tommy?"

"I've heard that before, I just can't place it. It'll come back to me later."

"Anyway, she goes up to her office and breaks right at noon. She walks down the street and has lunch at the Marriott every day, then leaves the office every day at six. Walks to her condo, might have her meals delivered or in her position someone there to cook for her, but we know she doesn't go out. Nothing makes the job easier than a creature of habit."

Michael Hanks piped in, "Listen up, she crosses six intersections on her way to work. That gives us two maybe three chances going and coming. It's risky though because of the morning and evening traffic. We get stuck, we're done. But if it's clear at noon, we can grab her off the sidewalk, drag her down the stairs to the street below, do her, dump the body in the Chicago river and be gone before the police have time to react."

"We've got five days and then we take our chances doing it right on the street. She can't be at that meeting on the morning of the 12th."

It was obvious that as rough and tumble as Charles Buntrik's upbringing and ascent to power had been, he had little experience with professionals when he called Thomas Petrone for the umpteenth time.

"I told you it would be done right and your calling me doesn't help."

"You came highly recommended and you had better produce?"

"Don't threaten us Mr. Buntrik. We're not your local thugs."

"I'm sorry, but it's imperative this be done as we discussed."

"It will, now don't bother us again."

The Petrone gang decided that tomorrow would be the day. They would get this job done, get on a plane before anyone was the wiser and be back on their way to Manila.

"Let's go back to the neighborhood, have a couple drinks and get back to the room early. We've got a busy day ahead of us."

Like criminals going back to the scenes of their crimes, they also go back to their old haunts. The half hour drive back to The Double Shot

Lounge up along the lake shore gave the four of them a chance to talk.

"I'm tempted to take care of that slime bag before we leave, just to make sure we don't have to look over our shoulders for the rest of our lives."

"We should think about it Tommy."

There was a sparse midday crowd at The Double Shot made up mostly of hardcore regulars.

"Hey Tommy?"

"Yeah Slim, what do you need?"

"A guy from the neighborhood came in about a half hour after you left."

"Really?"

"Yeah, he said he hadn't been here in years."

"Did you mention my name?"

"Well sure, I asked him if he knew you. He said he didn't, but he did say he may come back."

"Did you say anything about when I plan on leaving?"

"Yeah, I told him Friday."

To someone as experienced as Petrone, this was not a deal killer, but it had to be dealt with. He went to the booth in the back of the lounge where Johnson, Hanks and Gleason were waiting.

"I just found out that there was someone here looking for us. I don't know who the guy is that's snooping around, but what I do know is his showing up in this dump is not a coincidence."

There were only mild looks of concern on the faces of the three.

"We don't have time to jerk around trying to find out who this is. We stick to our plan. If he shows, we'll take care of him and the big mouth has to go."

Michael Hanks was staring at Steve Flanagan perched on his stool at the bar when he said,

"Tommy, the Sox are playing tonight. Let's invite your boy Slim to come along."

"Mike, that kind of thinking is why we all make such a good team. I'll go over and give him the invite."

Tommy Petrone walked over to the bar and squeezed between the bar stools.

"Hey Slim, we have an extra ticket for the Sox tonight. You want to go?"

"I'm really a Cubs fan Tommy, but it's hard to pass up a free ticket to any ball game, sure count me in."

"I'll tell you what, we'll be back for you in about an hour. We can stop in Bridgeport at a bar close to the park for a couple drinks and then go to the game."

"I'll be here waiting, thanks Tommy."

His three accomplices were already out the door and waiting by the rental car.

"We need to stop at a home center, pick up some concrete blocks, wire and a couple nine by twelve poly tarps. We'll be halfway back to Manila by the time the bodies surface in the Chicago river."

Nick decided to head back to The Double Shot. The more he thought about his recent acquaintance, Slim, the more he knew he had to do something to get him out of harm's way. I hope that poor guy hasn't said anything to Tommy Petrone about my being there. Tommy will get rid of him for sure. I better get him out of there if he's not gone already. He parked on Granville and walked south on Broadway to the lounge. Through the grimy front window, he could see Slim sitting in his usual spot at the bar. Nick hesitated at the door for a second, so he could see if Patrone or any of his men were inside. When he was sure they weren't, he walked in and went directly to the bar. "Slim, how are you doing tonight?"

"Ok Bill, I didn't think I'd see you again so soon. You know, Tommy Petrone was just here and he's coming back in a little while. He and his friends have an extra ticket for me to the Sox game tonight."

"Did you tell them about me?"

"I sure did Bill."

"Slim, do I look like someone who would feed you a line of bull?"

"No, you don't."

"Is there a back door in this place?"

"Yes, there is."

"Then you need to leave with me right now."

"But the game with Tommy?"

"Slim, if you go with them, you are going to die. They are here to do something bad and I can't be responsible for your death. We have to go right now."

"Alright Bill."

"Slim, I'm going to put you up in a motel a few blocks from here for a couple days. I'll get you plenty to drink and cover your meals while you're there. When those guys are gone Friday, it will be safe to come back here."

Slim's alcohol addled brain was having a hard time understanding what he was being told.

Call it 'The old neighborhood syndrome' when people think that no matter how awful a person has turned out they would never turn on their friends from 'the old neighborhood'.

Nick and Slim drove a couple miles west on Peterson Ave to the River View Motel. A budget friendly place where no one asks any questions and cash is the order of the day. He booked a room for three days to make sure he had Slim safely away.

"Slim, I have to run out to the liquor store. Stay in the room. It's paid through Sunday. Order all your meals in. Here's two-hundred dollars. I will be back with enough beer and whiskey to keep you through Sunday."

Nick got into the rental car knowing there was only a fifty-fifty chance that Slim would follow his instructions. Nick's assessment of the odds was way off. It should have been a one hundred percent chance that Slim would bolt.

Before the rear tires of the car had even cleared the edge of the parking lot, Slim was picking up the phone. I've got to call a cab and move before he gets back. He's gone and so am I, two hundred dollars richer. Got to get back to the 'Shot' so I can make the game with Tommy and his friends. That guy doesn't have a clue about the ties we have from the neighborhood. We all grew up together.

About an hour later Petrone and company were parking in front of The Double Shot Lounge.

"Do you see him anywhere in here?"

"No, I don't."

"Mike, you go inside and check the men's room. Jerome, see if he's hanging around outside."

Sean Gleason was the first to spot him.

"Tommy, he's coming up the street."

Slim had a smile on his face that Smokin' Joe Frazier couldn't wipe off with a right hook.

"Tommy you won't believe what happened. That guy came back and told me you were probably going to kill me for telling him how long you were going to be in town. He paid for a motel room for me until Sunday, covered my liquor and gave me two-hundred for meals. He doesn't understand being from the neighborhood."

"Your right Slim, let's get going. We're going to be late for the game."

Jerome opened the back door of the rental car.

"Slim, slide in between Jerome and Michael, I'm up front so I can give Sean directions to Sox Park."

307

"Ok Tommy, let's get moving."

Not two blocks south on Broadway Michael Hanks put his arm across Slim's shoulders while Jerome reached over and broke his neck.

"Keep him propped up so he looks like he's sleeping Sean. When you see an alley with no cameras, we'll pull in, wrap him in a tarp and stick him in the trunk. He won't be in there long enough to start smelling. We can dump both bodies in the river at the same time."

He made the trip to the liquor store, picked up everything Slim would need for his stay and drove back to the motel as fast as he could.

"Slim, I brought four cases of beer and two half gallons of Beam for you. Slim, are you in the bathroom?"

The only logical conclusion, He's gone, I'll bet he went back to the neighborhood as soon as I left. If he did, he's probably dead already. I had better check anyway. As he approached the lounge walking south on Broadway from Granville, he thought, I have slogged through some third world countries and back water dives in my life and this dump could rate up there with the best of them. Nick walked by slowly to see if Patrone, any of his men or by some stroke of luck

Slim were sitting at the bar. None were there so he went in and directly to the bartender.

"Have you seen Slim in here tonight?"

"Yeah, he was here for a little while and then left with Tommy Petrone and some other guys."

"Thanks."

"Hey, should I tell him you were here looking for him?"

"It won't be necessary."

Nick left the bar, walked to his car and drove back north on Sheridan Rd into Evanston to the Orrington Hotel so he could make some calls.

It was time to report in and to see how much assistance he was going to get.

"Nick, I have been expecting your call. What have you found out."

"They're in Chicago, basing out of the old neighborhood just as I suspected. Tommy Petrone had a visit from Charles Buntrik the other day and it had to be the payoff. He passed him a briefcase. I was told by one of his old neighborhood friends that they would be leaving on Friday, so I'm guessing they will have to act by tomorrow at the latest. It must have something to do with the union negotiations coming up on Monday."

"You know the target then?"

"I knew that all along."

"What are you thinking Nick?"

"I can't alert the Chicago police, he's President of the International Union. Buntrik is a very powerful man and has to be connected at the highest levels of state and local government. This is, after all, Illinois we're talking about."

"What about this local guy you mentioned? Could they have fed him wrong dates to throw off an investigation?"

"I don't think so. He and Petrone knew each other all the way back to grammar school. I tried to hide him out, convince him about how much danger he was in, but he apparently didn't believe me. He's vanished and is most likely dead."

"If they are leaving Friday, then they have to act tomorrow."

"There is no doubt they will attempt to kidnap and murder Pat Ricketts. Is there any way the FBI can get involved?"

"I have some contacts in those circles in Washington. I'll reach out to them right away and see what they can do and get right back to you."

"Thanks."

Nick Slater knew he had to start moving. He was running out of time. He gave General

Murray one hour to return his call. Fifty minutes later the phone in his room rang,

"Nick?"

"Yes sir."

"One of my contacts believes that Buntrik's soliciting of killers from outside the United States is the opening needed to get the FBI involved. If money changed hands and he is directly involved, we got him. However, it may take some time since he has to work around Mr. Buntrik in such a way that no one tips him off. There's no doubt he's bought and paid for politicians. We don't know how many and who."

"So for now, I have to go it alone?"

"Until something happens. Then they can get involved."

"Is there any possibility you could do some soft checking?"

"Such as?"

"See if Tommy Petrone or any of his men have rented a car under any of their names?"

"I think we can handle that. Beside Petrone, who do you have?"

"Jerome Johnson, Michael Hanks and Sean Gleason."

"I'll get right on it."

"I'm heading to his old neighborhood now. If you find anything out, let me know."

As he was driving back into the city, Nick knew he needed another set of eyes. He could handle the heavy lifting, but he needed to know where Petrone and his men were, so he could get to them. Nick Slater had been gone for so many years that he couldn't think of anyone in Chicago he could call for help when a name just came to mind. He checked the white pages and called.

"I'm looking for a Leon Higgins"

"This is his wife Meredith, can I help you?"

"I'm an old friend of Leon's and am just calling to say hello."

"Can I tell him who is calling?"

"Nick Slater."

"Oh my God! Colonel Slater, please hold on"

"Leon you have a call, it's Nick Slater hurry. I can't tell you how many times Leon has mentioned your name Colonel Slater."

"I'm just Nick Slater these days."

"Colonel, how are you?"

"I'm fine Leon, but more importantly, how are you?"

"Sir, I couldn't be better."

"It appears as though your stay in Colorado did some good."

"That's an understatement sir. I have a life thanks to you and that program."

"Leon, you just needed a break and you took advantage of it."

"What can I do for you sir?"

"Leon, I have to ask a favor of you, but I need to ask it face to face."

"I am just north of Loyola University right now just coming into Chicago."

"We are not far from you, we're in West Rogers Park, 2720 W Coyle Ave."

"I'll head that way right now."

Ten minutes later, Nick turned onto Coyle Ave and pulled up in front of 2720, a brown, brick bungalow. As he was walking up, the front door opened and out stepped a man who bore only a slight resemblance to the Leon he had put on the bus years before.

"Leon, it's good to see you."

"Same here Colonel, come in please."

"It looks like you finally have that life you wanted so badly."

"I do sir, this is my wife Meredith."

"It's good to meet you in person Colonel."

"I have a large favor to ask of Leon. If you say no, I will fully understand?"

"What is the favor sir?"

"I would like you to follow someone tomorrow in your car. There is going to be an attempt to kidnap someone and I need to have the car tailed so the proper authorities can arrest them."

"I am willing to help sir, but what about the Chicago Police Department?"

"Leon, there are very influential people involved. If they are tipped off, I'm afraid they will just kill her and take their chance escaping."

"May I ask who this person is?"

"Yes, it's Pat Ricketts, CEO of the North American Corporation."

"And this is more than just a job isn't it sir?"

"Yes, it is Leon."

"Sir, I lived on the street for years and learned how to read people very well, even you. When do we get started?"

"If we want to stay ahead of them, we start now."

Meredith Higgins called from the kitchen, "Leon, Colonel Slater, I have coffee on. Why don't you come have a seat in here while you go over your plans."

Leon asked his wife to sit in during the planning knowing she would worry less if she knew exactly what his part was.

"Leon, you will park one half block west of Michigan Ave heading east on Grand Ave. That should be far enough away to keep you from being noticed. Around noon is when I think they will attempt the kidnapping. It's the only place where a clean getaway is possible. There are four of them. Two will be up on Michigan Ave and two will be down below or on the stairs leading down. Whether they get her or not, you will follow their car at a distance and call their location to me.

I am waiting for a call to see if we can find out what they are driving. Don't get close. These are very dangerous people and if they do not get what they are after, there are no limits to what they will do to escape. I know the street will be very busy. Try to park as close to noon as you can. Before that, they may spot you. If I get the car information, I'll call right away. I'll see you tomorrow, and thank you."

As he walked to his car, he was confident he would succeed now that he had help from someone he could depend on. On the drive back to the hotel to finish preparations, his cell rang,

"Nick, Ron Murray."

"Yes sir."

"Your boys traveled here on their US passports and oddly, have booked seats for Vietnam using their Philippine passports for late afternoon departure Friday. They must have been paid enough that they think they can live in relative luxury and not worry about extradition, I also have the car rental information. It's under Michael Hanks, a 2005 Black Chrysler 300, Ohio license plate number JH3256."

"Thank you sir, I have to move."

He made the call to Leon Higgins and gave him the information he would need for his part.

At the hotel, Nick laid out everything he was going to need to carry out what he hoped to be the last operation of this kind he would ever take part in. He laid out his clothes and had his bags ready so he could check out first thing in the morning.

At 3:00 p.m., it was time to call Pat Ricketts and bring her on board.

"I would like to speak to Ms. Ricketts."

"I'm sorry, sir but Ms. Ricketts is not available for calls."

"Does she have a secretary or an assistant that I may speak to?"

"None of them are available for calls through Monday either."

"It's imperative that I speak to one of them."

"I'm sorry sir, but…"

"I will give you my name and a phone number. Please see that it gets to Ms. Ricketts. I guarantee she will call me back."

"What is your name?"

"Nick Slater, 305-432-1357."

"I'll leave the message with her assistant."

And to make his point,

"I will know if you don't in less than five minutes because if Pat Ricketts sees that name, she will call me immediately."

"Who are you?"

As fast as Nick ended the call, the receptionist was dialing the office of the CEO.

"Carrie Hartman."

"Ms. Hartman I just got a call for Ms. Ricketts from a man, he left a name and number he said it was very important."

"Nick?"

"Yes, how did you know?"

"Give me the number right away."

"Yes ma'am."

"Carrie, did you say Nick?"

"Yes, I did. He just called and left this number. I'm dialing it already. Get line two in your office."

A man's voice answered on the other end.

"Nick is that you?"

"Yes, it is."

"Where are you?"

"I'm in Chicago and we need to talk right now."

"Are you alright?"

"Yes, and please listen to what I have to tell you. Charles Buntrik hired men to kidnap and murder you before the union negotiations start tomorrow."

"How do you know this?"

"People familiar with us."

"What do you mean familiar with us? The last time we actually spoke was thirty-five years ago?"

"Some chatter was picked up coming out of the far east and I was asked to look into it. That's all I can say right now."

"Nick, I want to see you in my office right away."

"The best I can do is a quiet dinner tomorrow after this is over."

"What do you mean, when it's over?"

"Please listen to me Pat. The last person in the world I want to see hurt is you."

"Do you love me Nick Slater?"

"What?"

"Answer the question Nick. Do you love me?"

"Yes, of course I do, from the first time I laid eyes on you."

"Neal Moran was right."

"What?"

"Nothing."

"Pat, listen closely. There is no room for error. Your life depends upon it. Our life together depends on what we do in the next twenty-four hours."

Nick proceeded to bring Pat up to speed on what was happening and how critical it was that she follow his instructions.

"The only place they can grab you is at the stairway down to Grand Ave. off Michigan Ave. There will probably be two by the stairs and two below waiting to push you into their car. I will be watching and following you. I have to be careful, because they may recognize me. If you hear any commotion, don't turn around. Just walk to lunch the way you do every day. Everything will be alright. Will you do that Pat?"

"I'll be waiting for you Nick."

Friday morning on Michigan Ave looked like every other workday for Pat Ricketts. She walked out of her building and began to cross intersection after intersection until she reached North American Corporation towers. Watching her every move and reporting back to Tommy Petrone were Jerome Johnson and Michael Hanks.

"We just wait for lunch. Get coffee boys and don't look conspicuous."

At 11:50 a.m. Leon Higgins found parking on the crowded street and began his watch. When he spotted the Chrysler 300, he called in his first report to Nick. There were two people, one at the car, the other at the bottom of the stairs from Grand to Michigan Ave.

It was a busy morning in the office of the CEO preparing for the upcoming negotiations in three days. Noon came too quickly. A somewhat nervous Pat Ricketts dialed her assistant.

"Carrie, I am going out to lunch. Please call over to the Marriott and let them know I am on my way. I'd like a table for two today. I'll be back later."

In all the years Carrie had worked for Pat Ricketts, she couldn't remember when the last time she had requested a table for two at lunch. Down on Michigan Ave., Johnson and Hanks were in position waiting for their quarry. Promptly at noon,

"Is she moving?"

"Yes, right on time. She is walking out of the building and heading to the crosswalk."

"Is everyone in place?"

"Affirmative, the light just turned. She's crossing the intersection now. She should be here in a sec!"

A distressed call directed to Thomas Petrone from Michael Hanks.

"Jerome is down. Someone just hit Jerome. He must have been hit real hard. He's not moving!"

Michael Hanks was trying to pick out who or what had downed his partner on the crowded street, when a man wearing a baseball cap pulled down to obscure his identity walked up to him and looked directly in his eyes.

"Michael Hanks?"

"Captain Slater!"

"It's Colonel Slater and give my best to Tommy Petrone when you get down to the street."

Michael Hanks was neutralized by a move called a pierce to the throat prior to his being thrown down a straight two flights of steel stairs to the sidewalk below. His flying lesson ended as his remains reached the bottom of the staircase. Nick Slater's cell rang,

"Yes Leon?"

"They are on the move."

"Leon, they are probably going to head north as soon as they can. Keep me posted on their location."

"Yes sir."

"And keep your distance, these are desperate men."

"Yes sir."

He ended the call and immediately put a call into General Murray.

"Yes Nick."

"I have two down and two are driving. I have a man following them. Is there any way you can intervene now?"

"Yes, we can Nick. As we speak the FBI is picking up Charles Buntrik. We have the location of the motel they have been staying at and have a team waiting for them."

"I'll call my man off right away. What are you going to do with the rest of your day Nick?"

"Lunch and then a nice quiet dinner at Pat's."

"Goodbye Nick."

"Thank you for everything General."

"Thank you, Nick. It's been an honor."

One more call to complete his mission.

"Leon?"

"Yes sir."

"Mission accomplished, I can never thank you enough for your help."

"I hardly got to follow them at all."

"Enjoy your life. You deserve it."

"Yes sir and thanks."

Charles Buntrik was planning to stay late at the offices of the International Union anticipating a news alert announcing the kidnapping of Patricia Ricketts, CEO of North American Corporation. He invited several of his closest union officials to his office for drinks and after the news, they would all go to dinner to celebrate. When his secretary called.

"Sir, there are several FBI Agents out here in the lobby. They are on their way to your office right now with a warrant for your arrest."

Thomas Petrone and Sean Gleason drove under Michigan Ave on Grand and worked their way through the midday traffic. They headed north on Lakeshore Drive back to the old neighborhood. They never saw Leon following them, not that it mattered. They had failed and now had only one objective.

"We have to get back to the motel, grab the money and get out of the country. We're booked on a flight to Ho Chi Minh City on our Philippine passports. There's no extradition so it will give us time to get new identities before we go back to Manila."

"What about the body in the trunk?"

"We'll throw it in a dumpster somewhere along the way. If time gets too tight, we'll just park the car at O'Hare in long term parking. It will be days before they get to it."

"Who do you think it was that clubbed Jerome and threw Michael down those stairs?"

"I don't have a clue. Whoever it was, though, knew who they were and targeted them."

"Drive by the parking lot once to make sure no one is waiting."

They slowed down to get a clear look.

"It looks clear. Pull in Sean, hop out and open the door. I'm right behind you."
Once inside the motel room.

"Tommy, here's the briefcase. Just look at all that money."

"Sean, grab whatever you have to and let's move out. Get the Passports off the nightstands, we don't want to leave ID's behind."
Sean was distracted just long enough.

"Tommy, where did you get that gun?"

"In the briefcase, I asked Buntrik to put it there."

"What are you doing?"

"Sean a million dollars was never going to be enough to take care of four people. It's barely enough for one."

"Tommy don't do this. Just give me a couple hundred grand and I'll disappear here in the states."

"Sorry Sean."

Tommy Petrone shot the last of his accomplices dead, in the sleazy motel on the northside of Chicago. Through the ringing in his ears from firing the compact forty-five automatic in the motel room Thomas Petrone heard,

"Thomas Petrone, this is the FBI. All of the exits are blocked. Come out with your hands up."

Agents swarmed the room as he came out, hands on top of his head.

"There is one deceased in the room. That was the gunfire we heard. Here is the briefcase."

"Mr. Petrone, we are taking you down to the Federal lockup. You can lawyer up then if you so desire or you can talk to us. If you decide to talk to us, there is a possibility you will avoid the death penalty. The sooner you make that decision, the better. It is our guess that Mr. Buntrik will be casting as much blame on you and your co-conspirators as he possibly can to save his own skin."

"What about my men? They are all dead. Can you at least tell me who took them out?"

"A Nick Slater."

"Captain Nick Slater?"

"No, Colonel Nick Slater."

"We were told that he has been monitoring your activity for the last three days."

"Medium coffee with one teaspoon of cream."

"What was that?"

At the same instant Thomas Petrone was being cuffed and placed in the back seat of the unmarked FBI sedan, Nick was walking into the restaurant at the Marriott on Michigan Avenue.

"Can you direct me to Pat Ricketts' table please, I believe she is expecting me."

"And you are?"

"Nick Slater."

Emily and Mary Alice go to the Strip

On Thursday evening the 31st of May, at 10:00 p.m., Emily Greenberg was sitting in her living room looking out over the Las Vegas skyline and lamenting the loss of her husband Max ten years ago to the day. The thirty-five years they had together went by too quickly. They both married late considering the times, managed to raise two great children and see them off as adults. She still felt cheated because it all seemed to go by in the blink of an eye. To make the evening even more depressing was the thought of her seventieth birthday arriving promptly at dawn.

Emily intended to sleep in, so the blinds were closed, the room was dark when the display lit up and an annoying ring-tone put an end to a good night's rest. Her first thought was, it's 6:30, I wonder why Mary Alice is calling this early in the morning. "Mary Alice is there something wrong?"

"No, there's nothing wrong."

"Emily do you know what day it is today?"

"Of course, I do. It's our 70th birthday, but isn't it a little early to start celebrating?"

"Listen, I have the whole day planned, but you must get up and moving. It is going to be a very busy day, loaded with surprises."

"You know it's 6:30 in the morning. What time do you want me to be ready?"

"I'll be by at 7:30 to pick you up. Don't bother with breakfast. We'll stop for something light. I have appointments for both of us for 9:00 a.m. at Rampart, full spa treatment. We'll be there until at least 2:00 in the afternoon. Then, I thought we might go to the Mall to look for a couple of outfits to wear tonight when we go down to The Strip."

"The Strip, what are you talking about. We haven't been down there in years."

"Emily, that's just it. We haven't been there in years. We haven't had a decent martini or filet the way they make them there. As far as I'm concerned, we are both long overdue."

"You know, I was up until midnight last night thinking about my life with Max."

"I was doing the same thinking about Ron and what life without him has been like since he was killed in the plane crash with Max."

Em', it was the best thirty years of my life and my only regret was not being able to have children with him. Which is even more reason we must go out tonight. Get ready sis, I'll be there with the top down in Ron's old Jaguar in an hour."

At 7:30 a.m. Friday June 1st, Donnie Barlow and Kaylee Jackson were starting to put plans together on how to get the one hundred dollars they were going to need to feed their meth habits that night. Kaylee wasn't having much luck selling herself anymore. Her rotting teeth and meth acne was almost enough to turn off even the most hard-core sickos. Then they would want to haggle knowing she was desperate, so working the street was becoming a waste of valuable time.

After rattling off a series of possible ways to obtain the money as meth heads do, Donnie decided on mugging someone or worse if they got a good look at him in one of the parking garages without cameras along the Strip. Friday night there would be purses and pockets full of cash and if they got lucky, they might just come upon some old man or better yet some doddering old woman that would make for some easy money. Who knows, he mused, they might even get a car in the process that they could move at one of the chop shops in North Las Vegas.

The spa turned out to be just the remedy for Emily's birthday blues. Hair, nails, pedicure, massage, facial and Vichy rain therapy, in two words, the works. As it should have 2:00 p.m. came and went so they decided to run by Dillard's and pick up something to wear for the evenings birthday celebration. They both bought very stylish gray over black outfits that complimented their fit figures and exotic looks. Mary Alice dropped Emily at her home at 6:00 and told her she would be back to get her at 7:00. The ever prompt Mary Alice arrived exactly at 7:00, top down and as the old saying goes 'dressed to kill'. She honked the horn once and Emily appeared in the doorway equally stunning in her gray over black outfit.

Mary Alice announced they would be going to the SW Steakhouse at the Wynn for cocktails, dinner and a little gambling and if they didn't feel they could safely drive home, they would share a room for the night. They made their way to Lake Mead Blvd, headed east to 95 South to the ramp marked Los Angeles 15 South and exited at Sahara for the Strip, the start of a perfect evening.

The drug addled duo spent the entire morning and part of the afternoon deciding on the best garage to carry out their business. They decided on the Wynn. Even though security would be tight, the risk in their minds was worth the possible gain. They chose the third-floor midway back, an easy watch for roving security. They would allow themselves no more than sixty seconds to get what they wanted when a mark had been spotted. It was 7:45 p.m. when Donnie Barlow and Kaylee Jackson had themselves in position.

At 7:50 p.m., Mary Alice and Emily were pulling into a parking space on the third floor midway toward the back of the parking garage at the Wynn. Mary Alice put the top up closed the windows. The two of them stepped out of the Jaguar and started for the elevator to make an 8:00 p.m. dinner reservation. Emily immediately sensed something was very wrong, but before she could get so much as a word out, Donnie and Kaylee appeared in front and back of them. He wasted no time he moved forward, grabbed Mary Alice by the left arm and put a knife to her throat. Kaylee, also with a knife in her hand, kept a body's length from Emily and told her not to move. Donnie Barlow was ecstatic. He had what looked to be two well-heeled old bags that would probably provide them with enough cash to go for weeks.

"I want your purses, watches, rings, car keys, ATM numbers and I want them now or you irrelevant old bitches die!"

"It's my wedding ring and that is my late husband's car."

Donnie looked her in the eyes and sneered.

"Do you want to die old lady?"

As he continued to look her in the eyes, a transformation took place as she responded in a low sultry voice. "No, I don't."

The tone and calmness of her response was not like any he had heard in all the robberies and muggings he had committed. It caused him to hesitate for a fatal moment. Mary Alice moved within inches of him touching his sternum with her left hand so softly that he could barely feel it in all the excitement. She then moved her fingers slightly to his left. At the same time she pulled an ice pick from the side pocket of her purse and with her right hand, in a fluid motion like that of a great painter when starting a masterpiece, put the tip along the side of her fingers and in the same low soft voice as before said,

"Look at me. My sister and I are celebrating our 70th birthdays tonight. You just made our evening a once in a lifetime event, so even you should easily be able to tell we don't want to die. I'll tell you something else, we are not who or what we appear to be. We are not two irrelevant old bitches named Mary Alice Seigel and Emily

Greenberg. My name is Flamingo Jones and she is Sahara Jones. We've killed people for a living, very bad people not vermin like you, but tonight we're going to make an exception."

With that Flamingo Jones gracefully pushed the ice pick between the fourth and fifth ribs of Donnie Barlow into his heart four times killing him instantly, while leaving only a single-entry wound. As his lifeless methamphetamine wracked body fell to the floor, Kaylee turned and dropped to her knees with a look of disbelief, shaking Donnie and screaming hysterically. "What have you done to him?"

Stepping out of her shoes to keep from making so much as a sound, Sahara Jones, without hesitation, moved with the grace of a cat while pulling a long sturdy hat pin from her purse. In a movement which at the very least one would call well-rehearsed, she stuck the hat pin in the base of Kaylee Jackson's skull while pushing it up into her brain in a clockwise pattern, Kaylee was dead before her head hit the garage floor.

Sahara looked at Flamingo and asked, "Ice pick or hat pin?"

Flamingo's response, "Ice pick, a gift from Johnny Salerno long before we became respectable. How about you?"

"Hat pin, the one mother said belonged to our grandmother. The one she had made from hardened steel with a slightly larger diameter."

Sahara looked at her sister.

"You couldn't have made this evening better if you had planned it, we should move the car to the floor below before anyone comes."

Flamingo picked up Donnie's knife, cut the area she had touched out of his filthy tee shirt and pulled a small plastic zip bag from her purse. She put the knife and the piece of tee shirt in the bag.

"We've watched enough crime shows to know they will wipe down everything looking for DNA and anything else that can connect someone to this. I'll put this in the trunk behind the false panel Ron had installed to hide the large amounts of cash he picked up at the wrecking yards and recycle lots."

They wiped the blood and remains from their weapons of choice on tissues from their purses, put the tissues in the plastic bag with the other items, squeezed the air out and zipped the bag closed. While walking to the car Flamingo said,

"It looks like we can still make our reservation. What a wonderful birthday."

At 8:15 p.m., the head of Wynn security was on the phone with the Las Vegas Police Department. They were reporting that they had two deceased individuals, a man and a woman, midway back on the third level of the parking garage in the middle of the drive. There was a small amount of blood under the male victim and nothing to indicate what foul play caused the demise of the female. From the looks of the deceased, it was highly unlikely they were guests at the Wynn. Security also asked if it would be possible to be as discreet as possible when their units arrived.

At 8:16 p.m., Mary Alice was being served a perfect martini while Emily decided on something more contemporary opting for a rose martini. Mary Alice ordered the petite filet with black truffle creamed corn. Emily ordered the pan roasted sea scallops served on top of English pea risotto with pea vines and black truffle sauce. Mary Alice had a glass of Chateau Cantenac Brown while Emily ordered White Chateauneuf-pu-Pape. They split a Molten cake dessert and to say dinner at the SW Wynn on their 70th birthdays was unforgettable would be a gross understatement.

The third floor of the parking garage at the Wynn was closed by the time the first police cruiser arrived at 8:20 p.m. One of the first officers on scene noted that the bodies were still warm and thought he recognized Kaylee from North Las Vegas, but wasn't completely sure. The next to arrive were homicide detectives Greg Fuller and his partner Bill Bowling. The first thing they noticed was the missing piece of tee shirt and no weapon on the man. The woman lay partially over the man's legs and had a knife in her hand. The man more than likely didn't have a gun. The only reason there was no weapon is that the victim may have been cut or had physical contact with the deceased and didn't want to leave any DNA or blood evidence behind.

Short of a robbery gone bad, why would someone murder a couple lowlifes like these two in the parking garage of the Wynn? If these two were killed to settle some local score, it would be the usual sloppy job, this was not. There was no way this would warrant high price talent, so no matter how they looked at it something wasn't right. Detective Fuller had his partner go with security to look at any surveillance tapes they had from elevator traffic. He then requested officers be placed on all floors to question people leaving the facility about possibly seeing anyone 'running' from the scene or anyone suspicious looking.

Their forensics people were called in, looked the bodies over and called for a coroner pickup. There was a small amount of bleeding from the entry wound just to the left of the sternum between the fourth and fifth ribs on the corpse of the late Donnie Barlow. The medical examiner would have to look for a wound or whatever method was used to bring the life of Kaylee Jackson to an abrupt end, the point of entry was hidden in her hairline and at that was only a pin hole. Their prints would be taken and if they had arrest records they would get positive ID's on them within hours.

When Detective Bowling returned from doing an initial look at the surveillance, he said,

"Two older women got off the second-floor elevator and entered the lobby at 7:55 p.m. We will look for them when they come out, but only for routine questioning to see if they saw anyone or heard anything."

He commented to his partner,

"There won't be any problem spotting these two women. They appear to be in their early sixties or so and have the striking good looks of well-kept, old showgirls."

He also asked the security people to make a copy of the surveillance tapes that they could take with them. Detective Fuller was reluctant to search anyone but was contemplating looking in purses and asking anyone wearing a jacket to open it. Something about this just wasn't right.

Without saying a word after dinner, Emily and Mary Alice stopped at the women's restroom. Mary Alice entered a stall while Emily checked her makeup. She took the icepick from the purse, looked at the worn hot stamp on the handle that read, Salerno & Son Ice, Brooklyn, New York, smiled, slid a plastic tube over the pick and taped it to her thigh. When Mary Alice came out, Emily entered the stall and duplicated the procedure with the hat pin. It was though they knew no one would body search them or anyone else tonight. It was almost 10:00 p.m. and they decided they would take a drive south on I-15 to 215 west then back to Summerlin, a beautiful night for a ride with the top down.

Coming off the elevator, they were met by a uniformed police officer who asked them the routine questions they already knew he would. He did comment that they could be sisters, they looked so much alike. They said they were fraternal twins and were out celebrating their 70th birthdays. Emily Greenberg and Mary Alice Seigel knew they were in the clear tonight, but this was far from over. Experience had taught them that their planning must start immediately.

On Monday morning June 4th at 8:00 a.m. Ed Norkus recently retired homicide detective from the Las Vegas police department was just getting his day started when lead detective Greg Fuller from the Wynn murders stopped by to see his old friend for a quick visit. Norkus had been brought back to work cold cases.

"Ed, how's cold case going?"

"It's going ok. I have a room full of boxes to go through and I'll bet half of them are cases we both worked on over the years."

"How's your end doing Greg?"

"We had a strange one Friday night. Two dopers killed in the parking lot of the Wynn."

"I heard about it."

"One small hole in the chest the size of a nail and nothing visible on the other."

"How much bleeding?"

"Very little, that's just it. Usually chest wounds that appear to be from stabbing in the heart bleed all over. Did you ever work anything similar when you were in homicide?"

"Not personally, but my old partner Bill Thurman did back in the late 60's through the late 70's. He told me all about them. He was always intrigued by the relatively small amount of blood at the scene and never any trace evidence left behind. After the last killing no one ever saw anything like it again."

"Were the murders mainly here in Las Vegas?"

"No, only about a dozen here in Las Vegas. There were more around the country in Atlanta, Cleveland, Detroit, Chicago, New York, Boston, Philadelphia, Atlantic City, Miami, Dallas, L.A. and some big shot political type in DC. Everyone always assumed they were mob related. I'll tell you what, I'll go look for the files on the ones that happened here in Las Vegas. There will be coroner's reports and copies of the others from around the country attached to them. You can see if there are any similarities to the two you have."

"Thanks Ed, let me know as soon as you have them. Nothing about this follows any pattern. I asked the coroner's office to see if they could move this one through as quickly as possible."

At 4:00 p.m. Monday, Greg Fuller and Bill Bowling were coming back from a late lunch and found coroner's reports on their desks. There was also a voice message from Ed Norkus letting them know he had all the files for them to look at. They grabbed the reports and headed down to cold case to see what Ed had found. Three sets of experienced eyes on this would be a real plus. Ed had all the reports laid out on a long table when they got there.

"I made a mistake on the Las Vegas murders. There were fourteen not twelve plus six in Chicago, twelve in New York, four in Boston, four in Philadelphia, six in Atlantic City, two in Atlanta, two in Dallas, two in L.A., three in Cleveland, three in Detroit, five more in Miami and the one in DC. That's sixty-four over a ten-year span, plus your two from the other night."

As the detectives scanned the reports, it was obvious that the MO employed in all the murders were identical, either an ice pick, old fashioned hat pin or similar device. All either stabbed in the heart four times with one entry wound or a single entry wound at the base of the skull with the weapon turned in a clockwise motion when fully inserted into the brain of the victim. No witnesses and no trace evidence indicating who murdered these people.

Greg Fuller looked at his fellow detectives and said, "What the hell is going on here? If it's the original killer or killers, they must be at least in their seventies or eighties by now. If not, they have trained someone, because our two at the Wynn are carbon copies of the originals."

Ed Norkus put down one of the reports and said, "One name looks like it's mentioned in all the reports, John Salerno from New York. For every one of the murders, he had iron clad alibis but was always the main person of interest. His nickname was Ice pick Johnny. My old partner said he heard a rumor that only two people ever had the nerve to call him that and he allegedly killed them both with an ice pick."

Greg turned to his partner.

"Bill, could you check into the whereabouts of Mr. Salerno these days? See if he's still alive and if so, what kind of iron clad alibi he comes up with this time."

"OK Greg, I'll get right on it."

"Ed, you might as well leave everything out. Sixty-four murders in the sixties and seventies and then nothing until last Friday night. I know there's more to this than just chance."

When Greg Fuller walked into homicide at 8:00 a.m. on Tuesday June 5th his partner had some interesting information.

"Greg, John Salerno is in Las Vegas and he's staying at the Encore in the Wynn complex. What do you think about that?"

"I think it's too easy and however it looks it just doesn't fit. For some reason, I think it's just a coincidence that he's staying at the same hotel where two people were killed by a method he's known for. No matter how I look at this, the victims just aren't right. Let's take a drive over there anyway. I want to have a talk with Mr. Salerno and see what kind of a read we get from him."

Almost laughing he said, "You never know, we may flush a geriatric killer out of the shadows with his help."

Big John Salerno, as he was now nicknamed since ascending to the seat his father once occupied, was staying in a tower suite at the Encore in Las Vegas with two of his lieutenants and 'his go to guy' Paul Balbo. They were there to finalize a large drug deal for 100 kilos of pure heroin that had made its way from the middle east, by way of the Mediterranean, to Central America, then up through Mexico to Las Vegas. The plan was to complete the deal, ship the dope back to New York, then spend several days in Las Vegas before going back to the east coast to have the heroin cut and put into distribution.

John Salerno, like many of his counterparts in the criminal underworld, didn't leave town very often for fear he would come back to nothing or worse. John however had two sons, John III and Carmine who he could leave in charge. Both were as violent as their father, driven by the same quest for power and greed. They inherited the same brutish family looks and foul disposition, so a trip now and then wasn't a great risk to their criminal empire. Big John Salerno got up at 9:00 a.m., walked down the hallway to Paul Balbo's room and knocked twice. Paul came to the door already dressed.

"What do you need?"

"Pay those two whores in there and get rid of them. We have a busy day ahead of us. I need some privacy, so we can make a few plans and get out of here by tomorrow night."

"I thought we were going to stay through Saturday? The boys have been looking forward to some fun."

"Screw their fun. Send the two of them to Atlantic City when we get back. We have business, business that has to be taken care of now."

"Remember the two dopers who were killed in the parking lot Friday night?"

"Yeah, what about it?"

"Well, I know who did it. This goes way back and it's time to tie this one off. I'm surprised the cops haven't been here already to question us about the killings."

"If you're sure you know who did this, why not send Vito and Sal to take care of it?"

"It's not that simple. Like I said, it goes way back. We'll take care of this by tomorrow night at the latest, just the two of us. I don't want any other eyes or ears involved in it."

"Alright, what do you think we need? I'll get Vito and Sal going right away."

"I have an ice pick but need a snub nose 38 special loaded with real +P hollow points. You need a sawed off 12gauge double barrel with 00 buckshot and the largest caliber revolver you can shoot accurately."

"What, are we going to war?"

"Just do as I say. We both want to be on that charter."

"And call that piece of shit lawyer Sidney Lazar that we used to use, way back when. Tell him to get his ass over here right away if he knows what's good for him."

345

At the same time on the other side of town.

"Em', we knew the odds of this happening one day were high and if he hasn't heard from one of his contacts here, the police will have contacted him by now."

Emily quickly answered.

"How much time do you think we have and how many will he send?"

"If it was anyone else, they would probably send a couple of their flunkies to handle things. Since that pig's life is potentially at stake, he won't. He can't take a chance of anyone finding out that we did his hits back then. I know there were several we did that only Johnny and a couple of the big bosses were ever supposed to know about. If word ever got back to them that anyone else knew who ordered the hits, he and his whole family would pay."

Then Emily said,

"I'm guessing tonight or tomorrow at the latest for him to try. He was never one to drag his feet."

"How many others do you think he'll send along?"

"I say one other person. At seventy, there's no way he would do this alone."

"You're right Em'. My guess is he won't want to alarm us by showing up with a crew and besides, he has to limit his exposure."

"Remember, whoever he brings along, apart from maybe his mother, has to be gotten rid of when it's over."

"He's predictable. He'll come in as sweet as a piece of shit like him possibly can be and then turn on us when he thinks he has us off guard. His second man will be heavily armed and ready for anything that happens. Our greatest advantage is that I don't believe John will tell him that he's going after two women until they're almost in the door. It doesn't matter how cold blooded his man is. He's going to be rattled when he sees his job is to kill two 'old' women."

"It's been over thirty years since we've seen him and considering his lifestyle he probably hasn't aged all that well. But don't be fooled, no matter how bad he may look, he's still Johnny Salerno."

Flamingo and Sahara Jones put their bare feet up on the coffee table in front of the elegant oversize cream-colored leather sectional in Flamingo's living room. Silently sipping coffee, they looked west out over the Spring Mountains through the floor to ceiling windows.

At 9:45 a.m., criminal defense attorney Sidney Lazar arrived at the Encore tower suite. Paul Balbo let him in.

"Go on into the living room, get a cup of coffee and take a seat on the couch. Mr. Salerno will be right out."

When John Salerno walked into the room, he said,

"Don't get up. We don't have a lot of time. I just got a call from New York and the police are wondering about my whereabouts. They are probably on their way here to question me about the killings in the parking garage on Friday night. In case you didn't see it in the papers, it was two bust out dopers and the cops know I wouldn't waste my time on them. Since the hits here in Vegas resemble hits they have been trying to pin on me for years, they are going to hassle me." Squirming nervously on the couch Lazar said,

"Yes sir."

"That's why you're here. I don't want them thinking they can pull something off, so you are going to wait here until they finish their questioning."

At 10:00 a.m., there was a call from the front desk announcing there were two police detectives there to see Mr. Salerno. He told the desk clerk to send them up to his suite. He called Paul Balbo.

"Paul, the police are here and will be at the door in a minute. They're going to ask the usual questions about the murders, they'll want to know where I was that night and probably every night since then. We got nothing to be afraid of on this one, so I'll get them out of here as fast as I can."

There was a knock at the door and they heard a muffled voice saying, "Mr. Salerno, this is detectives Fuller and Bowling from the Las Vegas police department, open up."

He said, "Take it easy, we're coming." Paul Balbo opened the door.

"Come in, Mr. Salerno is in the living room."

The two detectives followed him to the living room where John Salerno was sitting in one of the arm chairs wearing a silk robe and holding a cup of coffee in his hand.

"You'll have to excuse me if I don't get up and offer to shake hands, but I don't think you're here for a social call. Do you know Mr. Lazar my attorney?"

"We know Mr. Lazar and you are right, this is not a social call."
Detective Bowling piped in.

"Mr. Salerno, we have a couple questions and then we will be on our way. First off, what are you doing here in Las Vegas?"

"I'm here to do a little gambling with friends and maybe catch a couple shows before going home. Is that a problem?"
It was now Greg Fuller's turn.

"It's a big problem if includes murder. Where were you this past Friday evening between 7:00 p.m. and 9:00 p.m.?"

"I was at the Italian American Club having dinner with some old friends. Would you like to know what I had for dinner?"

"You don't have to get smart with us. We can make your time here a lot worse than you can make it for us."

At that, Sidney Lazar stood up.

"My client has answered your questions honestly and will provide the names and numbers of the people he had dinner with. If you have no further questions and are not charging him with any crimes today, your time here is done."

"We expect a call within the hour with the names and numbers. Here's my card, come on Bill, let's go."
The lawyer turned to his client and said,

"Is there anything else I can do for you Mr. Salerno?"

"No there isn't. Paul, give Mr. Lazar a thousand dollars for his time on his way out the door."

Lazar took his cue, set his coffee cup on the table, followed Paul Balbo to the door and was handed ten crisp one hundred dollar bills for his trouble. When Sidney Lazar walked out into the hall, the two detectives were still waiting for the elevator. As he approached them, the elevator door opened. Greg Fuller looked at him and almost laughed.

"Come on, we promise we won't slap you around on the way down to the lobby."

After the elevator had started down, Detective Fuller continued the conversation.

"Off the record, you're a well-known defense attorney and probably have more business than you can handle, why do you work for someone like John Salerno?"

"Do you two know who he is? Do you know what kind of a person he is? What he's capable of? To be completely truthful and off the record, I don't care about seeing him anymore than you do and that is strictly off the record."

The elevator doors opened as they reached the lobby. Sidney Lazar didn't bother to excuse himself and scurried off toward the front entrance.

John Salerno spent the better part of the morning making changes to his plans. The drug deal for the hundred kilos of pure middle eastern heroin would take place on Wednesday night at midnight, after allotting two to three hours for getting rid of Flamingo and Sahara Jones, torching the bodies and driving to the executive hangars at North Las Vegas Airport. They would takeoff as soon as the drug deal was done and land at Teterboro around 7:00 a.m. EST. Since he was sure the police would be watching him for the rest of his time in Las Vegas.

They would need four additional cars to shake any tail the police would be setting up after questioning him about the murders at the Wynn. Big John Salerno instructed Paul Balbo to have Vito and Sal, his two lieutenants, rent the cars and park them in four different hotel garages, and get it done before the police had a chance to set up surveillance on him and his crew. He called his son John and told him he would be back in New York Saturday morning and to make sure there was a car there to pick him up. John III said,

"I'll take care of it, see you Saturday."

John then started making arrangements for a van to meet the charter when it arrived in the hangar at Teterboro on Thursday morning. He and Carmine would be there to meet their father.

After talking to his son, he called the traffickers to let them know when he would be at the airport with the money, which hangar to go to and who would be there. His last call was to 'The Pilot' to let him know what was happening and to make sure he was ready to go when they got there. Salerno also let 'The Pilot' know what he was planning for the Jones'. Years ago, another of his duties had been to fly the Jones sisters around the country. It was a safe bet he would see their pictures in the paper or on the local news after they were done away with.

The odds were good that 'The Pilot' would never rat the Salerno's out since he had run drugs for their organization for years and was complicit in all the hits. His life would be worthless if he did. On the other hand, just to cover all his bases it was probably time to tie this loose end off along with the others. 'The Pilot' would have to go after the shipment made it to Teterboro so there would never be any connection between John Salerno, 'The Pilot' and the drug running. Vito and Sal could handle that. Then John Salerno said to Paul Balbo,

"Make sure Vito and Sal are at the hangar so no one tries anything when we get there with the money. We do deals with these people, but I don't trust them as far as I can throw their sorry asses." Then, he handed Balbo four of the burner phones he'd been using, so they could be wiped clean and bleached leaving no DNA evidence in case any of their calls had been monitored.

He took out a fifth burner phone from the pocket of his robe and dialed Mary Alice Seigel's home phone. She didn't recognize the number, but knew almost instinctively she should answer the call,

"Flamingo, do you know who this is?"

"Yes, I do."

"Then, you know we have to meet. I'm planning on coming by tomorrow night about nine. Watch for me and make sure there's space in your garage. I want to see you and your sister understand?"

"She may be a little late. She's coming back from visiting her daughter, but I'll let her know she should be here as close to nine as possible."

"Where's her daughter live?"

"That's none of your business and never will be."

"Be careful when you get smart with me sweetheart. We may go way back, but when I ask a question, I want an answer. You know who I am."

"I do know who you are Johnny and I told you it's none of your business. Sahara will be here as close to nine as possible."

"That's not good enough. I want her there when I get there. You tell her to get her ass back to Vegas however she has to, understand?"

"Yes, I'll call her when we're done John. Come in the front door. I have remodeling work going on in the garage entry area and no one can use the door. Honk once when you get here. I'll open the garage, so you can pull in and park. When I see you on the walk, I'll close the garage door."

"Good, just make sure you are both there." The call ended as abruptly as it started. Mary Alice looked over to her sister sitting at the counter.

"Everything is now in play, it's time to get ready. He's coming to kill us."

Very few, if any, were not intimidated by John Salerno. If his somewhat simian like appearance when meeting for the first time wasn't enough, his reputation for violence and foul disposition more than made up the rest. Flamingo and Sahara Jones having been used and abused by the Salernos had no fear whatsoever, they knew them and their methods.

As detectives Fuller and Bowling were leaving the hotel garage after their brief meeting, they called in to set up a tail on John Salerno.

"It's my guess that Salerno and his people are here for more than just some gambling and a few shows. Our intel says he's been big into drug trafficking for years and I'm betting he and his people are here to score something really big. He wouldn't show for anything but."

"I think you're right Greg, but where and when?"

"Let's see what the tail produces. Make sure they get on him and his people as soon as possible. Check the airlines to see if he's booked for a return to New York or any other place for that matter."

"I'll get on it right away."

Jerry Weston a.k.a. 'The Pilot', had worked for the Salerno family since he was in his early twenties. He had been lured in by the big money and the lie that he would be part of the Family. The pay was good and even though he never got a cut from what he hauled, he fantasized himself a mobster, a heavy hitter, a player in the drug trafficking world. The money he made afforded him the opportunity to get his Airframe & Powerplant certification, pay for the flight training required for his airline transport license, buy several planes including a jet and set up a small charter business operating under the name Weston Aviation Service. In all the years flying drugs for the Salernos, he only had to ditch one load. They forgave him that one transgression, or so he thought.

In May of 2007, the tab came due for ditching the load of dope years before. The price dictated by John Salerno was to 'fix' Max Greenberg's King Air which led to his death and the unintended death of his brother-in-law Ron Seigel, Flamingo's husband, on June 1st, 2007, it was the cost for Sahara Jones leaving his employ without his 'blessing'.

Emily and Mary Alice were sitting down at Emily's for a light dinner when Mary Alice asked her sister,

"Do you think Max' and Ron's deaths could have been setup by John Salerno?"

"The NTSB report said engine failures due to fuel contamination."

"I know we have gone over this a million times. I just don't know how that could have happened, Max was borderline fanatical about maintenance and it's hard to believe other planes weren't affected. There were no signs of tampering, nothing on the airport security cameras to indicate that anyone had even been close to the plane other than authorized line personnel and they were all questioned thoroughly."

"That scum never openly made you pay for leaving, he made a point of telling me he and I were even when I had just come out of two weeks in a coma after being drugged, raped by him and passed around to his friends then beaten half to death. The surgeries gave me a new face, but we will never look like twins and worse the beating left me unable to have children. Even though I have done my best not to dwell on it and got on with my life, it appears that fate has set the stage for an act of retribution this piece of garbage is long overdue for."

"Em', have you ever even hinted about our life growing up, about mom or any of our past to the kids?"

"No, I have never told them anything. They think we were adopted at birth. I have no shame and in fact, am very proud of our heritage. But, as mother said, trying to explain away the ups and downs we all experienced over the years would not wash."

"Mom being mixed race in the early 1900's made life very difficult for her. She was not accepted anywhere. She worked tirelessly at educating herself and trying to have a decent life regardless."

"I've always wished we could have met our father. Mom said he was an incredibly handsome man of Chippewa Indian descent who also had a difficult time making his way."

"Mom said he was killed fighting in the jungles of the Philippines during the war. They planned to marry once he was discharged. He never knew she was pregnant with us when he shipped out."

"She said he was steadfast and would have never surrendered and I believe that is why we were always able to overcome any obstacle put in our path."

"Mary Alice, why don't we take a trip to the Philippines, at least it might bring some closure."

"Em', I think I'll start checking into it when this whole thing is behind us."

"Maybe we take the kids along and start the process of slowly letting them know who we and they are, with the one exception of our professional affiliation of course. For now, we have a great deal of work ahead of us if we're to survive the next few days and leave no loose ends."

Wednesday June 6th 9:00 a.m., the mobster and his associate were finalizing their plans when Paul Balbo got a call.

"Sal just left the parking garage on his way back to The Flamingo. He's been watching the car and said someone in plain clothes attached something to the bottom of the car."

"Tell him not to remove it until we get ready to pull out. I'll bet they have someone in the parking lot watching and if anyone goes near that tracking device, we'll never be able to shake them. There may be more than one on the car anyway. They don't want to take a chance on losing us. Besides, they'll have a helicopter following us for the first leg."

"What are the other cars they got for us?"

"A white Escalade and a blue Infinity QX80, both with dark tinted windows."

"Good, those are generic enough in this town. They will both be easy to get in and out of quickly when we change cars. Did they get everything I told you to have them get?"

"They did. I've got the shotgun, your snub nose and a seven shot 357 magnum revolver, a box of hollow point ammo for each and a box of 00 buckshot. There's five gallons of gasoline in the back of the two SUV's and a complete change of clothes for both of us. I have the bags and the two million ready to go."

"Meet up with Vito and Sal. Tell them to make themselves scarce, then do whatever is necessary to lose any tail the cops may have on them and tell them. Make sure they are not seen going to the hangar tonight. We're going to lay low here until dark, then we'll start moving around."

By 11:00 a.m., there were police officers in the parking lot, lobby and in several locations outside on the strip. There were officers in security watching live surveillance at the Wynn and Venetian in case they tried to slip away through either venue. Detective Fuller was in a public works van parked along the strip while detective Bowling, a former motorcycle policeman, was on a Suzuki Bandit near the exit of the garage. Greg Fuller called Detective Bowling.

"Has anyone gotten back to you about airline bookings for Salerno?"

"They did, but there's nothing, I am going to call in and have them check with charters flying out of McCarran or North Las Vegas. In fact, have them check all the airports in a one hundred mile radius that can handle business jets. I know he wouldn't be here unless it was something big. I am also going to check with drug enforcement and see if there is any noise out there about significant drug shipments."

The detectives were determined not to lose John Salerno and miss out on whatever he had planned. It was now a waiting game.

"Em', do you want to have lunch here or go out and grab something?"

"Let's go out. How about MiMi's? I could go for a cup of French onion soup and a salad."

"Light is exactly what I had in mind."

"We need to get out of the house to see if we are being watched anyhow. John could have someone out there, but that's not really his style and he doesn't want to let on at all who he's after."

"I don't really think the police suspect us of anything, but you never know."

"Em', we need to stop at one of the furniture stores to look at area rugs. I would like to buy two new ones and have them delivered by Saturday. I want to replace the 9 x 12 under the sectional in the living room and the 6 x 8 at the front door. They are both a little worn and I could use a change. I hate to use the term, but we do need to kill a couple hours this afternoon."

Lunch as usual was perfect, two cups of onion soup and dinner salads with a little French flair were just what they were looking for. Two new wool area rugs were purchased. Delivery scheduled for Saturday, June 9th no later than 10:00 a.m. Even though they would see them at early mass at St. Elizabeth Seaton, they called Joyce McPherson, wife of Superior Court Justice John McPherson, and Linda Winslow whose late husband Marvin was a prominent lawyer in Las Vegas to confirm their standing golf game at Eagle Crest for Sunday, June 10th at 12:00 p.m.

At 6:00 p.m., the Jones sisters pulled into the Enterprise car rental at Sun City Summerlin. Flamingo went inside and took care of all the arrangements for the rental, parked her car in the lot and they drove off toward her home. Before they left the lot, Sahara donned a sandy blond wig, flowery jacket and slouched down in the car seat. At 7:00 p.m., they pulled into Flamingo's driveway, opened the garage door drove in and immediately closed the door, before exiting the car. Since the alarm system had not been tripped while they were out, they could only guess that John Salerno was up to his neck in details himself this afternoon. It was agreed that they would handle this the same way they had the many other murders committed over the years, leave little or no evidence and never any indication there were two people.

"Em, I'm going to be John's focus when he comes in the door. He's going to make small talk before the rough stuff starts. You must look for an opening with his backup man. I'm sure he's good or he wouldn't be working for the Salerno's. They will both be armed. John's favorite was always a snub nosed 38 Special, even though he likes everyone to think he's a master with an icepick. I'm guessing the backup man will have a shotgun and a pistol. You'll know when the time is right to move."

Then Flamingo asked her sister to help tape an icepick to her back just above her waistline.

"I'm going to wear something that shows some cleavage. We may be getting on a little, but so is he. I know some skin will help keep him distracted. When I have my chance, I'm not going to waste a second."

"In a way, I wish we had picked up a couple 20gauge coach guns in case things get completely out of hand. Either way, I think it would be a good idea to pick up one for each of us for home protection after this is over."

The sun was still high over the Spring Mountains at 6:00 p.m. when John Salerno and Paul Balbo left their room. Paul was pulling a large briefcase with wheels containing just their dirty laundry. The surveillance people in the lobby of the Encore spotted them as they walked out of the elevator and made their way to the garage elevators. Detective Fuller was notified immediately, and the operation went full active. Surveillance cameras on the elevator caught the duo exiting on the third level. Plain clothes officers reported in as Paul Balbo loaded the briefcase into the back seat of the rented black Maserati Levante and again when both passengers were in and the car was backing out. John Salerno's father had always pressed his son to remain low key and not bring attention to himself, but the Maserati was a perfect fit for the plan he was putting in motion.

Paul Balbo backed out of the parking space on the third floor, headed for the exit ramp and made his way to the Strip. He turned right out of the drive and headed north on Las Vegas Boulevard to Sahara, turned right to Paradise Rd.

If the police had been able to track their movement by GPS, the course would have looked like a complex maze ending at Harrah's multi-level parking garage. When they got to the third level in the back, Paul parked the Maserati. They grabbed the bag and went directly to the elevator. When it reached the lobby, they walked across the mall to Harrah's and took the elevator to the fourth level. Midway to the back along the west wall the Escalade was waiting for them. Balbo unlocked the doors, opened the rear drivers side and put the briefcase on the floor.

John Salerno climbed in the back and laid across the seat. Paul put on a white flat brim baseball cap with a Raiders logo embroidered on the front. He backed out and headed for the exit. Reaching the bottom of the ramp they pulled out of Harrah's garage on to the street and were home free, their timing had been perfect. As they were making their way up the street, Bill Bowling was parking at the base of the ramp at the LINQ Hotel Casino and calling in to let Greg Fuller know he was in place.

It took less than fifteen minutes for the police to determine that their attempt to tail John Salerno and his men had failed. Bill Bowling hadn't seen anyone remotely resembling Paul

Balbo or his boss drive by his position. An unmarked car with two tactical officers was sent to observe the Maserati. They reported back that it was parked in the back of the garage and there was no one in sight. It would be a waste of manpower to have people out on the street looking for these people at this point. They would have to wait for the results of whatever they were up to.

Greg Fuller called off the surveillance teams and called his partner to tell him he would meet him at the police station. He also let Bill know that it had been a calculated risk to begin with. These were experienced criminals and as they could plainly see, had taken precautions to avoid detection. Then, as Bill was leaving the ramp area, he saw the Maserati in his rear-view mirror. He was in the right turn lane just past the entrance to the High Roller when the Maserati pulled up alongside of him. The dark tint of the windows and it being dusk made it impossible to see who was driving. He immediately called back to Greg Fuller, waited until the Maserati was through the intersection and a hundred yards or so down the street and started after it. The driver turned right onto Koval Ln, drove to Flamingo Rd and turned right. Detective Bowling followed him to the 15 north on-ramp. Detective Fuller told him to follow the vehicle to wherever the destination was and that he would get any necessary clearances once out of their jurisdiction.

For the next ninety minutes, Detective Bowling followed the car north to the Casablanca Resort and Casino in Mesquite. The driver pulled into the parking garage, drove up to the second level, parked the Maserati, took the keys he had been handed by Paul Balbo when he walked through the LINQ lobby and disappeared into the night. The Salerno people would say the police were had, if they knew they were being followed.

At the same time, John Salerno and Paul Balbo were pulling onto the street after their car change. Vito and Sal Candela on cue from their boss were walking out of their room at the Flamingo Hotel Casino. The two million dollars to cover the drug deal was in an identical rolling briefcase that had been passed to the longtime associates and nephews of John Salerno when they met briefly with Paul Balbo earlier in the day. They walked through the casino onto the Strip to the corner of Flamingo and Las Vegas Blvd and up the escalator to the crosswalk leading to Bally's. They passed through the casino to a rear exit door and took the stairs to the second level of the parking garage. The very nondescript dark blue

Honda pilot was still where they parked it. They put on black, flat brim Raiders ball caps and black Raiders tee shirts, backed out and drove to their next stop. Vito and Sal also managed to ditch their tail through the casino lobbies and the crowded Strip. They drove out onto Flamingo, turned right to Las Vegas Blvd, they made another right into a typical Las Vegas traffic jam while heading toward their next stop at Luxor. Almost before their turn was completed, Vito said to Sal,

"You know, we've never gotten a cut from any of the deals we have been a part of and we're the ones who have our necks out there every time we do one of these."

"Vito, what are you talking about?"

"I'm saying what's wrong with asking for a small cut? We have two million dollars in this bag and when this deal is done, and the drugs get cut, it'll bring in ten maybe fifteen million. I don't care what you call it, we deserve something for the risk we take."

"We are never going to be the top guys. Remember, Big John has two sons so the best we are ever going to be is a couple of flunkies who carry out their orders. So why not get paid for our trouble."

A stunned Sal looked at his brother and said,

"Vito, we have been doing this how long?"

"Fifteen years, why?"

"We have managed to stay alive for fifteen years. We have only done time for a couple years and our wives and kids were always taken care of when we went away. Granted, they didn't get taken care of all that well, but they didn't miss a meal. I'm not aware of anyone who is more violent than John Salerno and Paul is his guy because there is no limit to what he will do when John gives him an order."

"Sal, I'm not saying we ask and if he say's no, we run with the money. I know they would hunt us down and probably kill us, and our wives and our kids. I'm just saying we ask? Think about this. We're his nephews, we've worked for him for a long time and never crossed him, not once. We are his sister's sons and it doesn't have to be big just a little cut. This may be a big drug deal, but it's really just another routine deal and there's nothing else going on so if we're ever going to ask, now is the time."

"Vito, I'll be honest with you, I don't like being a flunky any more than you do. Maybe you're right, now might be the best time to test the water. We've never done him wrong, not once."

"I'll tell you what also pisses me off. We were going to get a couple days here after the deal to have some fun. Now, he says, we have to leave after the deal is done tonight. I'm surprised that cheap-ass didn't tell us we have to fly back to New York commercial and he and Paul get to stick around for a couple days. I flew my girlfriend out and put her up at Excalibur. She likes to go to Medieval Times and then hang out in the casino. We were planning on having some real fun."

"Why didn't you tell me what you were up to? What was I supposed to do, stand around like a jerk while you had a ball? I guess I'm lucky though, because if I'd have known, I would have flown my new girlfriend Raylene out here too."

"So, Sal what do you think? We don't have all night to do this. I have two burners. If we are going to call, we have to do it now?"

"Ok Vito, go ahead, let's see if we can get him to see it our way?"

John Salerno and Paul Balbo had made their way north to the parking garage at the Fremont Hotel & Casino. They drove to the fourth level, located the blue QX80 and switched out vehicles. They had a thirty-minute drive ahead of them. About ten minutes from their destination, John Salerno would brief Paul Balbo on what they were about to do and why, omitting little bits and pieces to keep from making him look bad. Just as Paul was about to back out one of John's two remaining cell phones rang. It could only be Vito or Sal, so he answered,

"What do you guys need? I told you not to call us unless there was an emergency."

Vito said,

"I just want to run something by you?"

"Run something by me, what do you think is going on here?"

"Come on boss, just give me a second." Knowing they had his two million dollars and sensing an unusual uneasiness in the tone of Vito's voice, he said,

"I'll do you better than that I'll give you two minutes, but that's it."

"Boss, we've been talking, and we would like to have a cut of this deal when it's done. Before you say anything, we have been with you a long time, always loyal, never done anything behind your back or anything that would come back on you. It doesn't have to be a big cut, we would just like something."

Big John Salerno had the speaker on from the time he knew it was Vito calling. He looked over at Paul who put his index finger to his throat and moved it from left to right. Big John shook his head in the affirmative,

"I wish you two hadn't done this in the middle of a deal like this, but if it was me, I would have done it just the same way."

Vito looked over at Sal and gave him a thumbs up.

"I'm not happy, but we'll work out a cut. Are you on schedule?"

"Yes sir, we are."

"Then, stick to the schedule we gave you." John ended the call.

It took twenty minutes to travel two blocks in the sluggish Friday night traffic. Sal turned to Vito.

"Do you think we made a mistake?"

"No, I don't. We were going to have to do this somewhere along the line and this was as good a time as any. Do you want to be an errand boy for the rest of your life?"

"If it means being a live errand boy."

"We could call the girls, have them get the kids and we all disappear with the two million. A million cash per family would go a long way. We just have to stay gone until he dies. He's seventy. His father died from natural causes when he was seventy-two. Chances are we'd only have to hide out for a couple of years."

"We've already talked about that. John would hunt us down wherever we went. He'd use his own mother as bait and knowing him, he'd probably have Paul kill her if she knew too much. Then he'd kill our mother, wives and kids in front of us before he did us."

"Stay sharp. When they show up tonight to do this deal if something doesn't look right, we kill Paul first, then John, then the traffickers and we go with everything. We could probably turn that much dope for another five hundred thousand before anyone knew what happened. Then we'd get the girls and the kids and disappear. On the other hand, if it looks ok, we get our cut and everything works out, no harm no foul."

Vito and Sal made their second change without any problems. They parked the Honda Pilot on the third level at Luxor started the gray GMC Yukon Denali and commenced the last leg. They used a street map to plot their course to the North Las Vegas Airport. Vito tossed the burner phone he used to call John Salerno earlier before starting the drive to the airport. They knew they would be dealing with 'The Pilot' after the heroin was in New York and they were back in Las

Vegas. Vito and Sal had also been instructed that they had to be cautious as the drug deal went down. Big John himself had briefed them about his distrusting the traffickers with a transaction this size. They were to kill the traffickers if there were any problems and it looked like they might be contemplating a rip-off. Two million dollars was enough to tempt anyone to try something. They would wait inside the hangar for everyone to arrive and stay off to the side keeping as low a profile as possible during the deal. There could be no mistakes or the chances of getting a cut of this deal would dry up faster than spit on a Las Vegas sidewalk in July.

To come up through organized crime, not be killed and end up running one's own organization requires a Machiavellian personality, luck and a great deal of street smarts. After the call from Vito and Sal, John Salerno decided he and Paul Balbo would take a short break to help slow things down a little. They would have dinner at a steakhouse in the Fremont Casino, play a little blackjack and be back in the SUV by 8:30 p.m. He still hadn't decided if he was going to let Paul take the two traitors back to New York or not. He needed insurance and didn't want to alarm his 'go to guy.'

"Paul, this deal is too big to have it screwed up by these two morons. We have to keep them in the loop until everything is done, but I don't trust them one bit. I'm going to get John and Carmine out here tonight. If we have to delay the flight back for a couple hours, it won't upset anything. The jet has eight seats, so there's no space problem. I want to be sure those two don't try something. There's no doubt in my mind that as the night wears on, as stupid as they are, they will figure out that they made a fatal mistake. I don't want us on the wrong end of this. Think about where you want to get rid of them. We have time and we'll have the boys here to help get everything done right. Let's relax and slow things down a little."

John Salerno then called his son John in New York.

"John, I need you and Carmine on a flight as soon as you can get one. Charter would be the best, it can get you right into North Las Vegas Airport."

Then his son said,

"Is there some kind of a problem, is the deal in jeopardy?"

Big Johns immediate response was,

"No, nothing like that. We just need you and your brother here like right now and come prepared. When you land, have the charter drop you at the Weston Aviation hangar. Paul and I will be waiting there with 'The Pilot', Vito and Sal. We're having a little issue with Vito and Sal, so greet them like you normally do and don't let them out of your sight, understand? As far as they are going to know, the plane is going to make an unscheduled stop at an airport outside Philadelphia in case we are being tracked."

"I'll get Carmine and we'll be on the way. It will take a half hour to get to Teterboro and whatever else to get to Vegas. You're sure everything's ok?"

"Yes, it's all ok. It will all work out as planned when you get out here. Just get moving. I'm pitching this phone when we're done. You do the same and make sure no one knows the two of you are leaving town."

John directed Paul to work his way to Charleston and the 15 north on ramp. They would take that to the 95 north ramp and up to Lake Mead. It was just 8:50 p.m. when they reached Lake Mead Blvd, twenty minutes from Flamingo Jones' home, when he decided it was time to bring Paul Balbo up to speed.

"Let me explain who we're going to see and what we are going to do tonight. We are going to see two old hitters. They are the ones who killed those dopers in the parking garage the other night. They worked for us back in the sixties and seventies and took out a lot of our enemies. The thing is, it's two women."

Paul was completely stunned.

"What do you mean two women?"

"Not two women like you normally think of two women, these were something special mixed-race White, Black, Hispanic, Asian and American Indian. I think the term is exotic looking, but that doesn't even come close to how good looking they were. There was no one they couldn't lure into a trap. They were identical twins which made them even more effective. The marks didn't know if they were coming or going. Their mother was getting old. She was stripping at one of the dumps in Times Square trying to make ends meet. They were living on the street when I picked them up. They were rough, but two of the best lookers I'd ever seen. A funny thing though, their mother must have almost killed herself doing it, but she saw to it that they had a good Catholic school education. They were well spoken and could travel in just about any company. Too good looking to hand over to one of our pimps just to be put out on the street, so we set them up with one of our operations as call girls. We made a ton with each of them. Alone they brought in fifteen hundred a night and for both, a businessman would pay four thousand. That was in the early sixties. One night, a client decided he wanted to live out some stupid fantasy and got really rough with Flamingo. She ended up stabbing him twelve times in the chest with an ice pick. I think this idiot thought since he paid big money for her that he could kill her as part of the deal."

"What happened to her?"

"Nothing, a couple bruises and that was it.

"What about the John?"

"We disposed of him."

"I saw a whole new potential in those two. They developed their own style and we put them to work. They worked all over the country, nothing like them then or now. Never left any evidence. The cops couldn't even figure out how many there were. They used ice picks and some kind of antique hatpin. Technique was always the same, perfect kills. They did sixty some hits and then about 1973, they just up and told us they wanted out. They wanted real lives and to become respectable."

With their upbringing, did they even have any idea what respectable was?"

"The one sister, Flamingo came by to give me the news. I drugged her did what I wanted with her for five days, because she would never go near me. She learned no one turns me down.

Then gave her over to the boys to have their fun with her for about a week. When they were done, I beat her half to death and really did a job on her face. When she came out of the coma, I told her that was the price for her leaving us. A few years later, I was wondering what they were up to. I knew they were originally from Las Vegas, so I had Lazar do some checking on them. The private detective he used said Flamingo had her face reconstructed. He said it was a good job, and she was married to some guy named Seigel in the scrap business, but she couldn't have children. I'm guessing that was from the beating she got.

Her sister, Sahara, skipped before I could get to her and do the same. I found out she was married to a guy named Greenberg in the mortuary business. I had 'The Pilot' 'fix' Greenberg's plane about ten years ago. It must have been my lucky day because Greenberg and Seigel were both killed in the wreck. The sisters never knew I ordered the job, but I plan on telling Sahara just before we kill her. They should have known better than to think they could walk away from us without our blessing."

"John, they've got to be at least seventy or so. They're two old women how hard can it be to get rid of them?"

"Listen, I told you they were unique. We aren't taking any chances with them. They were the best I have ever seen and in or out of practice they will kill you."

"I'm seventy and do you think I've softened much over the years?"

"Point taken."

"Well, they are times two, so remember that."

John Salerno knew he was going to get rid of Paul, he just had to figure where and when during the nights events. He had given him information only he should know. He also knew that Paul Balbo was smart enough to know that. It was time to bring him into his confidence, keep your enemies closer.

"Paul, they did several hits that I personally arranged for the big bosses. I was supposed to do those hits, so there would never be any way anything could come back on them or their organizations. I used these two, because I knew there was no chance there would be any witnesses. That's where that stupid Ice pick Johnny nickname came from, the girls never gave me a hard time about it, because they knew it was good for their cover. About the time they left, I was moving up in the organization and wasn't called to do hits myself anymore. I ordered them. So, whatever we use tonight on these two goes in the river when we get back out east."

"Jesus John, how did you manage to stay alive knowing anything that could bring those guys down."

"My father was high up and they trusted him as much as their paranoia would let them. When he died, I moved up into his spot. They were all getting older, so they gave me the same trust my father had been given. That's why these two have to go tonight."

Then, it was time to address another problem,

"Paul, you're going to take care of Vito and Sal, so decide if you want to do it here in Vegas tonight or when we get back to New York. They are going to be really cautious when we meet up, because of this cut they asked for. It's easier to dispose of them in New York and if you do it here, we're going to have to haul them out into the desert where we used to dump bodies years back. That will eat up our time. We're also going to have to get rid of their wives and girlfriends. As stupid as these two appear to be, I wouldn't take bets that they haven't told them."

Paul's brain was racing like an Indy Car.

"Alright, I'll do the two of them when we get back."

Paul needed to buy as much time as he could and killing the two flunkies in Las Vegas would take his value as a participant to zero.

"I'll work something out to get all of them on the same day. You will have to be out of town when it happens and so will your sons."

"Good thinking Paul, we'll get it planned out as soon as we get back. I don't want those jerks on the street a day longer than necessary. We're about ten minutes from her house. When we pull up to the garage door, honk once and she'll open the door. You pull right in, she said to come in the front door that there's remodeling going on and we can't get in through the garage. Flamingo said she will close the garage door as soon as she sees us on the walk."

Greg Fuller and Bill Bowling were sitting in a quiet back booth at an almost empty 24-hour Denny's on Sahara Avenue having coffee and discussing the failed surveillance operation earlier in the day.

"Bill, sometimes these things are hit and miss. I don't look at it as a complete failure by any means. These guys have been around for a long time and they all know the drill. As soon as John Salerno found out that we were coming to talk to him he put a plan in motion. What we probably did accomplish was force them to move much faster than they had planned and maybe even alter their plans which is when mistakes happen. Remember this, none of these guys, no matter how much they talk about being crime 'families', trusts each other. These cockroaches will kill the other off over nothing and if we can bring just a little confusion into their lives, they will turn on each other. It will be like rats leaving a sinking ship. And if we get real lucky, we may snag one that will rat the rest out to save his miserable skin."

"Greg, do we have a plan from here on out?"

"We sure do, we wait. I will go out on a limb and guarantee that things will start happening tonight. By tomorrow morning, we'll be all over this. Like I said from the beginning, this guy wouldn't be here if this wasn't a big deal. His story about being here for fun and games was nothing but BS. Bill, if you want to stop at home to say hello to your wife and get a couple hours sleep, now is the time to go."

"That's ok Greg. I'll give her a call. I'm buying your hunch about things starting tonight and I don't want to miss any of it."

"That's what I wanted to hear Bill. Miss could we get a couple of fresh cups of coffee, please. We have a long night ahead of us. I think we should have breakfast now."

At midnight eastern time, Chief Inspector Rick Hassman of the FBI was just falling asleep after a big retirement party for one of his long-time agents when his phone rang.

"Rick this is Assistant Director Bud Shepard over at The Hoover Building. I just got off the phone with the director of the Las Vegas office and it appears that there is something very big going on there. Quickly, there was a former congressman from New York turned lobbyist named Alan Happ. He was always involved in one shady deal after another, but no one would ever go after him. He must have had more dirt on more people from his twenty-five years in Congress than you could imagine. Anyway, he allegedly got involved with some organized crime people and like most of his ilk, thought he was above everything. He turned up dead in a parking garage in downtown D.C. thirty-five years ago. His wife was related to a partner at one of the connected law firms, I think Arnold, Benedict and McKinley. She had part of the investigation sealed, the part about his being with a high-priced call girl for the evening. He was stabbed in the heart four times with an ice pick, single entry wound."

"And you're saying that the MO is the connection?"

"Yes, two meth-heads were killed, one of them in the exact same way, last Friday night in the parking garage at the Wynn Hotel & Casino in Las Vegas and the other with a hatpin or similar device shoved up into the brain. Sixty-four murders were attributed to this killer in the sixties and seventies and then he stopped."

"But it's thirty-five years later and basically two nobody's were killed."

"That's what is confusing about what happened. It was always speculated that they were all mob hits and the son of Big John Salerno was the main suspect in every single one, but always had iron clad alibis. He even acquired the nickname 'Ice Pick Johnny' but nothing ever stuck."

Inspector Hassman was trying to make some connection between suspected mob hits and the current murders.

"So, now we have these two murders, thirty-five years after the former congressman's."

"Yes, and after a quick check, it turns out that the son of Big John Salerno who assumed his father's moniker after his death was in Las Vegas last Friday night and has been staying at the Encore at the Wynn complex. There's a catch though, Las Vegas Homicide has this sharp young detective working the case and he swears Salerno didn't do this one."

"At first glance, I would tend to agree with the Las Vegas detective."

"The Las Vegas people think John Salerno is there for something really big, possibly a massive drug deal. They had surveillance early today. Salerno and his people got away. They are convinced that there is far more to this than a simple murder of two drug addicts in a parking garage and frankly, so am I after listening to our people there. Salerno is known to be involved in drugs, prostitution, loan sharking, illegal gambling, extortion and money laundering."

"What would you like me to do?"

"First off, call a Captain Girolami at Las Vegas Homicide as soon as we're finished. Let him know you want to be kept in the loop on this investigation. I have already called for a car to take you to the airport. You'll be flying out of Dulles as soon as you get there. This guy has evaded us for well over forty years and putting him away would be unbelievable. While you're there, casually meet detective Fuller, if he's as sharp as they say, we want him."

"Yes sir."

"And keep me informed on what's going on."

"Will do, I'll get a quick shower and be waiting for the car to get here."

Greg Fuller and Bill Bowling had barely started attacking their Lumberjack and All-American Slams, respectively, when detective Fuller's cell rang. It was Captain Girolami. Greg's first thought was, 'What is he calling about at this time of night for?'

"Captain what can I do for you?"

"Greg, it's not really for me. I just got off the phone with Chief Investigator Rick Hassman at the FBI in Washington. Somehow, they got wind of the killings in the garage at the Wynn and because the MO matches a Washington heavy weight killed years ago, they want to be kept informed all along the way. They want a complete report of what we have found out so far, names everything."

"You know, you just ruined my breakfast. I'm sorry, but you know what runs downhill and if we don't want this case taken over by the FEDs, you'll give them what they want."

"We'll get on it as soon as we are finished eating Captain. I think things are going to start moving quickly very soon."

"You've been right on in the past Greg. Get something ready for the FBI to look at and keep me posted as this unfolds."

"Yes sir."

At 9:15 p.m. local time, John Salerno and Paul Balbo pulled into the driveway of Flamingo Jones' home. He had Paul honk the horn once to make sure she was waiting for them. The garage door began to open. The first thing he noticed was the late model gray Chevy Impala, which struck him as odd, parked to the right of a spotless red 90's Jaguar XJ convertible. They pulled into the empty space to the left of the Jaguar and got out of the SUV, John intentionally slamming his door into the side of the convertible. They walked out of the garage, turned right and started up the front walk. They could hear the garage door closing and see the front door being opened. Flamingo did not wait for them to enter. She turned and walked toward the living room. She was wearing black workout pants, lightweight running shoes and a loose silky top cut low in the front that mimicked the bright green skin of the Vietnamese Bamboo Viper.

She said as she was walking, "Please close the door behind you."

Paul closed the door, locked the dead bolt and took a position about six feet front and center of the door. John walked into the living room looking Flamingo over like he was inspecting a slab of meat while thinking, 'not a wrinkle on this woman. She's really held up.'

"It's been a long time, hasn't it?"

Flamingo's less than cordial response was,

"Not long enough John, what do you want?"

"Always the smart ass, aren't you? Where's your twin sister?"

In a tone meant to both aggravate and demean,

"She's on her way here."

"I told you I wanted her here when I got here."

Grabbing her by her arm and squeezing hard enough to get a wince out of her.

"Get your slimy hand off me. She'll be here shortly. Her flight had a slight delay and it was the only one out tonight."

"You know, we have a couple hours to kill and I told Paul here we might have a little fun while we're here. I was telling Paul on the way over that even drugged, I never had anyone like you, before or after."

"I'd rather sleep with Harry the Horse than a gorilla like you or your lackey over there by the door."

At that, John Salerno lost his temper, backhanded Flamingo Jones across the face and started spewing the vitriol he had been saving for both sisters.

"By killing those two dopers in the garage the other night, you brought the police down on us when we're here to do business. I have a deal for a hundred kilos of pure middle eastern heroin and two million dollars of my money is sitting at the airport waiting to pay for it. We had to waste valuable time losing the cops and anyone else that's out there looking for us. That's the first thing you are both going to pay for. My sons have to come to Las Vegas tonight to help clear up the mess you two caused potentially exposing them to great risk. By the way, that little bit of blood running out the side of your pretty mouth is nothing compared to what I'm going to do." Flamingo sneered at him.

"I understand your husband was burned in a plane wreck about ten years ago. Well I've got some news for you bitch. I had 'The Pilot' 'fix' that plane as payback for your sister walking out on us. Killing your old man was just a bonus."

At first, Flamingo's eyes opened wide as eyes will when someone is totally shocked. John Salerno stood face to face with Flamingo Jones looking from her eyes to her hands not taking any chances. She blinked her eyes once and he found himself looking into a pair of hate-filled eyes belonging to one half of what may have been the deadliest hit team ever created. There was dead silence throughout the house. Paul was just staring at his boss' shotgun in hand, waiting for an order.

The next sound John heard was a small exhale and the shotgun falling to the floor followed by the sound of a human head hitting the ceramic tile. The distance from the front door to the living was between thirty and forty feet. When he heard the body hit the floor, he knew they should have searched the house. Sahara Jones had been there all along. Turning his back on Flamingo would be fatal. He turned slightly, not letting her out of his sight, reaching into his pocket for the snub nose, but before he could wrap his fingers around the butt of the revolver, he felt a sharp needle like pain in the back of his neck and then, the sensation of weightlessness as his body collapsed on the floor.

Standing over the live but immobilized John Salerno were Flamingo and Sahara Jones. Sahara used her bare foot to roll Big John's head to the side, so he could see the crumpled body of his go to guy Paul Balbo.

"John, there is your dead backup man. I made sure there were no others and to be honest, am insulted that you only had one other person with you. I'm a little out of practice not having done this in over thirty-five years. I had really wanted you to be able to talk, but we'll settle for your only being able to move your eyes. You did enough talking before anyway and gave us what we need."

As Sahara let his head roll back, Flamingo noticed a familiar bulge in his pocket. She pulled out a pair of nitrile gloves from the waist of her pants, put them on, reached into his pocket and took out a Salerno & Sons ice pick. Flamingo looked John Salerno in the eyes.

"John you shouldn't have. Well, maybe I should say you didn't need to be so considerate because I still have the one you gave me years ago."

She went to the kitchen and returned with a plastic zipper bag, dropped it in and closed the bag. Then, Sahara bent over and came within inches of his face.

"We will be checking to see if you have any areas that have sensation for hot, cold or pain. You know the routine better than we do since torture was more your style. In case you are wondering what, I did, I stabbed my hatpin between your vertebrae and severed your spinal cord. Not enough to kill you, as you can tell, but enough to paralyze you. Now, Flamingo and I have a great deal of work and planning to do in a very short amount of time, so if you will just make yourself comfortable we will be back with you as soon as we can."

"I have the body bags Max kept at the house for emergencies. Let's slip his backup man into one now."

While they were bagging the remains of Paul Balbo, they continued planning. "Have you spoken to Ray?"

"Yes, I will give him a call and he'll come right away. We have to be at the airport before midnight if possible."

Before zipping the body bag closed Flamingo took John Salerno's ice pick from the plastic bag and stabbed the body of the late Paul Balbo enough times to get a good DNA sample. She then bagged the ice pick again. It took both Jones sisters to slide a bag under John Salerno.

Ray Hernandez was a young man on his way to a life of crime when shortly after being released from prison he was offered a job at the Whispering Winds Mortuary. He worked at the first of what would become a string of mortuaries in Utah, Nevada and California over the next twenty years. Max Greenberg saw something in this young man and told him he was going to teach him to work with his head, to be a businessman. Ray completed the requirements for his high school diploma, went on to get a bachelor's degree and then to mortuary school. He and his family grew and prospered with the Greenberg's. When Max was killed Sahara made him her full partner and set up an arrangement for him to purchase the entire operation over time. And so, it was, without hesitation that Ray said he would take care of this disposal problem for his trusted and dear friend.

Ron Seigel had a similar experience with his scrap and recycling business. The Siegel's and the Greenberg's were always taking in 'strays' they felt had great potential and giving them a chance to succeed when the world otherwise might not have. Flamingo made a quick call to World Scrap and Recycling's main office, the company her husband and the love of her life had built into a multi-state scrap and recycling giant.

She had a short conversation with Larry Rabren, the man she appointed President and CEO after Ron's death. Ron and Flamingo had seen something special in Larry and had helped him through direction and their unyielding friendship to overcome the effects of drinking, drugs and PTSD from combat while in the military. They would drop the rented Chevy at the scrap yard office while they were on their way to the airport. Then, drop the SUV at the scrap yard when they were done with their night's work and leave in the rental. By morning, the entire SUV would be shredded in pieces no larger than a shoe and mixed with other scrap in rail cars headed for the steel mills along the Pearl River in China.

They expected Ray at 10:30 p.m. in an unmarked van. He was instructed to back into the drive and come to the door. He would carry the body bags out through the garage entrance and slide them into the van. But for now, Flamingo and Sahara were going to have a one-sided conversation with Big John Salerno and then check him over.

Sahara was first.

"John, what you did, killing our husbands, is the evilest act of retribution I could ever conceive. When this conversation is over, we are going to check to see if you have any sensation anywhere, because here's what is going to happen. You are going to be picked up in the next half hour or so, transported to the Whispering Winds Crematorium where your backup man is going to be cremated first and then you are going to be shoved into the crematory oven and burned alive. In fact, the body bag you are partially in right now will be left open, so you can see the gas flame when it's lit."

John Salerno's eyes spoke of stark terror. Then it was Flamingos turn.

"John you raped, beat and rendered me incapable of having children and you murdered our husbands. Ron Seigel was the only man I have ever loved in my life and you stole him from me, you evil scum. So now, I am going to tell you the price for your misdeeds. We are going to kill the drug traffickers, your two nephews, your sons and

'The Pilot'. When the traffickers' associates find their drugs and money gone, and their people killed, they will take care of what's left of the Salerno crime organization and their families."

"John there is really a method to our madness. Years ago, you always said you didn't like to leave any loose ends I think the term you used to death was 'tie everything off' and that's precisely what we are about to do."

"We have no idea who you may have told about us over the years. We're guessing your 'go to guy' in the bag by the door, maybe your nephews, most likely your sons, we doubt your wife, but the traffickers will handle that one for us and since we worked with 'The Pilot', he knows. We will find out the names of anyone he may have talked to and we will 'tie them off' as well."
The doorbell rang as she was finishing.

"Sahara, I think that's Ray at the door I'll get it."

Flamingo showed Ray the door to the garage. He started dragging the body bag with the lifeless body of Paul Balbo inside toward it, while Flamingo and Sahara did their promised inspection of Big John's body. They used a lighter and icepick finding two areas that still responded to heat and pain ensuring a most gruesome end. As the Jones girls were preparing to leave, Sahara stopped by John Salerno one last time.

"John, we have to go now. We have a busy night ahead of us. Make sure you save some seats when you arrive in hell tonight. There will be plenty of company joining you later."
Big John Salerno didn't have a clue what cold blooded was when he first arrived for the evening's fateful meeting. Ray zipped the bag up to Big John's chin, so he would have plenty of oxygen to breath on his way to the crematorium.

When the bodies were loaded, he told Sahara everything would be carried out as discussed. Then he rolled up the rug by the front door, moved the sofa and rolled that rug as well. Both rugs would be disposed of in similar fashion. Flamingo bleached the spot where Paul's head had hit the tile floor. Regardless of how far down the ladder of suspects they were, they had always been thorough when it came to disposing of and eliminating anything incriminating. New rugs would be delivered on schedule and rolled out Saturday morning.

It was 11:00 p.m. when Flamingo backed the rented Impala out of the garage and was followed by Sahara in the QX80. They drove across town to the scrap yard. Flamingo called just before they arrived, Larry already had the gate open for them. She parked the Impala just out of sight under an overhang inside the yard, grabbed a small nylon bag from the passenger side, walked out to the SUV and climbed into the passenger seat. Larry closed the gate and told them he would be waiting for them when they returned with the SUV. The sooner the better, since they were shredding cars tonight and had rail service picking up the cars at 4:00 a.m.

When the two detectives had finished dinner, Greg called in and asked to have someone run some checks with local car rental companies to see possibly how many cars the Salerno people had rented. If they got some hits, they may get things moving again. Detective Fuller was determined to pursue every avenue available to break this case open as soon as possible to avoid the FBI deciding to take the investigation over. The good news was he had filed his initial report with the FBI and hadn't heard anything back from them. At the same time, Rick Hassman was halfway across the country with a small team of investigators bumping along in some mild turbulence trying to get sleep before landing at North Las Vegas Airport. The FBI decided on North Las Vegas because they could get hangar space and their people could work without interruptions.

The drive from the scrap yard to the airport was about twenty minutes which gave them time to organize their thoughts. Flamingo said,

"If the traffickers are like the ones that were around when we were working, they will have lookouts and a driver outside the hangar. I say we take care of them first. There will more than likely only be two of the drug people inside, two of Salerno's people and 'The Pilot'. I have two pairs of charcoal coveralls in my bag, so we can stay in the shadows."

"The only one we have to spend any time at all with is 'The Pilot'. The rest won't have any information we can use."

At 11:30 p.m. Flamingo and Sahara Jones pulled up in front of the Las Vegas Aviation Service hangar located one door west of the Weston Aviation Service hangar. They sat quietly scanning the area around the Weston Aviation hangar picking out their marks and looking for any cameras. The operators of the various flight services apparently saw no need for cameras because there were none visible. There were two lookout men, one next to a black late model Chevy Suburban parked in a handicap zone and the other standing just inside the dark at the east corner of the hangar between the buildings. They could only make out the driver through the tinted windows and could only hope he was alone. They put on the coveralls, put their hair up and put on baseball caps. They took off the nitrile gloves they had put on earlier and put on new ones. They were lucky it was nighttime. They could pass themselves off as nightshift line crew. The black nitrile gloves were difficult to spot at night and didn't clash because of their natural light brown skin color. Sahara walked by the front of the Weston hangar while Flamingo walked toward the parked Suburban.

She noticed the driver had the window open and was smoking. As Flamingo walked up to the driver's side where the lookout was standing with her hands in her pockets to project no threat and said, "Sir, unless you have a handicap tag, you will have to move to another spot."

This elicited a questioning look from the driver and a sour look from the lookout.

She thought 'perfect timing'. Flamingo pulled an ice pick from each pocket, stabbed the lookout man between the fourth and fifth ribs pushing the ice pick in and out four times while leaving a single-entry wound. The stunned driver reached across the seat to grab the UZI he was always supposed to keep on his person. She reached in through the open window, grabbed him by the collar of his jacket as his hand touched the micro UZI machine pistol, pushed John Salerno's ice pick into the base of his skull and turned the tip in a three hundred and sixty degree circular pattern, the driver was dead, slumped forward on the wheel, seconds after his comrade.

The second lookout man saw what was happening and charged out of the dark. Sahara Jones was waiting and just as he came into the light, she slipped behind him pushing the modified hatpin into the base of his skull. Twisting it in the same circular motion her sister used with the ice pick on the driver. She killed him instantly. As the body was falling to the pavement, she grabbed the collar of the late lookout's jacket and dragged his corpse back between the buildings far enough in so no one walking by would see it in the darkness. Sahara removed the Heckler & Koch MP5 slung over his shoulder and holding it to her side, she ran it out to the Suburban. Flamingo took two MP5's and the UZI machine pistol to the SUV and put them under the back seat. At the same time Sahara was pounding on the front door of the Weston hangar. A man they could only guess was one of the traffickers came to the door. Sahara asking him if the Suburban was his and if so, he should know his driver was unconscious, then said.

"I saw someone tampering with the SUV when I walked over to investigate."

The man yelled inside that he was going to check on their driver. As he left the building Sahara repeated the procedure with the hatpin. While Flamingo slipped into the lobby of the office as the door was closing. Sahara dragged the body of the trafficker into the space between the buildings and placed it next to the other. She checked for weapons, found an UZI machine pistol harnessed to his chest and like the other removed it. She carefully looked out from between the hangars and casually walked to the front door. Flamingo opened it and let her in. They only opened the lobby door wide enough to slip into the office.

There were four offices along one wall and two meeting rooms along the other and a large executive office at the very end with the door closed. The four small offices were all dark and probably unoccupied. There was a single table lamp lit in the big office indicating 'The Pilot' was probably sleeping on the couch. In the one meeting room sat a somewhat anxious man, probably the trafficker, wondering where his

second man was. In the other was Vito, Sal and
the briefcase containing two million dollars. The
brothers were sitting at opposite ends of the eight-
foot conference table. First stop was the room
with the lone occupant.

Flamingo and Sahara walked through the
darkened office along the wall as though they
belonged there and opened the door. Sahara
looked directly at the trafficker. Pointing the Uzi
machine pistol at him with one hand putting her
index finger to her lips with the other and moving
her head from side to side to indicate he should
remain very quiet. Flamingo followed her into the
room, walked behind the trafficker, grabbed him
by his collar and pushed Salerno's ice pick up into
his brain killing him instantly. She pulled out the
chair and let the body quietly sink to the floor. He
was the principle. He had no weapon on him.

Sahara opened the conference room door
and entered like they were part of the deal. Vito
and Sal were caught off guard. Flamingo moved
behind Sal while Sahara gave silent orders to
remain quiet and positioned herself behind Vito.
Like perfectly timed and choreographed
performers, they wasted no words on either of the
thugs and killed them both. They quietly lowered
the deceased to the floor and moved on to the

executive office where, through the glass picture window, they saw 'The Pilot'. His back was facing them as he slept peacefully on his dark brown overstuffed leather couch.

For the first time in their lives, the sisters almost let their feelings interfere with their work. Sahara quietly pushed down on the door handle and opened the door to the executive office where Jerry Weston, 'The Pilot', Owner of Weston Aviation Service, drug runner, saboteur and murderer of their husbands lay sleeping. Flamingo followed her sister into the office and walked behind the couch. Sahara moved to the front and proceeded to drive her fist into the back of Jerry Weston's rib cage painfully waking him. When Jerry saw Flamingo standing behind the couch and turned and saw Sahara in front of him he was struck speechless with fear. Flamingo grabbed him by his hair from behind while Sahara screamed.

"You murdered our husbands."

In a fear-stricken voice, Weston answered.

"I had no choice, it was that or die. You know the Salernos as well as I do, probably better."

It was Flamingo's turn.

"You could have come to us and warned us. You know we would have helped you. You were well aware we have been living here with our families quietly for years. No 'Pilot', you…are as guilty and evil as John Salerno."

"When are John's sons supposed to be here? How long you live depends upon it."

"Within the hour, they are supposed to meet their father here and I am flying them all back to New York as soon as the deal is done."

"How are they getting here?"

"They took a charter out of Teterboro several hours ago."

"Have you had any communication with them?"

"Yes, I have."

"And how soon before they land and where?"

"They are supposed to land right at midnight. They are flying in here at North Las Vegas and they will be dropped in front of my hangar."

"That's right now." Exclaimed Sahara looking at the bright red display on the digital wall clock.

"Call them right now and find out where they are. If you give so much as inkling about what's happened here, your life will be worthless. Do you understand?"

"Yes, I do."

"Do you have a speaker on that cell phone?"

"Yes, I do."

"Then turn it on as soon as the ringing starts. If they ask if their father is here, you tell them not yet, but you are expecting him any minute."

The cell rang twice, and John Salerno's son John answered.

"What do you want now?"

"I just want to know when you think you'll be in here."

"We're on final approach right now, hold on."

He yelled to the pilot.

"How soon will you drop us at the hangar?"

The pilot of the charter yelled back,

"Less than five minutes."

"Did you hear that less than five minutes? Make sure the door is unlocked."

"It already is."

The voice was almost a carbon copy of his soon to be late father. Jerry Weston's mind was racing almost as fast as a turbine on one of his jets. He was desperate to figure out some way to save his own pathetic life when he thought that giving up his employer might buy him some time.

"Here's something you should know before John gets here. He may be getting older, but age hasn't mellowed him one bit. John's 'go to guy', Paul Balbo, is not someone to be fooled with. He's young, very tough and as violent as I have ever seen."

Both Sahara and Flamingo looked at him with the same disdain as they did when they woke him. Sahara chimed in.

"I'll take your phony concern to heart 'Pilot' but for your information Mr. Balbo won't be getting any older."

Sahara Jones walked behind the couch and as she had done earlier in the evening stabbed Jerry Weston 'The Pilot' in his spine severing his spinal cord.
He fell limp on the leather couch able to move his eyes and surprisingly, able to speak.

"What have you done to me?"

"I have paralyzed you. I have severed your spinal cord."

"But why? I answered all your questions."

"Do you think you deserve special treatment for giving us some lousy information after what you have done?"

And at that Flamingo pushed John Salerno's ice pick into Jerry Weston's heart one time and delivered his prognosis.

"I have only stabbed you one time, you have already started to bleed internally, my best guess is that you will live maybe another fifty minutes. In that time, you need to reflect on your life and all of the sadness you have brought to the world."

Flamingo and Sahara left the dying criminal on his couch with John Salerno's ice pick lying on the coffee table next to him and went to the hangar area. At 12:10 a.m. they turned off the lights in the hangar, the only light was from the table lamp in Jerry Weston's office emanating out through the picture window overlooking the hangar area. They slipped into the shadows and began their wait. At 12:14 a.m. the door rattled as the knob was being turned and the door opened. In the darkened hangar John Salerno III and his brother Carmine walked into the arms of the avenging Jones sisters and as swiftly as they had come, they were gone.

At 12:20 a.m. Greg Fuller received a call from headquarters letting him know they had car rental information for him. The Salerno people, specifically Vito Candela, had rented five vehicles, a white Escalade, a black Maserati, a blue Infiniti QX80, a gray GMC Yukon XL Denali and a dark blue Honda Pilot. The Maserati was accounted for up in Mesquite. The Las Vegas police department had a flatbed truck on its way to get it, so it could be processed. Surveillance would start again immediately looking for the four other vehicles. Security at all the hotels along the strip and downtown was contacted. Each was asked to check their parking lots for any of the rented vehicles. All the patrol units were told to look out for the rental vehicles, but not to stop only surveil. They were given orders to check the parking lots at McCarran and North Lass Vegas airports. It was now just a matter of time before something came through.

At 12:30 a.m. Flamingo and Sahara removed the coveralls and nitrile gloves and put the articles, along with one ice pick and the hatpin, in the nylon bag they had brought along. Sahara started the Infiniti and began the ride to the scrap yard. They decided to head northeast on Losee Rd through the industrial and commercial areas, not knowing that the police were looking for the SUV they were driving. They passed an all-night restaurant where two patrolmen were just coming off break. As the officers were getting ready to pull out, Flamingo and Sahara Jones caught one of the luckiest breaks of their lives. A drunk driver drove into the parking lot and plowed into the patrol car. The yard was one mile ahead. Flamingo called Larry Rabren and let him know where they were and to open the gate, now. When they pulled in, Larry directed them to a crane in the yard with a grappling hook. They took their bag and the weapons out of the back seat.

Larry opened the access door, removed the gas cap, climbed up on the crane, started it, swung the boom over the top of the SUV and lowered the open hook. He let it drop onto the top of the QX80 and activated the hook, crushing the roof and sides inward while lifting the vehicle five feet off the ground. He stopped, made a call and had one of his yard men bring a fifty-five-gallon drum with a screened funnel. The yard man took out a sharpened spike, pierced the gas tank and drained the tank. When the tank was empty, Larry lifted the SUV up over a crusher and released it.

The crusher operator then proceeded to crush the rented SUV. It was pushed out on a conveyor and went directly to the shredder. In less than two minutes, the entire SUV was shredded and running down another conveyor to a waiting train car. Another conveyor was dumping shredded cars on top of the SUV within minutes. Larry climbed down from the crane and told

Flamingo that rail service would be there in a couple hours to pick up the cars of scrap. She asked Larry if he could dispose of the weapons they had acquired in their travels. He said he would personally take a torch and make all the parts unrecognizable. They put their nylon bag in the Impala and headed toward home.

Greg Fuller got a call that the Escalade had been located as well as the Honda Pilot. He knew they were a waste of time, but if there was any chance of them being used again, that was over. Within minutes, a call came in that the GMC Yukon had been located at North Las Vegas Airport, parked at the Weston Aviation Service hangar. The FBI was also monitoring radio calls and was stunned that whatever was going on was being done under their noses. Detective Fuller called Captain Girolami with the report. He then called Chief Inspector Hassman who informed him they were just several hundred feet from the vehicle and were on their way.

The FBI team ran to the hangar and noticed the obvious right away. They had one deceased in a Suburban and another lying next to the driver's door. A patrol car pulled up to the front of the building and its headlights inadvertently shined on the two corpses in the walkway between the buildings. Fuller and Bowling were the next to arrive and made the decision, along with their counterparts from the FBI, to not wait for a SWAT team and entered the building. In the first conference room, they found the trafficker lying on the floor dead and a large suitcase with, after counting, one hundred kilos of pure middle eastern heroin. In the next conference room, they found Vito and Sal Candela lying at opposite ends of the conference table and a large rolling briefcase, with, after counting, one million nine hundred ninety-nine thousand five hundred dollars. The police, then found Jerry 'The Pilot' Weston alive on his couch. His condition was, however, so critical that he was unable to talk or finger an assailant. He passed into the next life on his way to the emergency room in the ambulance. The Salerno brothers were found where they fell in the hangar area. One thing in particular caught the eye of both Greg Fuller and Agent Rick Hassman, the Salerno & Son ice pick on the coffee table. Since the FBI could process DNA samples far quicker than the Las Vegas Police Department, they conceded knowing they couldn't win that one.

Sahara called Ray Hernandez and asked for one more favor. It turned out, Ray was still at the crematorium, so they went to meet him there.

Sahara asked if he could possibly dispose of the coveralls and nitrile gloves. Flamingo asked if he had a pair of pliers or a vice grip he returned with pliers and Flamingo removed the ice pick from the handle. She then asked Ray if he would burn it with the other pieces. He told them the other task was almost completed and he would personally see to it that these items would be gone. Even though it was almost the middle of the night, Flamingo drove to the car rental lot, parked the Impala, put the keys in the drop box and they left for home with her car. She dropped Sahara at her house and drove out to Summerlin. The following morning, Sahara's phone rang at 6:30 a.m., she answered in an annoyed tone,

"What do you want now?"

"We need to take a boat trip and we need to do it as soon as possible. Ron used to tell me he had three loves in this world, me the Jaguar convertible and his fishing boat. I'll be there in one hour. Please bring a thermos of coffee." She hung up.

When she arrived to pick up her sister she asked if she had the nylon bag with the hatpin and remains of the ice pick, Sahara replied, "I have everything. We never left any loose ends in all the years we worked and now is not the time to start."

Then Flamingo let on, "I have a strange feeling we are going to be visited by Detective Fuller and his partner sooner rather than later. We were the only two people who got off the elevator in the few minutes before and after those two unfortunates tried to mug us."

"Mary Alice, you may be right. Let's take care of this right away. Just because we've gotten on a little doesn't mean we should get sloppy."

Dressed for a boat ride, they pulled on Welcome to Las Vegas ball caps, put down the top and headed for Lake Mead. When they got to the landing, there was Ron's boat ready to go. They idled out across the lake taking notice of one car that seemed to be paralleling their course along the shoreline. Flamingo decided it was time to make quick work of their admirer, whoever it was, and pushed the throttles full forward on the twin two hundred fifty horse Mercury outboards. After sufficient distance, Sahara took the honors of subtly dropping the tools of their trade and the nylon bag with a five-pound rock tied to it overboard.

The newspapers had a field day reporting the whole incident. Local news outlets hadn't had a good crime story to work for several years. It had almost every element to make great news:

violence, money, drugs, murder, mobsters and tons of unanswered questions. The DNA and finger print analysis came back. Big John Salerno's prints and DNA were all over the ice pick as well as several others. All the players were accounted for, except for of course, John Salerno and Paul Balbo. Rick Hassman and his team looked like superstars for their solving of the thirty-five-year-old murder of former Congressman Alan Happ. Everyone was happy except Greg Fuller and Bill Bowling.

They were back at their Denny's for breakfast at a normal time and discussing the case.

"There's no doubt Salerno was here to do this drug deal and I think that's all he was here to do. I think he got sidetracked somehow and everything just fell apart. His whole organization is gone. They say his wife, nephew's wives and kids, as well as his sister are all in protective custody. What do you think Bill?"

"I say he's dead and will never be found, not so much as a trace, and nobody will ever talk. There was no DNA other than the people murdered at the crime scene, not even on those guys dragged into the walkway."

"We know they were armed. Traffickers are some of the most heavily armed people in the world, especially when their doing a deal this size. There was only one weapon left behind, that UZI mini machine pistol in the second conference room and there wasn't so much as a print or trace of DNA on it other than the driver of the suburban."

"Greg, this is the biggest case I have worked as a detective or police officer for that matter. If you have any ideas, I'm with you."

"I actually do. I think your two women, the ones who look like old showgirls, who got off the elevator know more about this than they let on. I am going to talk to Captain Girolami about looking into them when we get into work."

"Did you get the message about the Captain wanting to see us at 10:00 a.m.? Yes, I did."

"Do you have any idea what it's about?"

"No, I don't, but we'll find out soon enough."

The phone rang in Captain Girolami's office.

"Girolami."

"Captain, this is Chief Inspector Hassman at the FBI."

"What can I do for you today Inspector?"

"I'm just calling to thank you for working with us on this case. We know it gets a little difficult to cross lines and you and your people couldn't have worked with us better."

"Well thanks."

"Also, I don't want to go completely behind your back, but we would sure like to get our hands on your detective Fuller."

"Have you talked to him already?"

"Just briefly and he said no. He told me he's a Las Vegas Homicide detective and wants to continue to grow with this town."

"Well, I guess you're not going to get him at least for the time being."

"It was good working with you Captain I'm sure we'll cross paths again in the future."

"I'm sure we will sir, goodbye."
At 10:00 a.m. Greg Fuller and Bill Bowling arrived at Homicide. Greg went to the captain's office and asked if he could see him for a minute,

"Come in Greg. What's on your mind?"

"Well Captain, it's this case. I think there's way more to this and I'd like to pursue it further."

"Before we go any further, I understand you turned the FBI down."

"Yes sir, I did. I told them I'm a Las Vegas guy and I think I can do an awful lot of good right here."

"I wish you would have let me in on what was going on. I'll be honest with you, they caught me a little off guard, but I didn't think it was that important that I had to tell anyone. I told them I just wasn't interested."

"Greg, we have another matter to discuss this morning."

"Yes sir."

"It's going to be difficult to pursue this case much further, because as a newly minted Lieutenant, your duties won't leave an awful lot of time for activities other than directing the people that work for you. Congratulations Greg, you earned this the hard way, just the same way the rest of us have."

"Thank you sir, but what about my partner Bill Bowling?"

"Bill is being promoted to lead detective and will be meeting his new partner in about an hour. Now, get out of here and go do something."

After docking the boat and making sure it was stored away properly, Flamingo and Sahara started their drive back to Las Vegas. As they were pulling out onto the highway, Sahara said,

"Did you hear any news reports about their finding one million nine hundred ninety-nine thousand five hundred?"

"Yes, I did."

"John specifically said two million. He was fanatical about his money. He would not have said two million if it was as much as a dollar less."

Flamingo looked over at her sister with a half smiling guilty look on her face and said,

"I confess. As we were leaving, I thought it was only fair to take five hundred from one bundle to cover dinner at the Wynn when we go back to The Strip."

It's a Dogs World

Truly Epstein, daughter of Morris and Maris
Epstein of Tenafly, NJ, was raised in one of the
most loving households one could ever imagine.
Morris and Maris had set out to have four children,
an easily affordable size family as Morris was a
successful manufacturer of women's
undergarments. Sadly, after the birth of Truly,
Maris was unable to conceive any more children
and though deeply saddened, the couple was
eternally thankful that they had been blessed with
such a wonderful child. On Truly's first birthday,
her father brought home a Cocker Spaniel to the
absolute delight of his little princess and named the
dog Sparkles. Truly and Sparkles took to each
other instantly and for the next twelve years were
almost inseparable until, that day.
As always happens in dog human relationships,
Sparkles passed away from old age leaving a
totally distraught Truly.

Morris seeing how sad his daughter was
started looking immediately for another dog.
Afraid that she would think he was attempting to
replace the irreplaceable Cocker Spaniel he came
home one afternoon with a Springer and Truly
quickly named him Charlie. Charlie took to her

kind loving nature almost immediately and once again dog and girl were almost inseparable. Truly grew into a beautiful young woman seldom seen without Charlie. She went off to college at eighteen and after completing her first year, her father rented an apartment just off campus that allowed pets. Charlie was moved in within days and again Truly's life could not have been better.

In her senior year, Truly met Ron Langdorf a handsome finance major and the two of them could not have hit it off better. They dated for the next two years and were married three days after Truly's twenty-fourth birthday. Shortly after they were married Truly was totally distraught for the second time in her young life.

As always happens in dog and human relationships, Charlie passed away from old age. After several months, Truly began to get over the loss of her beloved Charlie and talk about starting a family of their own took center stage. When Truly told her parents she and Ron were going to start a family, they were literally overcome with joy. They had visions of grandchildren running through their home on visits and holidays. They could not have been more excited.

Then, the first minor setback in their relationship came when Morris offered Ron a position with his company which would eventually lead to his taking over the business. Ron refused the offer and instead accepted a position with a bank in St. Louis. Even though Morris was hurt to say the least, he wrote the whole thing off to Ron's inexperience, and everyone got on with their lives. Then, in a second but major setback to their life together, Truly was informed after numerous trips to fertility clinics, specialists, and even a trip to a famous hospital in Switzerland that she was unable to conceive. It was devastating. Some believed that it took a toll in years from the lives of Morris and Maris Epstein too. When Truly finally accepted that she would never have children, she sat with Ron one afternoon and started discussing them getting a dog.

"Truly, I don't think getting a dog is really a very good idea."

"Ron, you are away at work all day and put in such long hours it would be company for me. I grew up with dogs and have missed them so much."

"Let me think about it. I'm really not a dog person."

"But I thought...?"

"You never really asked me."

"It wouldn't be a financial burden and I would take care of it."

"What are you thinking of?"

"I don't know yet, but not a big dog." Several weeks passed, more conversation and finally, Ron relented. Truly set about looking for her new dog.

Several days into her search, Truly came home with a surprise.

"Ron, isn't she the cutest dog you have ever seen?"

"What kind of a dog is it?"

"She is a Bichon Frise and I found her at a no kill rescue shelter. Isn't she beautiful?"

"If you say so."

"Ron, they have so many dogs that need homes, so many that have been abandoned just because their owners tired of them or were just unable to care for them anymore. It's such a shame. She is only a year old and Bichons live well into their teens. I haven't been this happy in such a long time."

"Well, alright, but don't try to bring another dog into this house. You know how I feel about dogs."

"I think I am going to name her Bindy. What do you think Ron?"

"I guess that will do."

"You're not excited are you Ron?"

"I am if you are. I don't know how many times I have to tell you, I'm not really a dog person."

As time went on, it turned out that Ron was just not much of a dog person, but also not much of a people person either. He didn't have nearly the relationship with his family that Truly had with Morris and Maris and openly didn't care.

"Ron, I would like to fly back to New Jersey to visit my parents. They aren't doing well, and it's been almost six months since I was there."

"I would prefer if you were here, but if you really must, go ahead. Who is going to watch the dog while you are gone?"

"She never makes a mess and all you need do is let her in the yard when you get home."

"I don't have time. You wanted her you take care of her."

"Alright, I'll board her while I'm gone."

"That won't work. It's too expensive."

"Is it that difficult to let her out?"

"Yes, it is."

"I'll take her with me then."

"That's too expensive."

"Then, I'll drive. It's two days and the trip will be no more than one round trip ticket."

Two days later, after driving through Illinois, Indiana, Ohio and Pennsylvania, Truly arrived at her parents in Tenafly with Bindy at her side. In her mind, the dog was far better company these days than if Ron had made the trip with her.

"Mom, Dad, how are you feeling?"

"We are doing alright."

"I'm not blind. You don't look well."

"Why can't you come more often? It's been six months?"

"Ron has fits when I come. I had to drive because he won't care for Bindy and he won't let me board her. He said it would also cost too much if I had to pay to bring the dog on a plane."

"Truly is there something going on that you want to tell us about?"

"Ron tries to control everything I do. He talks to me like I am of lesser intelligence. I am basically forced to drive what he says I can drive, buy the food he wants, decorate to his taste and sometimes, I think he is just waiting for you to die, so he can get his hands on the inheritance."

Upon hearing their daughters remark, Morris started walking toward the living room waving his wife and daughter along. Her parents sat on their couch while Truly sat across from them in a large comfortable overstuffed chair.

"Truly, we must apologize. We didn't think you were aware of any of this. Your father and I would never interfere in your marriage and in hindsight, we should have talked to you privately years ago."

"We hope you can forgive us for remaining quiet for so long?"

"There is no need for you to apologize, I should have confronted him years ago and we would not be having this conversation today."

"Regardless, we are taking steps to make sure your inheritance is safe, so please don't say anything to Ron."

"I won't, thank you for looking out for me. I wish I could be with you more often."
Now that everything was finally out in the open, Truly had the best visit in years with her parents and as it always seems when people are thoroughly enjoying themselves, time seemed to fly by.

"I should start back tomorrow, a week away and Ron starts to get testy. The house will also be a mess. It's as though he punishes me for visiting you."

"We understand, and we are so happy you brought Bindy. Will you bring her the next time you come to visit?"

"Oh yes, absolutely."

As always happens in the lives of humans once we were young, then middle age, then we are old, and no matter how we prepare, no one is ready for the sadness that comes with the passing of loved ones. Four months after her last visit, Truly got a call from the nurse's station at Tenafly General Hospital at 7:00 a.m. on Monday.

"Mrs. Langdorf?"

"Yes."

"This is Ethel Jones. I'm the nurse assigned to your mother and father. They were both admitted to the hospital last night and have both been asking for you repeatedly."

"I just spoke to them last night."

"I know, they told me. You must get here as quickly as possible."

"Please let them know I will leave immediately."

"I will, thank you."

She immediately called her husband at his office. They had to leave as soon as possible for New Jersey.

"Ron, my mother and father are both in the hospital. A nurse called and said we need to get there as quickly as we can."

"I can't leave. I have work."

"Ron, it's my mother and father. They bought our home and have helped us over the years. I don't understand. They are very ill. The bank will surely understand."

"I have work."

"Then, can I leave Bindy. Will you see that she is let out and fed while I'm gone?"

"I suppose."

"I'll be leaving as soon as I can get a flight."

"Try not to be gone too long."

"Ron, it's my mother and father."

Truly was able to get a flight out of St. Louis to Newark, rented a car, and arrived in Tenafly that day. She spent the next four days at the bedsides of her parents leaving only for an occasional meal in the hospital cafeteria. On Saturday morning, Truly made her first call to her husband since leaving St. Louis.

"Ron, my father passed away last night, and my mother passed away this morning."

"What are your plans?"

"What do you mean, my plans?"

"When are you going to bury them?"

"I have a meeting with the mortician this afternoon. I wish you were here if just for moral support."

"I can't get away."

"They were my parents Ron. They did so many things for us over the years."

"I suppose."

"How is Bindy?"

"The dog is just fine."

Truly had just finished her call with Ron when nurse Jones approached her in the waiting area opposite the nurse's station.

"Mrs. Langdorf, before you leave, if you would like to see your parents one more time, we can arrange it?"

"That is so kind of you. Yes, I would."

"Also, I have a letter your father gave me and asked that I give it to you. It is for you only."

"Oh, thank you so much."

My dearest Truly,

Your mother and I could never have asked for a more wonderful child. You brought untold joy into our lives. We know these last few years have become more difficult for you and we decided to take some steps to help insure your future. We have set up a trust that only you can break, and I sincerely request that you never do. It will pay a modest sum each month allowing you and Ron to live comfortably. Please keep the house in Tenafly, it may be a backup someday that you will be happy to have. It, too, will be controlled by the trust.

We will love you for all eternity.

Mom and Dad.

P.S. As much as you may want to keep this letter, you must dispose of it immediately.

Truly followed her parents' instructions and disposed of the letter they had left. She went back to her parents', now her home, and started preparations for their burial. She wanted to schedule the services to coincide with Ron coming to town, so a call to her husband was her first order of business.

"Ron, my parents will be buried on Tuesday. Can you be here Monday evening?"

"I don't see why it's necessary that I come for this. It's not exactly like they'll miss me and it's very busy at work right now. I have investments that require tracking daily. When will you be back?"

"On Thursday."

"Good."

"How is Bindy?"

"The dog is fine."

Truly was more than aware that she and Ron had become distant over the years. How distant became clear when their call ended, and she found herself missing her Bindy more than her husband. Truly left New Jersey on Friday morning from Newark and landed in St. Louis late in the afternoon and was back home just after Ron arrived home from work.

"Ron, I'm home."

"You said you would be here yesterday."

"Where is Bindy?"

"I don't know, I came home, the door was open, and the dog was gone."

"We must go look for her right now."

"I walked around the block and there was no sign of the dog."

"Well, we have to go and look some more then."

"You go, it's your dog."

"Ron!"

"What are we having for dinner? I'm tired of frozen meals."

"Well, you will have to make do with them for one more night or just go out."

While Truly was out looking for Bindy, walking block after block, the phone rang at the Langdorf home,

"Mr. Langdorf?"

"Yes."

"That dog you dropped here three days ago, are you sure you haven't seen it in your neighborhood before?"

"No, I haven't."

"You know sir, if no one claims a dog within four days, we put it down?"

"That's fine with me."

That was easy enough, I wonder how long it will be before she starts in about getting another one?

Ron was well aware that Truly's parents had left a sizeable inheritance for their only daughter, so the thought of working to a respectable retirement age was out of the question.

"Truly, I'm coming up on twenty-five years at the bank and think it's time to retire. We have a nice monthly from your parents and I will get a decent retirement from the bank. What do you think about Florida?"

"I have never given it much thought."

"We can easily afford Boca Raton. I have been looking at condos there online and I have found a very nice three thousand square foot unit in a club setting. I think it would be perfect."

"Isn't that a little big?"

"No, we would have plenty of space and the unit is right on the water. I will have my own private dock."

"But you don't fish."

"I will now. By the way, I want to talk to the lawyers that handle your trust to see if we can get more money from it. I have some investment ideas I would like to try when we get down south."

"I thought you were just looking?"

"Well, looking and moving forward at the same time."

"Ron, I don't know if I will like it there?"

"You'll like it."

Within days, there was a For Sale sign in front of their home in St. Louis. The market was good, and the house sold quickly. Ron had started the purchase process well in advance, so their new home is Florida was ready when the movers showed up at their old one.

"Ron it's big, and not exactly what I had in mind. Come out here and look at this dock."

"Ron there's a huge alligator crawling up the bank on the other side of the waterway. I'm not going near that dock."

"They don't come up here. You have nothing to worry about."

"I don't know Ron?"

"My boat will be delivered this coming Monday. Wait till you see it. Not as big as I would like, but good for fishing and short cruises." As was the case for most of their marriage, Ron had his activities and various diversions which for the most part did not include his wife.

"Ron, I want to get another dog. I am here all alone just about every day while you are out fishing and doing your investments, if you want to call them that."

"What do you mean by that Truly? You don't know the first thing about investing, I'm following the advice of an investment counselor I found on the internet and there is a fortune to be made in currencies."

"Ron, most of those people are regularly exposed as scam artists who just take people's money."

"Not the ones I am following."

"What is it that you're being advised to buy?"

"Syrian Lira and Zimbabwe dollars, these currencies are going to be revalued and I am going to make a fortune."

"Ron it's a scam. I hope you haven't put too much into it?"

"You don't know what you are talking about. I'll invest our money as I see fit."

"By the way, I am going out tomorrow to look for a new dog."

"I don't want any dogs here. Do you understand me?"

"I am getting another dog Ron. All I have ever asked for is a dog. You have your boat and your investments to keep you busy."

Truly was learning that as a rule, bullies back down when openly confronted, and Ron also knew which side of his bread was buttered. The search for a new dog was on.

"She is beautiful. I'm going to call her Puddles. It's been so long since I had a dog."

"Brittany's are great dogs Mrs. Langdorf. We are sure you will love her."

"Oh yes, I already do. Come on Puddles lets go home."

Puddles brought a new sense of purpose to Truly Langdorf's life.

"Ron I'm home, come see our new addition to the family."

"Just keep the dog away from my boxes of money. I don't want any of it spoiled, it's going to be worth a lot very soon."

Time flies when you are having fun, well most of the time.

Ron mulled the fate of the currency investments he made wondering when they would ever be revalued and becoming more cynical by the day. Truly, traveled back and forth from the condo in Boca Raton to the home in Tenafly with Puddles always perched in the passenger seat when she drove. So, it was only appropriate that Truly give Ron a call on her beloved Puddles' birthday to rub him the wrong way, just a little.

"Ron, Puddles is ten years old today and I have enjoyed every day we have had her."

"I wish you spent more time here in Florida and lots less at your parents' home in New Jersey."

"It's our home Ron and it is a beautiful home."

"Maybe to you."

"Ron, I don't feel well today?"

"What seems to be wrong?"

"I don't know exactly. I think I better see the doctor. I am going to see one here in New Jersey."

"What for? We have doctors here."

"Why do you always try to make my decisions for me?"

"Someone has to."

"That's insulting Ron."

"Live with it."

Truly went to a friend of the family who referred her to a specialist. After a quick exam, she underwent a battery of tests and was asked to come back in four days. When she arrived, she was escorted into the doctor's office and asked to have a seat.

"Mrs. Langdorf, there is no good way to tell you this. You have stage four cancer. I'm sorry."

"Doctor what are my options?"

"I am afraid there are none at this point. We can keep you comfortable and out of pain, but not much more. I would like to have you talk to one of our counselors if you have time today."

"Yes, I have time. I can do that."

After meeting with the doctor, Truly was escorted to the counselor's office. Mrs. Langdorf, my name is Verba Yates. I would like to talk to you about options available to you. Is there anyone at home that can help care for you when you are unable to?"

"I don't think my husband would."

"What do you mean, would?"

"Just that. He's not very helpful. Can you tell me what other options I have?"

"Skilled care or assisted living is the next best thing. There are some wonderful facilities available to you here in Tenafly and at your home in Florida."

"I would like to be close to my dog. She is in Florida, I flew here this time, because I didn't feel well."

"I understand. It would probably be best to go back and start making arrangements as soon as possible."

"I have to take care of having my home here closed up and then, I will be on my way."

If Truly was anything, it was polite. No matter how much tension there was at home she did her best to remain civil.

"Ron, I will be leaving for Florida in a couple days. I have several things I must attend to here before I leave."

"Did you see your doctors there?"

"Yes, and we have things to discuss as soon as I get back."

"Can't we talk about it now?"

"No, this is something we need to talk about face to face."

"Alright, if you say so."

Part of the process of getting her affairs in order was to meet with the Epstein family attorney, Morton Litwin.

"Mr. Litwin, thank you for seeing me on such short notice."

"Mrs. Langdorf, you are one of my most valued clients. I always have time for you."

"Mr. Litwin, I'm not well. In fact, my condition is grave."

"I'm so sorry to hear that."

"Mr. Litwin, I will come right to the point. You have had minor dealings with my husband over the years, but when I tell him of my condition, I am afraid he is going to attempt to break the trust my father set up through your firm, immediately. I would like to make some changes to my will while I am here today."

"And what changes do you have in mind?"

"First, I want to leave my husband comfortable and that is all. I have prepared a list of organizations who will be the recipients of the bulk of my estate. I do need to get back to Florida and would like to know if you can have the papers ready to sign by the end of the day today?"

"Yes, I can."

"Good, then please have your office call when I can come back in to sign everything. I want to make sure you are forewarned, Ron will come at you when I am gone and possibly before when he finds out how ill I am."

"Thank you for the heads up. We will be ready."

While Truly was making her arrangements, the phone was ringing at the Langdorf home in Florida.

"Mr. Langdorf, this is Bill Gleason at International Currency Traders."

"Yes Bill."

"I have an offer that I am only making available to a very select small group that have bought my investment guide and follow my podcasts. I will be receiving a new shipment of Syrian Lira in six weeks and am calling to give you an opportunity to buy in early before I open it to the general public. The minimum purchase is one hundred thousand dollars."

"When it revalues, what do you estimate it will be worth?"

"Right now, my analysts believe it will be in excess of fifty times."

"Will you have five hundred thousand dollars worth available?"

"Yes, I surely will."

"How soon will you be wiring funds after I have the Lira available?"

"I will need twenty business days after you have the Lira to free up that amount."

"I don't know if we can wait that long. We will have an anxious clientele waiting to buy in."

"Bill, I have never reneged on a purchase."

"You're right Mr. Langdorf. I'll hold the Lira in reserve for you. I'll call back in about six weeks."

She will never consent to requesting a five hundred thousand dollar release from the trust for me to invest.

"Alright dog, I'll take you out."

'She knows nothing about investing. How am I going to get her to give me the money? God, I'd love to be rid of her. That is one big alligator. Well here's a start'.

Barely able to make it to Newark airport, there was no way Truly could drive herself home.

"Ron, you will have to hire someone to drive my car from the airport. I'm just too weak and am on my way in a cab."

"Too weak, what do you mean?"

"I'll be home soon and we'll talk then."

"You can't tell me now?"

"No, I can't."

Truly was about to give the bad news to Ron about her condition and Ron was about to give her worse news.

"Ron, I have stage four cancer. I have to make arrangements to enter the Starlight Assisted Living facility tomorrow, and where's Puddles?"

"I'm sorry I have to tell you this when you aren't feeling well."

"Not feeling well, Ron? I am dying. Where is my dog?"

"I had her out for a walk yesterday and that huge alligator we have seen before came out of the water and grabbed her."

"Oh no, Ron, you weren't watching her. How could you let that happen? I loved that dog. How could you?"

"I was lucky that alligator didn't go for me, things happen."

Truly Langdorf, distraught and wracked with pain, had to go somewhere where she would not have to look at Ron's face and collect her thoughts. The closest place was her next-door neighbors and dear friends, Ken and Lorraine Rudolph.

"Truly what happened? You look terrible. Lorraine, I have stage four cancer and will be leaving for Starlight Assisted Living this afternoon."

Lorraine helped her dear friend in and sat with her holding her hand.

"I wanted to stop by and tell you how wonderful it has been living next door to you and Ken all these years. I couldn't have asked for better friends and neighbors and just wanted to talk to you before I left. Ron just told me about the alligator grabbing Puddles the other day. I just don't know with him. He must not have been watching her at all."

"Truly, that's not what happened."

"What do you mean?"

"I saw the whole thing."

"What?"

"Ron led her to the water's edge and kicked her in when this huge alligator came close to shore."

"How could he do such a cruel thing? He knows how much I loved her."

"Truly, he was looking around as though he wanted to make sure no one saw him."

"All the years of bullying and trying to control my life takes a back seat to this act. If it was anyone other than you, telling me this, I wouldn't believe them."

When she had settled down a bit, after her neighbor's revelations, she slowly walked back to the condo.

"Ron, I have an appointment to check in at Starlight Assisted Living in one hour. Do you think you could drive me to the hospital? My bag is already by the front door."

"Can you take a cab? I have a ton of calls to make this morning and can't miss any of them."

"Ron, I'm your wife and I'm ill."

"I told you these are important calls, Lorraine probably doesn't have anything to do. Give her a call."

Truly made the call to her friend.

"Lorraine, I hate to bother you again, but Ron can't drive me to the hospital and I was wondering if you could?"

"I will be there in one minute."

"My bag is by the front door and thank you."

She went to the garage where Ron was winding new line onto one of his fishing reels.

"Ron, Lorraine is driving me to the hospital. Will you be stopping by later?"

"Sure, I'll try to get there sometime tonight. I should be done with my business by then."

It was probably better that Lorraine drove Truly to the assisted living facility, since it gave her a chance to calm herself down a little. Lorraine stayed with her old friend through check-in, made sure she was comfortable in her room, and ensured her assigned nurse was in the room.

"Mrs. Langdorf we are going to give you something to help you sleep tonight. The doctor will be here to see you first thing in the morning."

"What about Doctor Goldberg? He has been my doctor for years."

"He asked us to keep you comfortable and he will also be stopping by first thing."

"Thank you, would it be possible to hold the medication for a while? My husband is coming by later."

"We can, but we would like to have you take it before it is too late."

"I understand and thank you."

Ron, as expected, never showed or even called to check on his wife's condition. In the morning, the nurse came to her room.

"Again, I am sorry Mrs. Langdorf, but we couldn't wait any longer last night to give you your medication."

"I understand."

Shortly after the nurse left her bedside, the phone rang,

"Ron?"

"No, this is Doctor Goldberg."

"Oh, Doctor Goldberg, they said you would be here first thing this morning. I had intended to, but spoke to one of the doctors there this morning and I believe he is better equipped to deal with your condition. I wanted to clear this with you before just telling him to come ahead."

"Thank you, doctor. When will he be coming to see me?"

"He said he wanted to visit with you as early as possible this morning, so you can expect him very soon."

"He is part of a specialty medical group that practices at Starlight."

"Thank you, Doctor."

"I'll check back with you in a few days."

While Truly was waiting for the specialist to show up, Ron was busy putting a plan together.

"Harrington & Harrington, how may I direct your call?"

"James Harrington please."

"I'll transfer you now."

"James Harrington, how can I help you?"

"James, this is Ron Langdorf."

"Hello Ron, what can I do for you today?"

"My wife came back from our home in New Jersey and has been diagnosed with stage four cancer."

"I'm sorry to hear that Ron."

"Thank you, James, I'll just get to the point of this call. I need your firm to see what it can do to break the trust that her father setup years ago or at the very least, have them release some funds. I have several investment opportunities coming up quickly and I want to take advantage of them."

"Have you discussed this with your wife?"

"No, she's too ill and would more than likely drag her feet trying to make a decision."

"At the risk of sounding offensive, do you know how much time she has left?"

"No, I don't, but if she lingers for more than a month or two, I could miss out."

"Understood, we will look into it right away. You do realize these things can be quite costly."

"Break the trust and cost isn't an issue. I just need it done."

"We'll take care of it."

Within a half hour after her conversation with Dr. Goldberg Truly had a visitor. As he was entering the room she saw his name on the badge on his lab coat. It read Dr. A.K. Ita. "Good morning, Mrs. Langdorf."

"Good morning."

"I'm Dr. Ita, I spoke to your physician this morning and we agreed that I may be better to attend to your specific needs."

"Did he tell you I have stage four cancer?"

"Oh yes, we deal with that quite often."

"Do you think you can do anything for me?"

"We have to run some labs, and then we can make a determination as to what course we will take. I would also like to ask you some questions, since our course of treatment requires that you be in a proper frame of mind."

"Alright doctor, what would you like to know?"

As she was preparing to answer his questions, the phone rang.

"Doctor, would you mind if I answered this call. It may be my husband."

"No, not at all."

"Truly it's me."

"Yes Ron, I wish you would have come to see me last night."

"It wasn't possible. I was on the phone all night."

"Will you be coming to visit today?"

"No, I don't think so, I have to track currency markets and I have a two-hour live podcast starting at 3:00 p.m."

"I wish you would come by. I don't believe I have a great deal of time left and you are all the family I have left."

"I'll try tomorrow, get some rest."
A dejected Truly hung up the phone.

"That was your husband?"

"Yes, it was."

"And from what I gather, he has not been here to see you and won't be today?"

"That's correct doctor."

"If I may ask, how is your life?"

"What do you mean?"

"Your life, your marriage, your relationship with your husband?"

"We have been married for forty-five years and he has been a good provider."

"That's not an answer. I will be more direct Mrs. Langdorf. are you happy and if not, how long has it been since you were?"

"I haven't been happy since Charlie died."

"Charlie?"

"Yes, my Springer Spaniel."

"Tell me about that time in your life."

"Well, I had Charlie from the time I was twelve years old until after Ron and I were married. I had him all through college and for the first two years of my marriage. We were all so happy together, or so I thought."

"What do you mean?"

"Well, when Charlie died, I was so sad and when I told Ron I wanted to get another dog, he said no. He said he wasn't really a dog person and didn't want any around."

"Tell me more."

And so it was, Mrs. Langdorf proceeded to tell her life story about the dogs she had so loved from childhood throughout her adult years, the strange disappearance of Bindy, and ending with the horrific accounting of the murder of her beloved Puddles.

"Mrs. Langdorf, I would like to thank you for your candor. I sometimes come off as a little too direct and think at this stage, it would be in your best interest if I had one of my associates come to speak to you. There is no one that doesn't get along with him famously, I must consult with him briefly and he will be right in."

"Thank you Dr. Ita".

After about a half hour Dr. Ita's associate entered her room. As the doctor entered the room she looked at the badge on his lab coat. It read, Dr. L.A. Brador.

"Mrs. Langdorf?"

"Yes."

"I am Dr. Brador, are they keeping you comfortable?"

"Oh yes doctor, they are."

"Good, Dr. Ita and I discussed your condition and the conversation you had with him. From that, I hope that what I have to say will interest you?"

"Does this have something to do with treating my cancer?"

"Yes, in a way. Mrs. Langdorf, what if you could have a second chance?"

"A second chance at what?"

"At life."

"You mean like start over?"

"Not quite over."

"I don't' know. At first glance, I would say yes, but then without the love my dogs gave me and the joy they brought me throughout my life, I don't know?"

"I would like you to think about this overnight and we will talk again, first thing in the morning."

The following morning, Dr. Brador was there bright and early.

"Mrs. Langdorf, how are you this morning?"

"I'm not feeling well doctor."

"Are you in pain?"

"No, they are keeping me comfortable."

"Did you think about our conversation yesterday?"

"Yes, I did as a matter of fact, I was up for the better part of the night."

"And?"

"I have decided no. Life without my dogs would not be much better than it is today. Is that the right answer Dr. Brador?"

"There are no right or wrong answers Mrs. Langdorf, but answer this hypothetical if you would please?"

"If you had your dogs and were offered a second chance, would you take it?"

"Yes doctor, I would."

"I'll be right back."

The door opened and in ran four very familiar furry faces. "Sparkles! No that's not her. But, that's her collar. How did you get her collar doctor? Look, she moves just like Sparkles and lays her head on my lap just like Sparkles. Doctor what is happening? Charlie, Bindy and Puddles this can't be them, doctor what is this?"

"Mrs. Langdorf, I would like to leave you with your dogs for a while. We'll talk this evening."

"But doctor what…?"

"We have much to talk about later."

Dr. Brador returned later in the evening.

"Mrs. Langdorf have you decided?"

"If I can live my life out with my dogs, the answer is yes."

"Thank you, Mrs. Langdorf, that is the answer we hoped you would give us."

"There is a great deal we must do in a very short amount of time."

"Doctor I can hardly get out of bed."

"Right now, I need nothing more than your word that you won't change your mind?"

"You have my word."

"Then, you must get some rest. We begin in the morning."

With the prospect of a second chance with the company of her dogs, it was virtually impossible for Truly Langdorf to get any sleep.

"Good morning Mrs. Langdorf, I see you are up and about."

"I was up all night with my dogs and hardly feel tired at all. Doctor what is happening? I feel so different, but still look the same as I did when I was admitted."

"You have to trust, that everything will be alright. Now, we are going to see some lawyers. They will begin to put your affairs in order. If you will take a quick look at this packet, I will get an aid to bring you down to the van."

"You will be going to Berman, Kingese and Vasz, they handle all our legal issues. You will find them to be a topflight law firm."

The thirty-five mile trip from Boca Raton to Miami on a bright sunny morning was exactly what Truly Langdorf needed to get her in the right frame of mind for the day's business at hand. The van pulled up in front of an impressive building sheathed in white marble with Berman, Kingese and Vasz above the double glass doors in one-foot high polished brass letters. At the top of the stairs was a large bronze statue of a German Shepherd with a plaque that read, 'Man's Best Friend'. Truly Langdorf felt totally at ease for the first time in years as she walked into the building.

"Good morning Mrs. Langdorf, I am Ms. Pug. We have been expecting you. You will be meeting with Mr. Berman, one of our senior partners."

Ms. Pug led Truly down a long hall to one of the three offices. The placard on the door read D.O. Berman, Ms. Pug knocked and opened the door.

"Good morning Mrs. Langdorf, I am Donald Berman, I will be taking over your affairs, temporarily, and then will pass you to one of the other partners."

"Mr. Berman, I have a large trust that was established by my father and is currently administered in New Jersey by Morton Litwin, the attorney who has handled my affairs for years."

"We have already contacted Mr. Litwin and he is more than willing to work with us. He mentioned you had made some substantial changes before returning to Florida and that your husband has initiated a legal action to break the Trust."

"How can that be? I know nothing about that. He must have some investment scheme that he needs funds for. He couldn't even wait until I was gone?"

"Mrs. Langdorf, I will be in court with his lawyers later this week and will do everything in my power to persuade them that it is not in their best interest to pursue this action."

"I don't know if you hear this very often Mr. Berman, but I have confidence you will work in my best interest."

"Thank you, Mrs. Langdorf, you can rest assured, I will."

Mr. Berman then told Truly he had to run to a meeting with his partners and led her back to the reception area after their brief meeting.

"Ms. Pug, how long do you think it will take Mr. Berman to settle my trust issues?"

"Usually, one court visit. He tends to be very intimidating in the courtroom."

"Which one of your other attorneys will I be dealing with going forward?"

"Well, it could be Mr. Kingese, everyone just loves him, he is so smart and so nice, but depending how complex your affairs are it could go to Mr. Vasz though. We sometimes joke with him about being so protective and loyal to his clients. Either way, you will be in good hands. Now, I have several contracts for you to sign. If you could sign on this line, now this line and this line."

"I haven't read anything yet."

"Oh, that's ok. Mr. Kingese can give you an overview before you leave. Now let me show you to Mr. Kingese' office."

A short walk down the hall to another office. The placard on the door read, P.E. Kingese.

"Mrs. Langdorf, I am Peter Kingese. I am here to go over the contracts you signed here this afternoon."

"Yes sir."

"Oh, we're not that formal, please. Essentially, what you have signed is this, when your treatments are over, you will physically be about fifty-five years old and in perfect health. Your life span from that point will be normal as long as you take care of yourself."

"I don't understand?"

"I believe either Dr. Senji or Dr. Hnauzer will be explaining how the process works. Anyway, your looks will be somewhat altered, so no one knows who you really are, and you are legally bound to never tell anyone."

"What about my dogs? If I am fifty-five and live a normal lifespan, I will outlive them. To lose them one after another, I'm afraid that will bring sorrow I don't believe I could bear."

"Now for the dogs, Mrs. Langdorf, the dogs' life cycles will adjust to yours. You are all going to live your lives out together and when the end comes, we hope, many years from now, you will all go peacefully and be together for all time.

Now, I have to run. I have a meeting with my partners. It was a pleasure meeting you."

"And you Mr. Kingese."

"Ms. Pug will be here in a moment to get you to your next meeting."

Almost as fast as the lawyer had left, Ms. Pug appeared in the doorway.

"Mrs. Langdorf, you have one last meeting today. It will be with Mr. Vasz. Now, he may seem a little gruff when you first meet him, but remember he has your best interest at heart. I can tell you that over time, you will come to view him as a most trusted friend."

She was led down the hall again to a third office. The placard on this door read K.U. Vasz. Ms. Pug knocked and opened the door.

"Mrs. Langdorf, good morning, I am Kirk Vasz."

"It's a pleasure to meet you Mr. Vasz."

"I am here to discuss your new name."

"I have to change my name?"

"Yes, you do. With a second chance, comes a new name. No one can know what you have been given."

"I almost feel selfish."

"Please don't. Very few meet our requirements. Look at this as being blessed. Your new name is Betsy Moore. All the arrangements are being made for the transfer of property. Mr. Berman has power of attorney and will be signing for the transfer of your trust to your new name. I will be taking over the management and making appropriate changes to the trust as soon as the papers are signed."

"And Mr. Litwin?"

"He is approaching retirement and has full confidence that we will give you the same care he has over the years. Do you have any questions?"

"No, I don't."

"Then I have to run. I have a meeting with my partners."

"Thank you, Mr. Vasz. Thank you for everything."

"Ms. Pug will be here shortly to take you back to the reception area."

Again, almost as soon as the lawyer had walked out of his office, Ms. Pug appeared in the doorway waiting to take Betsy Moore back to the reception area. As they were walking down the hallway she said,

"Ms. Pug, how can I thank you for all you and your firm have done for me?"

"Just enjoy your life with your dogs. I can hear the van pulling up in front right now. Get used to your new name and your new life and have a safe trip. Mrs. Moore we'll talk to you soon." Mrs. Betsy Moore left believing, in her heart of hearts, that she was in good hands. As each mile passed on the drive back to the hospital, Betsy's feelings of optimism about her future became greater and greater. The doctor was waiting for her when she arrived.

"Dr. Ita, am I not going back to my same room?"

"No, we are moving you to the other side. The rooms are larger and will accommodate you and the dogs much better."

"How long is all of this going to take?"

"Dr. Hnauzer will explain all of that to you."

"Thank you, Doctor."

She was wheeled to the other side of the hospital and into her new room where a doctor was waiting. She looked at the badge on his lab coat, it read Dr. S.C. Hnauzer.

"Mrs. Moore, welcome to my side of the hospital. I am Dr. Hnauzer and I will be completing your procedure."

"Doctor, how long will this procedure take?"

"Several days, but the time will just seem to fly by. I will need to take your dogs but will return them in a couple days. In case you have questions about their care, I give you my personal guarantee that they will be returned as you see them today."

"Can I pet each one before they go?"

"Oh, by all means."

Three days into the transition from Truly Langdorf to Betsy Moore and even after being notified that his wife had passed away, Ron, as usual, was in pursuit of his own selfish interests, during the one time he should have been paying attention to his wife. He had a day of fishing planned. Mourning and making arrangements for his deceased wife came in a distant second. As he was carrying his gear down to the dock.

"Kenneth come over here quickly. Look at all of the dogs down by the Langdorf's dock. Ron is out on his pier and they are all barking at him."

"Lori, that looks like a Pekingese and a Pug,"

"Ken, there are more, look."

"Lorraine there's a Giant Schnauzer and an Akita."

"Kenneth that one's a Labrador, Ron looks like he's throwing something at them. He's charging at them. It looks like he's trying to scare them off."

"Oh, my goodness, just look at the size of that Doberman."

"Kenneth what is that big white dog?"

"It's a Kuvasz and a big one. You know they are originally from Hungary."

"Lorraine grab the dog book. There's a smaller one that looks like a Basenji?"

"They're all blocking the end of the pier now. Ron looks like he doesn't know what to do. I hope he doesn't panic."

"Kenneth look at that huge alligator swimming across the channel from the other bank. It stopped at the end of Ron's pier."

"Kenneth, get the phone and call the police right now!"
Lor, that thing has to be twenty feet long if it's an inch."

"Kenneth those two big dogs just pushed through the pack to the front. They are starting to charge down the pier at Ron."

"It looks like he's trying to jump into his boat. If he can make it onto the deck, he can lock himself in the cabin."
Ken Rudolph yelled through the window,

"Ron, watch your step, the bait bucket. Lorraine, he tripped over his bait bucket. He's falling into the water. He'll be ok if he gets to the ladder."

"Dear God in Heaven, Kenneth, that alligator just grabbed him in its jaws and is rolling over and over. Oh my God, it tore him in half."

"Look it just went under. No, it is coming straight up and it has Ron in its jaws chomping and swallowing him. Look at his face, oh that scream."

"Now, it's going straight for his legs. It's chomping and swallowing them too. Look at the legs flopping like a rag doll sticking out of the sides of its mouth."

"I have never seen anything like this before. I won't be able to forget this for the rest of my life."

"Kenneth, here's the phone. Call the police and the department of wildlife!"

"Lorraine, all those dogs are gone. It's almost as if they just disappeared."

Kenneth and Lorraine Rudolph gave their complete and accurate account to the police and the department of wildlife. A search was initiated immediately covering twenty miles in either direction. There were four sheriff's boats, five Department of Wildlife boats, two more from the Florida Fish and Wildlife Conservation

Commission, and two kayaks from Save the Alligators replete with camera equipment, protest signs and handout materials for spectators. When word got out there was a man-eater on the loose, more than one hundred alligator hunters from Florida to Louisiana converged on the site causing a massive traffic jam that took the sheriff's department four days to break up.

The search for the twenty-foot alligator lasted for two weeks, but to no avail. Not a trace of Ron Langdorf or the alligator was ever found. It took several more weeks for the excitement to calm down, leaving the neighbors left to wonder who would purchase the Langdorf condo and what would they be like. Late one warm Saturday afternoon, there was a knock on the door of Ken and Lorraine Rudolph's condo.

"Hello, I just wanted to stop by and introduce myself. My name is Betsy Moore and I'm your new neighbor."

"I'm Lorraine Rudolph and this is my husband Ken. We're so glad to meet you. Are those your dogs?"

"Yes, all of them."

"Oh, Kenneth and I love dogs. We had a Brittany years ago named Molly that looked just like yours."

"Well, this is Sparkles and this is Charlie, Bindy and Puddles."

"Puddles? That was the name of our old neighbor's Brittany and she looks just like her."

"I have had her since she was just a puppy."

"Betsy are you married?"

"No, my husband passed away recently and went on to his just reward."

"I'm so sorry to hear that."

"I heard a very sad story about the former residents."

"Oh yes, Ron and Truly Langdorf, she was a kind and wonderful friend. I know it's not right to say, but Ron was not. He didn't even attend Truly's memorial service when she died. Telling you any more would just be tawdry gossip and add insult to injury."

"I'm so glad to be here. I thought that the unit would be too big, but it turns out that it's the perfect size for me and all of my dogs. They are going to be so happy here."

"This may sound odd, but there is something vaguely familiar about you."

"Really, and what would that be?"

"I can't quite put my finger on it. You seem so happy and full of life."

"That's so kind of you to say that."

"Would you like to come by for dinner tonight? Ken is getting ready to start the grill."
"Why yes, that's so nice of you to ask."
"And Betsy, please bring your dogs."

Christopher Oelerich

Chris Oelerich is an author, businessman, husband and father. His first venture into writing was 'Merry Christmas and a Happy PTSD'. Published after reading the unacceptable statistics about veteran suicides in America. His own experiences as a combat helicopter pilot in Vietnam provided him with the necessary insights to convey to those suffering from PTSD as he puts it; How as a former front-line combat soldier I have dealt with PTSD and managed to have a very, very good life.

As a businessman he has traveled extensively throughout the United States and Far East.

His new book, 'A Senior's Bedtime Reader' Volume I, was written with a little more mature reader in mind; One novella, two novelettes and four short stories to help while away your evenings. Mystery/Suspense, Conspiracy, Paranormal and a couple love stories.

He lives with his wife Norine in Las Vegas. **Watch for Volume II, in late 2018.**

Made in the USA
Columbia, SC
07 January 2020